Praise
Second St

"*Second Story Man* is a down and dirty game of cat and mouse, only this time there are two cats and the mouse hasn't yet seen the trap that can touch him. Are two cats better than one? Read it and see."

—Reed Farrel Coleman, *New York Times* bestselling author of *What You Break*

"Terrific. And the riveting *Second Story Man* is also a master class in voice and dialogue and storytelling. This cat and mouse caper about three men—two cops and a burglar—reinventing themselves for the second stories of their lives is unique, textured and even hilarious. Charles Salzberg has perfected the existential crime novel—and this one will break your heart."

—Hank Phillippi Ryan, Award-winning author

"I dare you to try and put Salzberg's *Second Story Man* down after you've read through the first two chapters. From one absorbing character to another, *Second Story Man* is a gripping and totally rewarding read."

—David Swinson, author of *The Second Girl*

"With *Second Story Man*, Charles Salzberg works his magic on the old cat-and-mouse game: he adds an extra cat, a (Michael J.) foxy mouse, and a mousetrap you won't see coming until it snaps shut."

—Tim O'Mara, author of the Raymond Donne mysteries

"Charles Salzberg's *Second Story Man* is a fast-paced, character-driven pursuit novel. Three interwoven voices reveal the story of a hunt for a master thief, but each man is also searching for something more—a return to who they think they ought to be, or once were. Salzberg is a superb wordsmith, with an honest ear for dialogue, and a delight in plot twists. If you're not already a Salzberg fan, read this book; you will become one."

—Michael Sears, Award-winning author

"Charlie Floyd and Manny Perez are a new and most welcome team on the investigative scene. Now that they've dispensed with master burglar Francis Hoyt—or have they?—I'm expecting, and looking forward to, more of their unique take on how to bring down evil-doers."

—SJ Rozan, Award-winning author

"*Second Story Man* is a cat-and-mouse thriller. But not the Tom and Jerry kind. More like if the mouse was carrying the plague and a sizable gambling debt and the cat, scabies and a drinking problem. Traversing my old stomping grounds, from Connecticut to South Beach, I loved the local touches and flavors. But what hit me hardest is how much this plays like a re-envisioned Michael Mann's *Heat*, like if we'd been treated to nothing but Pacino and DeNiro. The terse dialogue, two men on opposite sides of the law but oh-so-much alike, the chess match. I would've liked to see that movie. With *Second Story Man*, Salzberg socks it to us."

—Joe Clifford, author of the
Jay Porter thriller series

SECOND STORY MAN

ALSO BY CHARLES SALZBERG

Henry Swann Mystery Series
Swann's Last Song
Swann Dives In
Swann's Lake of Despair
Swann's Way Out

Stand Alone
Devil in the Hole

Novella
Triple Shot (Twist of Fate)

CHARLES SALZBERG

SECOND STORY MAN

Copyright © 2018 by Charles Salzberg

All rights reserved. No part of the book may be reproduced in any form or by any electronic or mechanical means, including information storage and retrieval systems, without permission in writing from the publisher, except by a reviewer who may quote brief passages in a review.

Down & Out Books
3959 Van Dyke Rd, Ste. 265
Lutz, FL 33558
www.DownAndOutBooks.com

The characters and events in this book are fictitious. Any similarity to real persons, living or dead, is coincidental and not intended by the author.

Cover design by JT Lindroos

ISBN: 1-946502-55-3
ISBN-13: 978-1-946502-55-1

Francis Hoyt

"Where's my fucking money?"

"Francis, these things take time, man."

I pounded on the table. Ice clattered against the sides of glasses.

"It's been three fucking weeks, Artie. Are you running a business, or what? I want my fucking money and I want it now."

I moved my chair around until I was sitting right next to him and then I got all up in his face, so close I could smell his cheap after-shave. Old Spice. I hadn't smelled that since I was a kid and my old man used to pour it on to cover his nauseating stink of alcohol and cigarettes.

"Listen," I whispered, "you do not want to fuck with me. I can be nice and I can be not so nice. Trust me, you do not want to deal with the not so nice Francis Hoyt. That would be a very big mistake, my friend."

We're sitting at a table by the pool at the Fontainebleau Hotel in Miami. Artie's wearing one of those obscene-looking, loud Hawaiian shirts and a bathing suit to match. He looks like he's some fucking fat tourist from Iowa on vacation for the first time. I'm dressed like a human being: khakis and a pale blue polo, Gucci loafers. One of us looks like a complete asshole and it's not me.

I'm not registered at the hotel and I doubt Artie is either. I'm the one who can afford it. He's not. But this is where he hangs out and this is where he likes to act like a big shot by conducting business by the pool surrounded by a bunch of old, overweight, greased-up Jews spread out on chaise lounges, staring up at the sun while they bake. Guys like Artie don't have offices. They just exist somewhere in time and space. But they wouldn't exist at all if it wasn't for guys like me.

Artie is a fence. I'm a thief. Not just a run-of-the-mill, knock-you-over-the-head-and-steal-your-wallet thief, but the best damn thief in the whole goddamn world. Artie owes me money for goods delivered. The good stuff. Only the good stuff. Antique silver. Three heists' worth. I figure I should clear at least a couple hundred grand after Artie takes his cut. That sounds like a lot but it's only a fraction of its real value.

"Francis," he whines, "I don't think you understand how my business works. You bring me high-end items like what you give me and I have to find unique buyers. And it ain't here in the States. It's much too risky to dispose of that kind of stuff here. I have to reach out to my European contacts. That takes time. You want me to get the best price, don't you?"

"Listen to me, Artie," I raised my voice a little, just enough to raise the stakes slightly. Just enough to let him know I meant business. "Because I'm not going to say it again. I'm leaving town soon and I need that money. I'm not interested in your business problems. You're a fucking fence. Do your fucking job. If you can't, I'll find someone who can."

Artie loves to look like a big man so he's ordered lunch for us. Pastrami sandwiches on rye. I don't want lunch, I especially don't want a pastrami sandwich because I don't eat meat. Artie would have known that if he'd bothered to ask, but he didn't. He just wanted to look like a fucking big shot. I don't care about his fucking lunch. I just want my fucking money. Besides, it's hot, so hot I'm starting to sweat through my shirt, even though I hardly ever sweat. As it gets closer to one, it's getting hotter. I look up and see why. There's not a fucking cloud in the sky. Just the sun. A big, yellow ball in the sky, suspended in an ocean of blue. That's why people come down here. For the sun and the heat. So, they can jump in the pool to cool off. Makes no sense to me. You want to cool off stay the fuck where you were up north. Or stay in your air-conditioned room.

"Whoa, Francis, we go back a long way. I don't want to lose an old client like you. Besides, you're more like a friend than a client."

I laughed. I don't think of myself as a client and I certainly don't think of myself as Artie's friend. I break into people's homes and take what I want. Artie sells what I take. We have what they call a symbiotic relationship. It's as simple as that. Only Artie isn't making it as simple as that. He's making it difficult. It's my job to get him back on track. To remind him who the fuck he is and why the fuck he exists.

"I'll give you two days. You understand? Two fucking days. No more. You either come up with the dough or you give me back the goods. I'll find someone else to fence it or I'll fucking melt it down and sell the shit myself."

"Don't do that! Please. Some of those pieces are part of history, man. American history. They go way, way back."

"I don't give a fuck about American history. All I give a fuck about is the money. And don't fuck with me when it comes to the money. I know the value of those pieces. I researched them. It's not just the silver it's the provenance. You know what that means?"

"I do, Francis. I really do. And that's why I'm being so careful. Whatever you bring me is high-grade stuff. I have to take special care. But you'll get your money, I promise you."

I move my chair back a couple steps. I've been too close to him for too long. That stink coming off him is starting to make me sick.

"In two days."

"I don't want to set unrealistic expectations," he said, as he reached for his sandwich. I grabbed his wrist before he could get it up to his mouth.

"Let me put this as simple as I can. If I feel like you're trying to cheat me, or if I feel like you're shining me on, or if I think

3

you're doing this just to Jew down the price, I'm going to deal with you in ways you don't want to even think about. I may be physically small but I am very deadly. See that pool over there?" I gestured toward the enormous swimming pool filled with chlorine blue water and screaming kids.

"Yeah. Sure. I see it."

"You don't want to wind up floating in it, face down."

"There's no need for threats."

"It's not a threat. It's a statement of fact. I'm a man who can see into the future. That's your future. Two days."

I got up.

"You haven't even taken a bite of your sandwich."

"I don't eat meat, Artie. Get yourself a doggie bag."

Fucking moron.

Charlie Floyd

"Good morning, Charlie Floyd. Do you know who this is?"

The voice was vaguely familiar. Slight hint of an accent. Hispanic, probably. But I needed more.

"Should I?"

He laughed. Not one of those thin, phony laughs, but one that reflected genuine amusement. I leaned back in my recliner and stretched my legs out onto the ottoman. I'd already had breakfast, finished the morning paper, and had nothing better to do till lunch rolled around, so why not play along?

"Did I say something funny?"

"No. Not funny, though I am amused. I thought you would remember me. I am told I am a very memorable man. Frankly, I am a little disappointed, Charlie Floyd."

He'd said enough. I did know him. I'd spent a couple days with him in Miami Beach a while back, while I was down there looking for a killer named John Hartman. Murdered his family, wife, three teenage kids, mother, and the family dog, then disappeared. Cuban-born Miami detective Manny Perez did his best to help me out. That was back when I did that sort of thing for the state of Connecticut. Not anymore. For the past year or so I've been on my own, looking for ways to pass the time, hoping for divine inspiration on how I might spend the rest of my life. No word yet.

"How are you, Manny?"

"I knew you would remember me, Charlie Floyd. Am I not, as I said, a very memorable man?"

"That you are. How've you been?"

"I have been very good. Thank you for asking. Miami is a much better place than Havana, Cuba."

"You've changed your tune since I saw you last."

"Yes. I am for sure singing a different tune now." He hummed a few bars of "God Bless America," then that laugh again. "I do not wish to return to Cuba. Let Castro and his thugs have it and let them do with it what they will. Now Miami is my home sweet home."

"I'm happy you've become assimilated, but my guess is this isn't a social call."

"Ha! I know you are not a very social man, Charlie Floyd. No, you are not one for idle chitchat. Me, on the other hand, I am very social. I like to meet new people. I like to go to night-clubs and have a good time. I like to dance. I like to sing. I like to drink rum and Coca-Cola. I like to talk to strangers on the street. But you are very correct, my friend. That is not why I am calling."

I loved the way Manny talked. Very few contractions, lots of sophisticated words, and every so often he'd throw in a collo-quialism or cliché that if it were used by anyone else would be cringe inducing. Not so with Manny. With him every word counted. The English language was never frivolous or haphaz-ard when he used it. I also loved the way he repeated a person's full name at the beginning or end of a sentence. Some might think it's an annoying affectation, but I think it's to show respect and I'm betting it also turns out to be a very effective interroga-tion tool. Fact is Manny's a very good cop. He knows how to work people. He's got a good head for detail and a memory sharp as a Ginsu knife. If I like him, and I do, it's better than even money everybody else pretty much feels the same. Even the guys he's trying to put in the slammer probably find him charm-ing and likeable. That's not something that can be said about me.

Although Spanish is his native tongue, Manny revels in the

6

English language. He taught American studies back in Cuba before he defected to the U.S. He loves all things American and there's no reason to contract words when to Manny they're so beautiful in their full-blown version. His style of speech reflects his style of police work. Slow, methodical, logical, he picks up every nuance, every comma, every semi-colon, every exclamation point, every period. Not like me. Seat of the pants, instinctive, sometimes impatient, some have even called me rash and impulsive. But it gets the job done, and in the end, that's how we're all judged. Results. That's the difference between the winners and the losers. While Manny is ingratiating, I'm just plain grating. But we both take police work very seriously. I suppose you could say both of us are a little on the obsessive side.

"To what do I owe the honor?"

"I am calling because I need your help, Charlie Floyd."

"In case word didn't make it down there to Miami, I don't work for the state anymore. I took early retirement about a year ago."

Every time I say the word *retirement* it sticks in my craw. I'm only forty-nine years old. Healthy, productive forty-nine-year olds aren't supposed to be retired. But when you start to work in the system when you're right out of college, then twenty-five years later, no matter how old you are, you're eligible for retirement. It was time for me to move on but I hadn't yet decided where I was moving on to.

"This is not good. You are much too young to retire. You have a lot of life ahead of you. Retirement is for the senior citizens who reside down here in Miami. They play pinochle. They play shuffleboard. They go to the jai alai matches. They take naps in the afternoon. They line up for the early bird special at four-thirty in the afternoon. I do not picture you playing pinochle or shuffleboard, going to jai alai matches, taking naps in the afternoon, or lining up before the sun sets for your evening meal. Take it from me, Charlie Floyd, retirement is not a life for a man such as you."

"Hunting people down for committing capital crimes can take its toll, Manny. It *did* take its toll. I don't have the stomach for that anymore. It's someone else's problem now."

"Then how *do* you spend the many hours of your day if you are not chasing down criminals and putting them behind bars?"

Good question. Nearly eight months off the job and I still hadn't figured out what I was going to do with the rest of my life. Now Manny Perez, a man I hadn't laid eyes on in close to five years, was forcing me to come up with an answer.

"I seem to find ways to pass the time," I said. Notice, I didn't say, *productively.* Anyone can pass the time. It's easy. You find silly, inconsequential things to do. Like getting a haircut every three weeks instead of every three months. Or fixing something around the house that doesn't really need fixing. Or signing up for Netflix and binging on programs you can't even remember the next day. Never had much time to make friends outside of work. I was never bitten by the golf bug. And so, what am I left with? Passing time till time passes me.

"That is not how a man like you should live. A man like you needs purpose. A goal. A man like you should not merely be 'passing the time.'"

"Why do I have the feeling you're calling to change that?"

"See, Charlie Floyd, you are, just as I always knew, an excellent detective."

"Not any more I'm not."

"You know what they say. 'Once a cop always a cop.' Do you still dress like John Wayne?'"

I laughed. "I never dressed like John Wayne."

"The cowboy hat, the boots…"

"I still have 'em, and I still wear them from time to time, if that's what you mean. But I never did learn how to ride a horse."

"I have a picture of you in my head, Charlie Floyd. And in that picture you are wearing a cowboy hat and cowboy boots. Just like John Wayne."

I wasn't going to argue with him. That's what I mean about

8

Manny Perez. He doesn't give up. Once he gets something in his head it's hard to shake it out of there.

"Maybe you should get to the point, Manny."

"Of course. The point." He chuckled. "My wife calls me long-winded and perhaps she is right. Have you ever heard of a man named Francis Hoyt?"

"Can't say I have. But I'm sure you're going to enlighten me."

He laughed. I liked Manny's laugh. It was full and hearty and brimming with life. I could imagine him smiling, his head thrown back, his perfect white teeth set off by his dark Latin complexion. The opposite of my pale New England pallor.

"That is what I shall most certainly do, though I am sur- prised you have not heard of Francis Hoyt, because he is one of the most renowned thieves in the world today."

"I never worked robbery, burglary or run-of-the-mill street crime. Homicides and white-collar crimes, that's what interested me. Those other things, much too low-class for me to waste my time with. No challenge in chasing down petty crooks. You re- member me, right? I'm a high-stakes kinda guy."

"Yes, I know that all too well and that is precisely why I am calling. And what you say explains why you do not know any- thing about Francis Hoyt. But if you have a moment or two, and since you are now a man of leisure, I am sure that you do, I shall enlighten you. Francis Hoyt is a genius. A talented, artistic, criminal genius. There has never been anyone like Francis Hoyt before and we should pray to God there never will be one like him in the future."

I pictured Manny crossing himself as he mentioned the Almighty.

"I'm sure you didn't call me to give me a history lesson on this guy Hoyt."

"No. That is most surely not the reason I am calling you. The reason I am calling you, Charlie Floyd, is that it is the month of May. Do you know what that means?"

"April showers bring May flowers."

He laughed. "Yes, that is very true. But it also means something else. It means, the snowbirds head back north."

"And the significance of that would be?"

"When the birds go north so do the predators."

"Manny, I know you well enough to know you're a man of way many words. And believe me, no one enjoys hearing them more than I do. But I hate talking on the phone. This sounds like it has the makings of a very long conversation and for that I prefer face to face. And since you're down there and I'm up here that's going to be impossible."

"I am very glad you said that, Charlie Floyd, because you are absolutely correct. And that is why I am making a trip up to Connecticut to meet with you. In fact, I have a plane ticket that leaves Miami International Airport early tomorrow morning and arrives at Kennedy Airport at 11:42 a.m."

Jesus, he was really serious about this.

"I hate to see you waste your money, Manny. Or the city of Miami waste theirs."

"If I am successful in my quest, it will be money well-spent."

"Truth is, I could probably use the company. But you might be wasting your time, so why don't you give me a hint as to why you want this face-to-face with me."

"I shall provide you with far more than a hint, Charlie Floyd. You are going to help me capture Francis Hoyt with enough evidence to put him back where he belongs."

Manny Perez

I love America. It is the land of the free and the home of the brave. America has been very good to me and when people are not good to it I become a very angry man and this is not a very pretty picture. Ask my wife, Esther, and she will tell you this is true. This is why I decided to join the Miami Police Department when I arrived here from Cuba almost twenty years ago. It was an opportunity for me to give back to a country that took me in and hugged me to its breast.

I like order. If I see a thread dangling from a sweater or other item of clothing I need to pull on it. My wife, who is a born and bred American, originally from Chicago, calls me a "neat freak." She says I am very close to having obsessive compulsive disorder. I do not believe that is true. I just like to see things in their proper place and I like to see people behave in a proper manner. That, I am sure, explains why I do what I do and why I love what I do. It is not the job I dreamed of having when I grew up as a child in Havana, but now it is my dream job.

The idea to call Charlie Floyd, a man whom I came to admire because once he starts a job he does not stop until it comes to a proper end, came to me in a dream. Yes, a dream. I had not thought of Charlie Floyd in years but when I went to bed thinking about Francis Hoyt and how I was going to apprehend him and bring him to justice, I woke up thinking about Charlie Floyd. I do not believe in coincidences and I do not believe in visions. But yes, I suppose you could say that Charlie Floyd came to me in a vision.

We are two very different people, Charlie Floyd and me. But I think that if Charlie Floyd saw a dangling thread he would also pull on it. Francis Hoyt is a dangling thread and that dangling thread must be pulled. But I needed help to pull it and that is why I called upon Charlie Floyd.

There is no doubt in my mind that Charlie Floyd and I can bring this situation to a satisfying conclusion. That explains why I already had my airline ticket in my hand when I called my old friend. I knew that once I met with him and I told him the story of Francis Hoyt and what he has done and what he will do if not apprehended, how he insults every person who believes in law and order, how he laughs in our faces because we cannot catch him, he could not refuse to help me find him, capture him, and bring him before the bar of justice.

When I disembarked from the airplane at Kennedy Airport Charlie Floyd was waiting for me at the baggage claim area. I had not seen him in almost five years but I recognized him immediately. He was wearing the very same cowboy hat and cowboy boots he was wearing when I met him in Miami five years ago. He claims he does not look like John Wayne and perhaps he is right when it comes to his facial features, but as far as I am concerned he is John Wayne, and that is probably something I would think even if he were not wearing a cowboy hat and cowboy boots.

We greeted each other with a hug. We must have made a strange pair, since I am five-foot-seven in my stocking feet and Charlie Floyd is at least six-foot-two. When I informed my wife I was going to see him she smiled and said, "Mutt and Jeff." I was not familiar with what she meant but when she explained the reference I had to smile, too.

"Good to see you again, Manny," he said.

"The feeling is very mutual, Charlie Floyd. And I am very sorry I got you up so early."

"That's okay. I'm an early riser. It's a habit I can't seem to break. Car's parked in the lot, not far from here. But I should warn you it's a bit of a drive back up to Connecticut. This time of day we shouldn't hit much traffic. Still, you can count on about an hour and a half. I guess that'll give you plenty of time to fill me in on why you're here and how you think I can help you. But maybe you ought to visit the head first."

"That sounds A-okay to me," I said, making a circle with my thumb and forefinger, something I learned from my son, Javier, when he was only three years old. "And not to worry, I have already visited, as you call it, 'the head.'"

"You drive a very nice car, Charlie Floyd," I said, as we buckled up and pulled out of the parking area.

"I like to make a good impression, Manny. No point driving around in a piece of shit when you can afford a nice ride. You been up here before?"

"Once. I came with my wife, Esther. We stayed for a long weekend. We went to the top of the Empire State Building, to the Statue of Liberty, down to Ground Zero, to Radio City Music Hall, into Central Park. We even saw a Broadway show. *Cabaret.* It was very entertaining."

"Sounds like you just about covered everything."

"It is a wonderful city though a little too noisy and messy for my taste. But my wife, who comes from a big city herself, Chicago—" he winked, "—that toddling town, found it quite enjoyable. I promised her I would bring her back some day. But today is not that day. Today I come alone to see you."

As we pulled onto the highway Charlie Floyd turned to me and said, "Okay, Manny, now's as good a time as any to tell me exactly why you're here. Tell me more about this Francis Hoyt guy, why you're looking for him and where I fit in?"

"Francis Hoyt is nothing less than a master thief, Charlie Floyd. He has been taking things that don't belong to him since he was a child. Candy from candy stores, bicycles from neighborhood children, wallets from pocketbooks of unsuspecting ladies. If there was something of value, something he wanted, he did not purchase it like the rest of us, he stole it. Over the years, he worked his way up from candy and bicycles to jewelry and now to antique silver. After years of practicing his trade he became so proficient that he was stealing hundreds of thousands of dollars' worth of jewelry a night. His modus operandi was one of genius. He would break into the homes of the wealthy at the perfect time. Dinnertime. When the wealthy homeowners were home, downstairs, enjoying their meal."

"Sounds a little crazy to me. Why the hell didn't he wait till after they went to sleep or better yet, when the house was empty? Less chance of being caught in the act, no?"

"When it comes to stealing, he is smarter than we are, Charlie Floyd. If the house was empty then perhaps all the jewelry would not be there, especially the most desired pieces. Instead, they would most likely be worn by the owners on their night out, or packed away in suitcases with them if they were on vacation. But if they were home, ah, then he knew exactly where the jewelry would be. Upstairs, in the bedroom, of course. In the early evening the family would be downstairs having dinner, watching television, playing board games, whatever families do at that time of night. The upstairs would be empty. And at dinnertime, it was far less likely that the alarm system would be activated."

"I see what you mean, Manny. This guy is obviously a thinking man's thief."

"Precisely, Charlie Floyd. And that is what makes him so successful, so dangerous, and so difficult to apprehend."

"How does he gain entry?"

"In addition to being brilliant in the art of crime, Francis Hoyt is an extremely athletic man. He climbs like a monkey, runs like a jaguar, and he is strong like a lion. To get into the houses he would climb a drainpipe, a column or a trellis. And if there were no drainpipe or trellis he would use his skills as a free climber, using mountain climbing apparatus. He is not a big man. He is only five feet four inches tall, and he weighs no more than one hundred and thirty pounds and most of that weight is comprised of muscle.

"Once inside the house, on the second floor, he knows exactly where to go and exactly what to take. He does not bother with jewelry that is fake or of dubious value. He only takes what he knows he can sell. And since most thieves are fortunate if they get ten or twenty cents on the dollar, he is very discerning as to the quality of the jewelry he steals."

"I'm impressed," said Charlie Floyd, and I could tell that he was. But there was so much more to tell him.

"He leaves absolutely no forensic evidence, Charlie Floyd. Not a fingerprint, not a hair, not a thread. He appears dressed like a ninja, all in black, with a black mask covering his entire face, except for slits for his eyes and holes just largest enough for him to breathe where his nose and mouth would be. He never comes armed. All he carries is a diamond tester to check the jewels, a long screwdriver to pop out windowpanes, and a small pen-size flashlight. He slips through second-story windows, almost always in the master bedroom and after he is done, he sometimes run for miles to get to where he parked his getaway car. Sometimes, he has been known to even take public transportation."

"If he's never been caught in the act, how do you know how he dresses, what he brings with him, how he gets away?"

"No plan is perfect, Charlie Floyd. On occasion, he has encountered his victims and they have given what description they could. And when he has encountered his victims he has always been the gentleman. When a woman once complained that he had tied her hands too tight with her husband's neckties, he loosened them. When another woman began to suffer an asthma attack, he gallantly handed over her inhalator."

"A gentleman bandit, huh?"

"Make no mistake, Francis Hoyt is no gentleman. Under the right circumstances, he is capable of violence. He has been brought in for questioning on suspicion several times. He has even spent a night or two in jail. But there has never been enough evidence to hold him for long. It is possible he never would have spent time in prison at all if he had not made one crucial mistake."

"Which was?"

"He stopped working alone."

Francis Hoyt

How many times have I said to myself, *Francis, this is the last job you're going to pull. You got enough money to last you the rest of your life. You don't have to do this anymore.*

Too many times to count. But the answer is always the same. *This is what you do, man. This is who you are. This is what you're good at. This is the one thing that distinguishes you from all the other assholes out there. This is what makes it worthwhile getting up in the morning. If not this, what?*

It's not only the job itself. Oh, no, it's much more than that. It's the planning and preparation that goes into it. And of course, most of all, there's the thrill of the actual heist. The incredible adrenaline rush I get as I enter someone else's house, uninvited. I am a shadow moving silently from one room to another, through hallways, lit and unlit. Not always knowing who or what I'm going to find. Then there is the even greater rush I get when I exit the house, a small fortune in my pocket, knowing that once again I've proven I'm smarter than the people who live in that house. Smarter than the cops who are trying to stop me. Fucking smarter than just about everybody. No matter how much money they have, I'm better than they are because I will end up with what's supposed to be theirs. And I've done it the old-fashioned way. By stealing it.

Let's be honest. That's what keeps me coming back.

It wasn't rocket science to figure out that dinnertime, when everyone was home, was the best time to strike. Counter-intuitive, sure, but it made perfect sense to me. I could climb up to the second floor with no fear of alarms going off, and little fear of anyone being anywhere but downstairs at the dinner table, enjoying their meal, conversing with family and friends. I could only imagine that because it's not like that kind of scene ever happened in my house growing up. No way. The old man grunted his way through meals. The only time he spoke was to complain about something. "Not enough salt," he'd growl. "Too much salt," he'd hiss. "The meat's tough as the sole of my shoe," he'd say as he flung it against the wall.

That kind of shit.

And my mother? Well, she kept her mouth shut and I can't say as I blamed her. She didn't want to risk saying the wrong thing, setting off the old man who more likely than not would launch into one of his tirades, bitching about us, his boss down at the construction site, local politicians, or just the whole damn world. And maybe later, after a few more drinks, if you got on his bad side—and that was just about every side he had—he might even take a swing at you. Maybe that's where I learned to be quick. My sister and me learned how to eat fast and keep our mouths shut except when asked a direct question. But that didn't happen much. Nothing normal like "what did you do in school today?" My father, he didn't give a shit. My mother, well, the dinner table, with my old man sitting across from her and with us sitting within striking distance of the back of his hand, sure wasn't the place she was going to ask questions like that which would just get a grunt or maybe a "who gives a fuck?" from him.

In the homes I "visited" as an uninvited guest, that wasn't the case. People talked to each other. They listened to each other. They valued what was being said. At least that's the way I imagined it. In the beginning, I'd sometimes crouch at the top of the stairs and try to hear what was being said. I don't know why I did. I knew every minute longer I stayed in the house upped the chances I'd be seen. I guess I just wanted to hear what normal dinner conversation sounded like. People connecting with each other in normal ways. No shouting. No sullen silences. The only connection that happened in my house was when my old man landed a smack.

I got a kick out of imagining what it would be like the next night, after they realized their home had been invaded and their valuables taken. Then they'd really have something to talk about. I had violated them. I had upset their perfect lives. What I'd done to them would reverberate in so many ways. Things would never be the same. They would never come into that house again without wondering if they were alone. What I had done would leave a lasting impression. That's the part I especially liked. The part where I'd become an integral part of their lives. Someone they would remember forever. I would be a story they would tell their friends and family. In a way, that would make me immortal.

The goal, of course, was to avoid people, avoid confrontation, avoid the risk someone would get a look at me and could pick me out of a lineup. I wasn't there to hurt anyone. They never did anything to me. They just had what I wanted.

Not that I couldn't handle myself if trouble came my way. Sure, I'm on the small side, but you mess with me you're gonna be sorry you did. I did a little wrestling in high school. I was too small to do anything else, like baseball or basketball, even though I could have. But in wrestling they had weight categories and even at a measly hundred and twenty pounds, I fit right in.

I worked out and practiced hard because I wanted to be good at something. No. Not just good at something. I wanted to be the best. I wanted to stand out. I wanted those fuckin' high school snobs to look at me and say, "That's Francis Hoyt. The wrestler. He's fuckin' state champ." I loved it when I pinned some asshole and heard "one, two, three," and that slapping sound on the mat that signaling victory. I even got good enough to go to the state's. Got all the way to the semifinals and then got beat by this kid. Not because he was better than me—I should have whipped his ass—but because he had better coaching. But I held my own and figured the next year I'd just work that much harder and then I'd pin that sonuvabitch or anyone else I faced and I'd hear that slap of victory again.

There was no next year for me. I lost interest. I quit school. Make no mistake, I was good. Good enough to win it all, if I'd kept at it. Good enough to be the best damn wrestler in the damn state. But I had other things to occupy my time. Something I had a natural knack for. Something I could be the best ever at.

Listen, I know I've got a lot of anger in me—I don't need a shrink to tell me that—but I'm not a violent guy by nature. It's always a last resort. But sometimes you got to go there. You might have to prove a point or get an advantage, or protect yourself. That's when violence is necessary. And when it is, I'm not afraid to use it.

I'm not stupid. Violence can wind up backfiring on you by raising the stakes and calling attention to yourself. That's not something you want. You want to be invisible. You want to blend in, not stand out. So, I don't go out of my way to get into a fight. But if I have to, I can hold my own against anybody. I don't fight clean. I take any advantage I can get. I hurt the other guy before he can hurt me. That's what got me through my time in the joint. I think quick, I act quick. No one messed with me once they found out it they might lose an eye or get a nose busted. Respect. That's what I got. That's what I earned.

When I first got to the joint some low-life wise-ass said, "Hey, Shorty, welcome to my world." I can read between the lines. I knew what that meant. But I wasn't going to be anyone's doll-baby, so the first chance I got I confronted the dude in the yard, who was maybe half a foot taller than me and twice as wide, and said in a nice even voice, but in a tone everyone around me could hear, "Don't you ever fuckin' call me Shorty." Then I ripped into him and wound up kicking the crap out of him. No one ever called me "Shorty" again.

I remember the look on my old man's face the first time I

stood up to him. I was what, maybe fifteen, sixteen, and I'd done something to piss him off, like maybe look at him the wrong way. That's all it took. He was drunk, as usual, so his reflexes weren't the best. I saw his hand ball into a fist and he started to bring it up. I was way too quick for him. Instead of running away, like I usually did, I just stood there. I watched his hand, which seemed to move in slow motion. When it was no more than six inches from my face I ducked to the side. He lost his balance and as he fell forward I socked him on the cheek with a right, then, as he started to fall like a fucking tree in the forest, I punched him back with a left.

I didn't hurt him much, even though I wanted to. But the shock of my fighting back was much worse than the blows themselves. From that day on, the sonuvabitch never raised a hand to me and I learned a valuable lesson. Fear is the best offense *and* best defense. You don't necessarily have to use force, you just have to make sure the other guy knows you're not afraid to do whatever it takes to win. That's how you established dominance and control.

Once inside the house I'm careful to make sure I'm not heard or seen. But you can't make the mistake of thinking you can control everything all the time. The unexpected can happen. Like the time that little girl, hell, she couldn't have been more than seven or eight, popped out of her room dressed in her pajamas holding onto her little Barbie doll. She probably thought I was the fuckin' boogeyman of her worst nightmares. She takes one look at me and screams. I already had the goods, so all I had to do was get out of there quick, and the quickest way was diving through an open window at the end of the hall. I landed on my feet, on the roof of the porch, then shimmied down the column and in the darkness, I ran the mile and a half through backyards and empty lots to where my car was parked, jewels worth a quarter of a million dollars stuffed in my pockets.

You're nothing if you don't learn from your mistakes and from then on, I always wore a black ski mask.

I'm always a gentleman. I'm not there to frighten or intimidate anyone. I'm a professional. I'm there to do a job, to get the goods and get out. I don't carry a weapon. That only leads to trouble. If you carry you've got to be prepared to use it and someone's bound to get hurt.

That time in Florida where I wound up getting pinched just proved my point.

After I got out of the joint, I swore I'd go straight. I probably meant it at the time. But a week later I was at it again. Only now, evolving like one of those creatures that slithered up from the ocean to dry land, I drastically changed my way of doing business.

Charlie Floyd

I'm an early riser. Probably the result of way too many years getting to work by 8:00 a.m. That's when the office was quietest, a time when I found I could get the most work done because no one was around to distract me. That or staying late, after eight o'clock in the evening, when you could fire a cannon in that place and hit no one except maybe me. Focus. I needed complete focus. Time to think, to plan, to get into the mind of whoever I was chasing after. Time to understand what they did, how they did it, why they did it, and what they might do next.

I showered then headed down to the kitchen. Manny's door was closed. I figured he was still asleep and there was no reason to wake him. I'd just started the coffee brewing when Manny, dressed in a seersucker suit and polka-dot tie, his black hair even blacker than usual, as if he'd applied some product or it was still wet from the shower, appeared at the doorway. His attire was in stark comparison to my faded blue sweatpants, a maroon UConn T-shirt with small holes at the shoulders, my hair rumpled, my face reflecting two days straight of not having shaved. Maybe Manny was right. Maybe I did need something to get me the hell out of the house. I was probably one step away from getting a cat to keep me company and we all know what that leads to.

"Ah, there is nothing quite like the smell of fresh coffee in the morning, Charlie Floyd. Good morning, my friend."

"And good morning to you, too. You know, Manny, we usually don't dress for meals around here. Every day is casual Friday at casa Floyd."

"Today we are going to work. This is the way I dress when I go to work. When I play, maybe I dress like you, but today is a momentous day. It is the first day of our investigation."

"Okay, I hear you. Sit down. How about something to eat? I can rustle up some eggs. Or I think I've got cold cereal up there in the cabinet. An English muffin? If you've got a hankering for fruit, though, I'm afraid you're in the wrong place."

He smiled. "Just coffee, thank you very much."

"My grandma used to say breakfast was the most important meal of the day."

"I am sure your grandmother was a very smart woman, Charlie Floyd, but I am just not very hungry at the crack of dawn. I must work up a hunger before I am ready to eat."

"To be honest, she wasn't all that smart. She just had an awful lot of advice to hand out, most of it pretty useless. You could've slept in. We don't punch a time clock around here."

"No. We have work to do. The sooner we start the sooner we will catch Francis Hoyt and I can return home."

Before I turned in last night Manny handed me a folder. "Bedtime reading," he called it. It was filled with pages of information about Francis Hoyt and his illustrious career. It went all the way back to petty thievery when he was a kid. Manny had put this dossier together all by himself and it was quite impressive.

At first, I was reluctant to get involved but after reading up a little on Hoyt—sleep sabotaged me before I could get halfway through—I was hooked. It wasn't even for the reward from the insurance companies that Manny mentioned before he turned in. I didn't even ask Manny how much it was. I didn't care, even though Manny insisted it would be all mine. I protested but he explained, "I am on the job, Charlie Floyd, therefore it would not be proper for me to have a financial gain for simply doing the job I am paid to perform."

There was no arguing with Manny. I tried, but he kept shaking his head and saying, "The money is all yours, Charlie

Floyd. All yours. For me, it is enough to put an end to Francis Hoyt's life of crime."

Truth is, I could use the money. The dough I was getting from my state pension wasn't all that much. And there were things I wanted to do, like travel, maybe even purchase a small boat. But Manny was right. Even more important, I needed something to get me out of bed every morning, other than reading the headlines in the newspaper and watching Matt Lauer interview the latest movie star who spends his or her off-screen time feeding the hungry in Africa. Manny, my little Cuban angel from heaven, was giving me that reason.

And you know what? Seeing Manny standing there in the kitchen, all dressed up and ready to go, suddenly made me lose my appetite for breakfast. And so, instead of eating, Manny and I sat across from each other at the kitchen table over coffee and hatched a plan of action.

"It seems to me there are three ways we can go. One, we catch him in the act. Unlikely, from what I've read and what you've told me. Two, we pick up his trail via breadcrumbs he leaves around. And three, we find someone to roll over on him."

"That is all very true, Charlie Floyd. As for your number one, let me tell you a story. It is not my story, but it is one told to me by a police officer in New Jersey who became all too familiar with Francis Hoyt. There were a number of robberies in a very wealthy neighborhood in his town. All of them bore the unmistakable imprint of Francis Hoyt. This, by the way, was before he went to prison, before he changed his m.o. So, the detective on the case managed to convince the local chief of police to assign a team of officers to stakeout the neighborhood one evening, thinking they would catch Francis Hoyt in the act. It was a Thursday evening and for the past three Thursday evenings Francis Hoyt had broken and entered houses, making off with hundreds and thousands of dollars' worth of jewelry. That, as you know, Charlie Floyd, constitutes a pattern. Human beings are creatures of habit and they assumed that since

Francis Hoyt is human he would strike again on a Thursday evening. And so, a dozen or more police officers were positioned throughout a twelve-block radius. The night passed quietly, seemingly without incident. There were no signs of any illegal activity. Evidently, or so they believed, Francis Hoyt had moved on to greener pastures. And yet, the next morning three different homeowners reported to the authorities that their houses had been broken into and that all together almost a quarter of a million dollars' worth of jewelry was missing. The homes were all within that twelve-block radius where the police were waiting for Francis Hoyt to appear."

"Jesus H. Christ. What is this guy, the Invisible Man?"

"No, Charlie Floyd, Francis Hoyt is no superhero and he does not have super powers. This is just one example of how good he is at what he does, how meticulous and adept he is."

"Which brings up something you said early on. The part about Hoyt spending time in the can. I'm afraid I didn't get through all the paperwork you handed me last night, so I didn't quite make it up to that point in his career. What was that all about?"

"It was the one time he did not work alone. That is what did him in."

"The story, Manny. The story."

"Francis Hoyt became involved with a New York City fence who was connected to the mob. The mob was, of course, in due time informed of his amazing exploits and naturally they came to admire not only his style but also his remarkable productivity. They asked him to mentor two of their own people. At first, Francis Hoyt wisely refused. But it did not take long for him to realize that it was not in his best interest to refuse the entreaties of the mob, to bite the hand that was feeding him, so to speak. And so finally, albeit reluctantly, he gave in to their demand.

"He agreed to take along two young thugs on one of his jobs, to tutor them in the fine art of high-end burglary. Unfortunately, he was not aware that one of them arrived armed. As I have mentioned, Francis Hoyt himself never carries much more than a screwdriver and a flashlight, neither of which he would ever use as a weapon. However, on this particular night something went terribly wrong. If he had been alone there is little if any chance the homeowners would have known he was on the premises, but having two unskilled thugs with him, well, it was inevitable that one of them would clumsily announce their presence. Perhaps he knocked something over. Or stumbled. Or spoke in a voice louder than a whisper. In any case, the owner of the house must have heard something and he came upstairs where he found them in the bedroom, just as they were helping themselves to the contents of his wife's jewelry box. He grabbed for a shotgun he kept in the closet. There was a struggle. One of the men with Francis Hoyt panicked, pulled out his revolver and shot the poor fellow."

"Jesus," I said.

"There is no doubt in my mind that if Francis Hoyt had been alone he would not have been heard. But even if he had been he would simply have made his escape, with or without the jewelry. No one would have been injured. Fortunately, the wound was not fatal, but upon hearing the sound of the pistol going off, the man's wife, who was still downstairs, set off the alarm and within moments the police arrived. The two men with Francis Hoyt panicked. While he went out the window they ran downstairs and went out the backdoor. In less than an hour the police tracked two of them down. They arrested them and one of them not only implicated Francis Hoyt but also provided them with enough information so that they could find him and arrest him as well. They also agreed to testify against him for a lighter sentence. At first, they tried to throw the blame on him for the shooting, but the homeowner knew exactly who had pulled the trigger and that it was not Francis Hoyt. But now, for the first time in his life, the police could make a case against him. He was tried and convicted because, as you know, he was held responsible for the shooting even though he did not pull the trigger. He spent almost two years in prison for that offense."

"That's not a lot of time for manslaughter."

"It was a first offense and although Francis Hoyt had been arrested several times he had never been convicted of anything, so he had a clean record."

"Obviously, his time in the slammer did nothing to convince him to go on the straight and narrow path."

"No, it did not. When he was finally released on parole, he swore he would never rob again. But that was a lie. Instead, he simply changed his modus operandi. He gave up his plan of breaking into homes at dinnertime. His days of stealing jewelry were behind him. He began a whole new career, a career that has been so successful he has never been apprehended."

"And we're going to change that, aren't we, Manny?"

"Yes, Charlie Floyd, we are most certainly going to change that."

Francis Hoyt

I've been to prison and, news flash, I don't want to go back. Yeah, been there, done that.

That didn't mean when I got out I was going to stop doing what I do. It just meant I was going to learn how to do it *better.* Only a fool or an insane person doesn't learn from his mistakes, and I may be many things but fool or insane person isn't among them.

Besides, why give up something you're so damn good at? Something that makes you stand apart from everyone else. Something that gives you...status. Hey, that's what America's all about, isn't it? Excellence. Being the best you can be. Winning. Making money. That's it in a nutshell. Being the best and money. That's how people judge you. That's how we judge ourselves. Isn't that in the Declaration of Independence? Yeah, we learned that in school. "Life, liberty, and the pursuit of happiness." Stealing shit makes me happy. I'm just following what the Founding Fathers wanted me to do.

So, there wasn't a chance in hell I was going straight, not that I was going to tell them that. I sat there in front of that parole board and lied my ass off.

"Yes, sir, I know what I did was wrong. I know I hurt so many people and I'm sorry for it. Real sorry. I know I'm capable of being a better man. I am a better man. There is no way I ever want to see the inside of a jail again."

What a load of shit. Hey, can you see me putting on a suit and tie and going to a fucking office every day? Yeah, right.

That wasn't going to happen. Stealing was what I did and what I did good. Now I'd just have to learn how to do it even better.

The problem was this: how to keep taking other people's shit while at the same time minimizing the possibility of someone coming in on me while I'm in the act. That's what happened when I hooked up with those two fuckin' mob clowns. Amateurs. They fucked up and I paid the price. Not once, in all the years I'd been doing this, even when I was first starting out, did I ever call attention to myself and run the risk of being seen. That kid who came out of her room that night, well, I couldn't help that. Shit happens, right? But even then, no harm no foul. You know why? Because I was prepared for things going wrong. I'd gone over every possible contingency in my head. Nothing was going to take me by surprise. There was nothing I didn't anticipate. I knew chances were someday I'd get caught in the act, but I knew I'd keep my cool and deal with it. Not those mental defectives. Even after I did everything I could to train them they still didn't know what the fuck they were doing. And dammit, I knew they'd screw up. But in the end, it was me who screwed up by letting them tag along. I didn't have a choice. They had me by the short hairs. I needed the mob to fence my swag. Besides, you don't want to cross people like that or you'll find yourself a bloated body floating in the East River, or dumped in the Jersey or Florida swamp. So, against my better judgment, I took them along. I paid the price.

I told those assholes over and over again not to bring weapons. What was I supposed to do, fucking frisk them when we met up? If I'd known they were packing they never would have got out the fucking door. There's a reason I have a strict no weapons policy. Someone once said, if you show a gun in the first act it has to go off in the second act. And if you pack heat, chances are eventually you're going to use it. Or someone else will. That's what happened. And I was the one who wound up paying the price.

There's a time and a place for violence, but not in someone

else's home. Not when it can blow back on me like it did. That wasn't going to happen again. From now on, no more fucking partners, and no fucking weapons. Armed robbery isn't my thing. I'll leave that to the brainless, no-neck punks who don't know any better.

I put hours and hours into my craft. I research my targets. I know more about them, what they do, and how they live have than they do. I know the layout of the house. I know where they keep their valuables. I spend hours and hours casing the house before a heist. I know who lives in the house. I know who goes in and who goes out of the house. I know when they go in and when they go out. I'm no low-life, degenerate, small-time, drug-addicted crook.

After I got out of the joint, I realized I had to limit the possibility of any contact with my victims. That meant no more dinnertime robberies. No more climbing up the side of a house to gain access to the second floor. I would miss that part, the athleticism of it, but I still had to keep in shape. I'm over forty now and, like any athlete, my prime is in the rearview mirror. But the truth is, and I ain't bragging, I'm in better shape now than I was at twenty-five. That coupled with experience made me a very effective thief.

When I was a kid I read a book about the great Houdini. "Now you see it, now you don't." And what you see isn't always what's there. I saw a lot of myself in him. He was the best at what he did. No one could touch him, no one could figure out how he did what he did. He was always in fucking A-plus shape, right up till the time he died from that sucker punch in the gut. Houdini is my idol, and like with all idols, my goal is to learn from him and surpass him. He let his guard down and that's what did him in. That ain't gonna happen to me.

I would strike in the dead of night, when everyone was asleep. I would never venture up to the second floor again. That meant I had to forget about jewelry. Instead, I had to find something valuable that was kept downstairs, something I would have easy access to, something that was left out in the open.

The answer was simple: silver. It was easy to spot and easy to move. I could either have it melted down and got the value of the silver, or even better, if it was antique silver with a pedigree, I could peddle it outside the country for big bucks. I'd still need a fence, but with better merchandise I could demand a better split.

I spent days researching silver. Once I was finished I knew everything there was to know about this precious metal. I was an expert at telling the good shit from the plated. I knew which pieces had value beyond the silver content and with them I would be stealing history. The first time I got a Paul Revere piece in my hands I felt an honest-to-God electrical jolt.

And by the time I finished teaching myself all I needed to know, I was ready to begin a new life.

I was a born-again thief.

Charlie Floyd

My mom used to say, "Man proposes, God disposes," which was just her way of saying you can make plans all you want, but they usually mean shit, so you'd better be prepared to think on your feet and go with your instincts, so there's always the risk of failure.

A man who is afraid to fail is a man who never succeeds. That's not my mom, it's me.

I hate to fail. It doesn't happen often but when it does you don't want to be around me. I snap at people. I throw things. Sometimes I go to a dark place, a very dark place in my head. But I've learned to stay on top of it and on those rare occasions when I do fail it only spurs me to try harder. I failed plenty when I was working in law enforcement, especially in the beginning when I didn't know what the hell I was doing. But failure and learning from that failure only made me a better investigator.

Always give yourself options. Figure out all the possible scenarios, then choose the most likely and start there. If that doesn't pan out, move on to the next option. It's not rocket science, just good, old-fashioned, tedious, often boring, police work.

I grabbed a legal-size yellow pad and wrote while Manny and I chucked ideas against the wall to see what stuck. We wound up with several options and scenarios. We were confident one of them, or maybe a combination, would wind up in us putting Francis Hoyt where he belonged.

By the time we'd finished, we had a pretty comprehensive list along with a tentative division of labor. In the beginning, we would work on our own. But as we got closer to the target we'd team up. Two separate lines eventually intersecting and becoming one headed in the same direction.

First, I would check with my sources in the state attorney general's office. I still had a few friends over there. Not many, but a few. And maybe they weren't exactly friends, but they were still talking to me. It's not that I was gone long enough for there to be a lot of turnover. More like I wasn't exactly a favorite son over there. I guess I'm an acquired taste that wasn't acquired by too many people. I stepped on toes. I pissed people off. I drove some of them crazy. I was a loose cannon who refused to do things according to procedure. Did I sometimes cross the line? Sure. But I got results. The way I figured, proper procedure was what I made it. Sometimes, I'm sure I came off as an arrogant son-of-a-bitch. That's probably because at times that's what I was. Did it bother me? Not really. I knew I was good at what I did so why shouldn't everyone else? But I thought that because I *was* good at what I did. Make that very good. But I'm not one of those full-of-himself, douchebag megalomaniacs. There were some things I was piss poor at. Not a lot. But a few. Like paperwork. Like working as part of a team. Like bowing to my superiors. Probably because I didn't think there was anyone superior to me. But the proof was in the pudding. I was an ace at nailing people who deserved to be nailed. I worked harder than everyone else. I gave a shit. Some-times, that's all it takes and you'd be surprised at how many people don't.

To begin with, my job was to obtain as much information as I could on Hoyt's activities in this neck of the woods. Hoyt had worked the area previously, so he had roots here, as well as in New York, New Jersey, and Massachusetts. This meant there was a file on him in all these states. I'd look for anyone who'd worked his cases. Manny claimed that if he wanted access to that kind of information he'd have to go through all kinds of bureaucratic red tape and he didn't want to waste the time or the effort. I couldn't blame him. That's the part of the job I hated. The red tape. The petty bullshit. Lazy, frightened people protecting their asses. State authorities don't always cooperate with each other. Jealousy and spite can rear its ugly head. That's where I came in. Manny was sure I could get the kind of cooperation he couldn't. At least in Connecticut. He was probably right. I knew the right buttons to push and I wasn't afraid to push them.

While I worked my sources, Manny would head down to the city to see what he could sniff out. We knew Hoyt doesn't work in a haphazard way. He chooses his targets very carefully, which means hours of research. Manny, who was far more used to this coming from the world of academia, would check out the libraries, where Hoyt was likely to go to find information about the richest families in the area. According to Manny he used sources like *Who's Who* and architectural magazines, as well as periodicals like *House and Garden, People*, and *Entertainment Weekly.* Anything that ran information about the life-styles of the rich and famous. These are the kinds of people I've dealt with people my whole life. The privileged and the entitled. They're vain and they're stupid and most of them, especially the ones with "new" money, like to flaunt their wealth and status. I have a hard time feeling sorry for them when they get robbed, unlike the poor, working slob who's living from paycheck to paycheck. Violent crimes against them piss me off, but I can't get all hot and bothered about these rich people who advertise their wealth and are shocked when someone wants to take it from them. Still, they're victims of crimes and they deserve to be protected and the people who commit these crimes, people like Hoyt, aren't heroes. They're just a little smarter than your average hit 'em over the head or shoot 'em stick-up artists. But that doesn't mean they get a free pass from me, and certainly not from Manny.

"Why wouldn't he use libraries in the towns he's planning to hit?" I asked.

"Because, my good friend, Francis Hoyt is smarter than that. He would more likely use libraries far from the areas he plans to work. Somewhere he would be anonymous and could blend in with the crowd."

"New York City."

"Yes, New York City," Manny echoed with a big, fat Cuban smile on his face. "But he will never steal from apartments, only houses. That is why he has never been active in New York City, though he spends a lot of time there. New York City is where we will find people who know him."

"Women?"

Manny nodded.

"Over the years, he has had many girlfriends. He wines them and he dines them then he leaves them. But only after he has made sure they are loyal to him. I have found several over the years, but none of them will speak of him. Most will not even admit that they knew him. We will try to find the ones he has up here and perhaps, between the two of us, we can persuade them to help us."

He winked.

After we'd filled five legal size sheets with notes, I made a copy for each of us, plus one more for a file I started, then I drove Manny to the train station.

"Do you think perhaps I should rent my own vehicle, Charlie Floyd?" he asked as we pulled into the parking area.

"Not necessary, Manny. I don't mind chauffeuring you around."

He flashed a smile. "I have never had a chauffeur before. But I like the sound of it. Something tells me we are going to work very well together."

"You think?"

"Yes, I do think."

"I should have asked this before, but do you have any solid evidence Hoyt is actually up here yet?"

He shook his head. "Nothing solid. But he is either here or

he is on his way. Of that, we can be sure. We are all creatures of habit, Charlie Floyd, even Francis Hoyt. He is either here or on his way here. I feel it in my bones. Even the unpredictable are predictable in their unpredictability."

"Careful, Manny, you're coming dangerously close to confusing the hell out of me. I have to tell you, I'm not all that good with abstract thinking. Nearly flunked philosophy in college. And don't ask me why I even bothered."

He laughed. "Even my wife says that sometimes she does not understand me, even when I am speaking English."

"A common problem among married couples. My wife didn't understand me, either. That's probably why she's not my wife anymore."

"There is no danger of that happening to me. I love Esther and she loves me in return."

"Don't get me wrong. I wasn't saying there was. I'm sure you're very happily married and you're going to stay that way. Sometimes it's best if there isn't too much understanding between men and women, if you know what I mean."

He nodded solemnly. "I am afraid I do."

I pulled up in front of the station and Manny hopped out. He had a briefcase with him in which I assumed he had all kinds of information about Hoyt, including photographs he'd probably show around. He also had a list of likely libraries Hoyt might visit to do his research. The Mid-Manhattan Branch at 41st and Fifth Avenue, and the Main Branch across the street were on the list, as was the 68th Street Branch off First Avenue, and the Society Library on 79th Street, off Madison Avenue. I doubted Manny would get to all of them in one day. But there was no hurry. For the next five months at least, according to Manny, Hoyt would be up north.

"Give me a call and let me know what train you're making back and I'll pick you up."

"There is no need for that, Charlie Floyd."

"You're my guest. We're in this thing together now. It's like we're an old married couple."

He grinned, flashing those pearly whites.

"You mean I will have to call if I cannot make it home for dinner."

Manny made a joke. The first one I remember him making. So, I laughed. "Exactly."

"I can stay at a hotel. I do not want to impose on your privacy."

"I've got more than enough room. You're staying with me. End of discussion."

He smiled. "Thank you."

"One more thing before you go."

"Of course."

"When we find him, and we will, who's going to be good cop and who's going to be bad cop?"

"With Francis Hoyt, we will both have to be bad."

Francis Hoyt

Time to head north. Following the pigeons, I like to call it.

But this time there was another reason to get out of town. A cop. Some dumb-ass Miami cop named Perez. He got a bug up his ass for me. Who knows why? He almost got me last week only I was too quick for him. Still, he got his hands on me and I could see it in his face. He knew exactly who I was and what I do. And he had one big, fat hard-on for me.

I don't need that shit. I finally got my dough from Artie, so it was time to saddle up and get out of Dodge.

I've got a soft spot in my heart for trains and buses. Sure, planes get you there faster but when you fly you leave a big, fat paper trail. What with the fucking Muslims and their 9/11 bullshit, Homeland Security is all over everyone's ass, so you can't just buy a ticket and pay for it in cash. Or else, red lights go off and bells ring. You've got to use a credit card. Breadcrumb. The ticket has your name on it. Breadcrumb. It has when you left, when you'll arrive and where you land. More breadcrumbs. Jesus, you might as well provide the cops with your fuckin' itinerary.

I could drive but I don't own a car. Never have. Not even as a teenager. My old man wouldn't let me near his wreck, a 1979 Chevy pickup. What he thought I'd do to that old heap that hadn't already been done to it beats the hell out of me. He was a mean sonuvabitch and he loved denying me things. You think that's the reason I take things without asking? Maybe. Who the hell cares? I do what I do and let some asshole shrink try to figure out why.

My old man got a kick out of saying no. When I was a kid, I cried and I cried even harder when I saw that big, stupid smile on his face when I wanted something and he said no, I couldn't have it. It didn't matter what it is, the answer was no. Even before I got the words out of my mouth, I knew what the answer would be. And he'd laugh at me. Like it was some kind of big joke.

When I got older I got revenge.

"I'm not letting you near that fucking truck," he said whenever I asked to use it, in that deep voice of his, loud enough so you could hear him halfway down the block. He'd even say it twice, in case I didn't get the point.

I got the last laugh, though. Stole his keys after he came home drunk as a skunk one night. Soon as he hit the couch, I grabbed those keys, took the car, and ran it into a fucking ditch. *On purpose.* I brought the keys home, put 'em back on his dresser where he always kept them, and he never knew the fucking difference. You should have seen the look on his face when he went out the next day to drive it to work and it wasn't there. "Who the fuck stole my truck," he yelled. This time it was me who was laughing.

Cops didn't find it till the next day. Cost him almost a grand to put it back together. My old man got even meaner for the next few days, but it was worth it, man. He never did find out I was the one who stole it and ran it into that ditch. But you better believe if I'd been at his deathbed just before he was ready to croak I would have told him just to see the goddamn look on his goddamn face.

Owning a car means paying for insurance. Another breadcrumb. They break down, you gotta fix 'em. That's a responsibility I don't want or need. Another breadcrumb. I don't rent cars, neither. You need a credit card for that and they take down your driver's license info.

That doesn't mean I don't have access to motor vehicles. I do. They're just not mine, at least on paper they're not. I have

40

one of my girlfriends buy them, with my dough, of course, and they're registered in their name.

Women. I can get them to do almost anything. Okay, call them girlfriends if you want. That's what they'd like to think. And listen, that's how I treat them. Good. Real good. Like girlfriends should be treated. I've never had any complaints in that department. At least they haven't complained to me. Maybe that's 'cause they know if they did they'd be put back out on the street, where I found them. Let's face it, they're pretty much disposable. I mean, it's not like I'm gonna settle down with any of them. They are a means to an end. None of them knows about the other, none of them live in the same city. I make sure of that. I try not to have more than two at a time. Too confusing. Besides, women are trouble and more than one woman doesn't mean double trouble it means four times as much trouble. I know this makes it sound like I'm an asshole, like I hate women, but you know what, I wouldn't argue with you there.

I don't buy cheap crap or used cars. Brand-fucking-new cars, that's all I buy. Evie's even got one of those new hybrids. That's what she wanted so that's what she got. I believe in quality. You buy shit it turns to shit. Cars aren't the only thing I give them. Clothing, jewelry, we eat at the best restaurants, and, oh yeah, maybe the most important thing, drugs. They are dependent on me for many things, but good drugs may be the most important. I know, that makes me even more of an asshole, but the truth is who's getting hurt? It's not like I stick needles in their arms. Some guys buy their women drinks, I prefer to supply them with the kinds of drugs that give them a buzz, make them happy. They're happy, I'm happy. Yeah, sure, it's a way of controlling them. I don't deny that. And it's not my fault if sometimes it goes beyond recreation. Don't put that shit on me. It's not like I'm the one who got them hooked. That's on them. You gotta have self-control if you're going to get anywhere in life and if they don't have it, well it's too fucking bad.

They're recreational drugs. None of the real dangerous, hard shit like meth or crack or maybe worst of all, horse. Do I really want to hang out with some strung-out junkie with holes up and down her arms?

Me? I don't do drugs at all. I don't drink anymore, either. Gave up that and smoking a long time ago, too. Not because I didn't enjoy those things, and not because they were "bad" for me. It's because they were getting in the way of doing my job. I need all my senses sharp. I need to be at my best at all times. My mind has to be clear, my body ready to do anything I ask it to do. You get messed up with that kind of shit and it affects your performance.

My girls let me use the cars whenever I need them. If there's trouble and I have to dump the car, I just tell them to report it stolen. I'll clean it up, make sure there are no fingerprints or anything else can lead back to me, then I leave it someplace where it won't be found right away. Once, I even got a little creative and torched one of them. Hell, let some damn insurance company pony up the dough to replace it.

I have false identities, plenty of them, and I use them if I have to. But I don't like to go to that well too often because the cops, the smarter ones, eventually pick up on that and the identities become worthless. They can also make up a trail easier to follow than if you use your own name. To make them work for you, you're best having dozens of them. And who wants to keep up with that? But I have to admit I do like coming up with aliases. Ricky Miranda. Saul Goodman. Tony Leonetti. Philip Armstrong. Paul Nowicki, Kenny Walsh, Mikey Leiman. Those are some of them. I like to hit as many different ethnic groups as I can. Sometimes I just use a variation of my name, sometimes by giving myself a middle initial. And I like playing around with different poses for the driver's licenses. But one thing I don't fool around with is fake passports. First off, that's getting tougher and tougher to pull off because of 9/11 and Homeland Security. You don't want to fuck with those dudes. Besides, because I've done time I'm pretty sure I'm on some kind of fucking "can't leave the country" list.

I'm not a big fan of disguises, which isn't to say I haven't used a few over the years. But if I do, they're usually simple. Sunglasses. A moustache. A beard. A hat. The simpler, the better. You'd be amazed at how one little thing, if it's prominent enough, can change your appearance enough so no one can recognize you without it. The human brain is fallible. It can be played with. Magicians know that. Houdini knew it better than anyone. Today, Penn and Teller and that Copperfield asshole who made the Statue of Liberty disappear know it. Thieves know it too, at least the good ones do. Now you see it, now you don't. Something as simple as a moustache, beard, sunglasses, or hat can draw a potential witness's attention enough so that's all they see. The more they see, the less they really see.

Bottom line: I'm not a slug. I don't leave a trail, paper or otherwise. My footprint is nonexistent.

I left Miami Thursday, May 14th. Coincidentally, it was my old man's birthday. The son-of-a-bitch croaked nearly fifteen years ago, but the bastard is seared into my head and May 14th doesn't come without me thinking about him. He's the demon that keeps on giving.

Birthdays were never a big deal around our house anyway. The old man said parties were for girls, not that he ever threw one for my sister, either.

I once asked my mother why I never got a birthday party and she said, "Francis, your birthday is in August. All your friends were away in August. That's why we didn't throw you a party. But don't you remember that party we gave you when you were three years old?"

"Yeah, sure, Ma, I can remember everything that ever happened to me. You know, I'm one of those genius savants that can remember stuff all the way back to the womb."

"Don't you remember? You had a wonderful time. You had a party hat and you had one of those blowing noisemaker things and you had a cake and you even tried to blow out the candles." She laughed. "I had to help you because you couldn't reach the candle on the other end of the cake. Don't you remember that?"

"You got any pictures, Ma?"

"I don't think we had a camera back then, Francis. But I wouldn't lie to you."

Yeah, right. She wouldn't lie to me. That's a laugh. Like no one ever lies to a kid.

I travel light. Minimal amount of clothing and I never carry my work tools with me. When I get where I'm going I buy a whole new wardrobe and anything else I need. I don't boost any of it. I'm a thief but I'm no two-bit, petty crook.

The trip north takes around twenty-eight hours. I ride the bus till I get bored. Then I hop off and find a motel for the night. The next day, same thing till I get where I'm headed. But I got no schedule. I got no one to answer to except me.

My bus left from Collins Avenue at 6:59 a.m. The route goes up through Florida, Georgia, South Carolina, North Carolina, Virginia, Washington, D.C., Maryland, New Jersey, and into the city. I read. I sleep. I listen to music. Maybe I strike up a conversation with the passenger next to me. When they ask me what I do for a living I make shit up. That's the fun part. Let's face it, I'm a damn good liar. Why shouldn't I be? I've had plenty of practice.

Charlie Floyd

I live around fifty miles outside Hartford in a little town called Sedgwick. It's what some people might call "picaresque." So picaresque it even has a town square. It also has a history, as do most small towns in New England. There was even one of those Revolutionary War battles close by. I chose it because it's near the water and because it wasn't Hartford, where I was based. There's probably more crime in Hartford than any other place in Connecticut, except maybe for New Haven, only a lot of it is the kind of crime for which we don't keep statistics. It's the kind of crime where your pockets are picked and you're nowhere near the scene of the crime. That's because Hartford, as the state capitol, is where the politicians are.

Driving up I-91 then CT-77S, depending on traffic, it can take anywhere from an hour to an hour and a half to get from Sedgwick to Hartford. One of the benefits of retirement is I can choose my time of departure, meaning I don't have to fight commuter traffic.

I was used to breezing straight through security, into the building where I had my office. Everyone knew me so I never even had to flash my ID or badge. But now that I'm just an ordinary citizen and it's been a year since I retired, the gatekeepers have changed. That means whenever I go back there, and it isn't often—usually just to drop by and chew the fat with old friends—I'm not special anymore. That means I have to go through the same rigmarole as everyone else. What hasn't changed is my ability to talk myself into (and out of) just about anything.

I didn't take it personally that the guard eyed me suspiciously. Maybe it was the cowboy boots. Or the Stetson. Whatever it was I've learned long ago not to take anything personally.

I explained who I was to the bored guard at the security station. I knew what he was thinking. He was counting the days to retirement. Been there, done that. I showed him my old ID, explained why I was carrying, and he waved me through the metal detector.

Instead of going to my old office I headed straight to the attorney general's office. I was looking for George Facinelli or, as we used to call him fondly, Georgie Porgie. He didn't seem to mind. In fact, I believe he kind of liked it. I was the one who gave him that name when I spotted him in the diner across the street digging into a big bowl of chocolate pudding. Sure enough, Georgie likes his pudding and pie. I also liked to refer to him as the oldest living assistant attorney general because he's held that position nearly twenty years through three different administrations. Georgie is a low-key, under-the-radar kind of guy, but he knows exactly where all the bodies are buried. You want to really know what's going on in the AG's office you talk to Georgie. That doesn't mean Georgie'll talk to you, though. He's discreet, which is why he's lasted so long on the job.

"What the hell are you doing here, Floyd?" he asked when he spotted me strolling toward his desk. His jacket was hanging on the back of his chair. His shirt sleeves were rolled up, the top two buttons were open, and his tie was loosened. His hair, or what he had left of it, which should be gray like the rest of us who work in this business, was dyed a weird shade of reddish brown. Somehow it looked okay on Georgie. When he stood up I noticed his belly had grown substantially in the year since I'd last seen him.

"Come here, Charlie. I'm gonna give you a great big hug, whether you like it or not."

He did. And you know something, it felt good, so I hugged

him back, not because I wanted something from him but because I actually missed the fat man. Or maybe it was the office I missed. Or the job. Well, it was something I missed, so let's just leave it at that.

Georgie's hug lingered well after he completed his embrace. Something else lingered. It was this sweet smell around his desk. Was it cinnamon?

"I've missed you, Porgie. I was in the 'hood so I figured I'd stop by and say hello."

"And feed me a line of bullshit?"

"That, too."

"As I recall you were pretty good at that."

"My specialty. What's that smell?"

He looked blank for a moment. "Oh, that. It's cinnamon."

"I thought so. What's that all about?"

He leaned in close. "I read somewhere women respond to the scent of cinnamon. It's supposed to drive them crazy. So, I went out and found this cinnamon spray and I've sprayed myself and the area around my desk for the past couple days."

"Does it work?"

He frowned. "Not yet. But I'm gonna give it some time. I'm kinda getting used to it, though I have to admit I've developed a constant urge for toast."

He looked at his watch.

"Almost time for lunch, Charlie."

"Always time for lunch, Porgie. I'm buying."

"Somehow I'm sure I'll wind up paying for it."

"You know me too well."

We wound up at Dino's, the diner across the street from the office. When the waitress, Greta, spotted Georgie and me, she broke into a wide grin. "Well, as I live and breathe, Charlie Floyd is back in town. Must mean the rodeo ain't far behind."

"Slumming," I said.

"You're in the right place for it. I just happen to have your old table available."

"I guess all those years of over-tipping is finally paying off," I said.

"Funny, that's not the way I remember it. Let's see how you do now that you're retired, Mr. Big Spender. How come you're not down in Florida at one of them century cities, with the rest of the old folks?"

"They wouldn't let me in. Said I was a menace to society."

She laughed. So did Georgie.

She led us to a table at the back of the diner. It was where she used to stash us back in the day. It wouldn't be quiet once the lunch rush arrived but it was now, since we were the only ones seated back there.

"You boys need menus?"

"Unless you've changed anything in the last year, Greta, I think we're good."

"I'd tell you boys about today's specials only we haven't got any."

"Everything's special at Dino's," said Georgie.

"Aren't you the sweet talker?" said Greta, squeezing his arm.

I ordered the turkey club. Georgie the shish kabob or as he preferred to call it, "chicken on a stick."

"So, what brings you to Dante's third circle in Hell, Charlie? I thought once you retired we'd never see you again."

"No such luck. I'm here on a…" I didn't know quite what to call it so the word that came out of my mouth was "case."

"You out on your own now?"

"I suppose I am. Ever hear of a dude named Francis Hoyt?"

"Are you kidding? Everyone around here knows him."

"I didn't."

"Let me amend that. Anyone who had anything to do with burglary and robbery knows him. I guess that was a little below your pay grade. Francis Hoyt, man, he's a fucking legend around these parts."

"How come if everyone knows who the fuck he is and what the fuck he does he's still running around free as a bird?"

Georgie smiled. "Because he's fucking Francis Hoyt, that's why. He's the crème de la crème. Why you interested in him?"

"I've been asked by someone to help find Hoyt and put him where he belongs."

"Who?"

"I can't say." I don't know why I said that. Manny hadn't asked me to keep his part in this under wraps, but I didn't think it was a good idea to broadcast his involvement.

Georgie leaned forward. "Charlie, this is Georgie Porgie you're talking to. Anything you tell me stays right here." He tapped the side of his head. "I'm a vault. Plenty of arrivals, no departures."

"I'm sorry, Georgie. I just..."

He threw his hands up. "Say no more. I understand. What are you, a private investigator now?"

I hated private dicks when I was working for the state. They just got in the way. And there was something, I don't know, disreputable about them. But I guess sometimes we become the thing we hate most. Maybe this was one of those times.

"This is totally unofficial, Georgie. I've got no professional standing now."

Georgie winked and put a forefinger to his lips. "So, how can I help?"

"I've got good reason to believe that if Hoyt isn't already here he's certainly headed this way. I need to find people who know him. His fence. His girlfriends. Anyone he works with."

"As I recall, he works alone."

"That's what I hear. But he's got to be in contact with other people. He's a thief, not a ghost."

"You know that story about that Jersey thing, right?"

"I do."

"Pretty ghost-like, if you ask me."

"Has he been active around here the last couple years?"

Georgie laughed. "He's active wherever there's money, especially old money. New York, Connecticut, New Jersey, and

Massachusetts, especially the Cape and the Vineyard. Hell, pretty much the entire Northeast coast, although I've heard stories about some Midwest break-ins that have his stamp on them. Trouble is, you never know where he's going to hit and when. He hops around like a friggin' kangaroo. But I'm no expert, Charlie. I just know what I hear."

"Know anyone who is?"

"There's a cop in Jersey who's had a number of run-ins with him. I can track down his info. And I'll dig around and see what else I can come up with."

"I'd appreciate it, Georgie."

He grinned. "It's getting to you, isn't it?"

"What?"

"Retirement. You're not the type to sit home clipping coupons. This is good for you, man. It puts you back in the game. And if I can do anything I to make that happen I will."

"Thanks, Georgie. I've gotta admit I was getting a little worried about all that free time on my hands. And let me tell you something. It isn't free. There's a price you pay in your soul for that so-called free time."

"You don't have to thank me. And you know, we really do miss you around here. You could always change your mind."

"No, I can't. I burned that bridge and there's no going back. Maybe this is my second act. But I really do appreciate you're getting that information for me."

I wasn't shining him on. I appreciated it so much that when it came time for dessert, I made Georgie order a big bowl of chocolate pudding and I even threw in a slice of pie for him to take back to the office.

Manny Perez

I am and always have been intoxicated by the aroma of libraries. They offer up the same sweet fragrance no matter where you go. It is the aphrodisiacal aroma of books, of words, of thoughts. As a child back in Havana, I found refuge there. My parents always knew where to find me after school or on a weekend. Never on the streets, playing with the other children, but rather wandering through the stacks, seeking out interesting books to read, books that would take me far away, to other places, other worlds. When I found the right one I would take it and sit in a quiet corner of the library where I would devour it. Often, I would lose track of time and my mother would have to send one of my sisters to find me. It was an easy task. They always knew precisely where I could be found.

Most of the books were, of course, in Spanish, but occasionally I would find an alluring book in English and I would sit in a corner thumbing through the pages, delighting in the sound of foreign words that elicited images of America, the America I sometimes saw in the old black and white movies, the America of my imagination. I had never visited the forbidden land, only ninety miles to the north. It was the land of our enemy, we were taught in school. Our heroes were Fidel and Che and Raoul and Lenin. But at home that was not the case. America was the Promised Land, a land where dreams came true, a land where you could be anyone you wanted to be, do anything you wanted to do. We were, in my family, capitalists trapped on an island of socialism. We dreamed of democracy. We dreamed of freedom.

My father visited the United States once. He was the guest of a person I now know to be an American gangster. How my father came to know a man such as that is simple. He worked as a waiter, then desk clerk, then night manager at the grand Hotel Nacional de Cuba. There, in the late 1940s and 1950s, he met and served men and women like George Raft, Betty Grable, Rita Hayworth, Ernest Hemingway, the Duke and Duchess of Windsor, Cesar Romero, Gary Cooper, Fred Astaire, Tyrone Power, Lucky Luciano, and Meyer Lansky, whose photograph, I am told, still graces the bar at the hotel. Those were the days when Cuba was the stopping off point for all the cruise ships from the United States. It was a romantic time, a free-wheeling time when Cuba was the playground for Hollywood celebrities and high-level members of the mob.

Like me, my father was a very social man. Like the great American humorist, Will Rogers, he never met a man (or woman) he did not like. His talent for making friends is what led him to make the rapid climb up from bus boy to hotel manager. All this changed, of course, when Fidel successfully overthrew the tyrannical butcher, Fulgencio Batista. But when Cuba's revolutionary government took over the hotel my father was relieved of his position. Cuban guests and small farmers replaced Hollywood stars, foreign royalty and American gangsters. Instead of catering to the wealthy and celebrated the hotel became the setting for the foundation of the National Revolution Militias and of the Committees for Defense of the Revolution.

In the years that followed the Revolution, the world's first cosmonaut, Yuri Gagarin, stayed at the hotel, along with Paul Sartre, Simone de Beauvoir, and Josephine Baker. But by this time my father was "retired," and therein began the long days and nights of plotting to escape the island of his birth, the island he used to love so dearly. Sadly, he never accomplished that dream. He died in 1975, when I was only five years old, leaving my mother to care for me and my two sisters.

It wasn't until 1992 that I finally fulfilled my father's dream by escaping to America along with my two sisters, only months after the death of our beloved mother.

Libraries continue to remind me of the land of my birth, but at the same time they reaffirm my love for America and democracy, where books are not banned and thought is not controlled. Someday, when Fidel and his brother, Raoul, have departed this earth, perhaps I shall return to Cuba. But then I will return only as a visitor, because America is my home now.

The first library I visited in New York City I search of a trail for Francis Hoyt was the main branch on 42nd Street and Fifth Avenue. I could have remained in those hallowed rooms for days, but I was on a mission, a mission to see if Francis Hoyt was in town and, if so, what kind of research he was doing so that we might predict where he would begin his latest reign of terror.

I moved from room to room questioning the librarians, showing them a photograph of Francis Hoyt, a mug shot taken shortly before he was incarcerated. There was not a glimmer of recognition from anyone. I even showed it to the guards and other employees of the library, but none of them remembered seeing the man in the photograph.

When I had exhausted all possibilities at the main branch I crossed the street to the Mid-Manhattan Branch, where I went from floor to floor, showing the photograph. The result was the same. No one recognized him.

It was lunch time and although I was tempted to keep to my mission I heard my wife Esther's voice inside my head, "Manny, you know how you get when you don't eat. Your blood sugar falls and your temper rises." Esther is always right and that is why I listen to her, even if it is only to her voice in my head. I found a coffee shop where I ordered my favorite, a bacon, lettuce and tomato sandwich on white toast, with extra mayonnaise. I like ordering a BLT, which to me sounds so American. It is the perfect combination of vegetable, fruit, and pork and when it is visited by the proper amount of mayonnaise the perfect sandwich is created. I even like the crunchy sound it makes when you bite into it. Does it sound like I enjoy my food? Indeed, I do.

By one-thirty I was on the bus up Madison Avenue, headed for the Society Library on 79th street, between Madison and Park avenues. It is a library I had never visited, only heard about, but as the bus rumbled past 72nd street, I felt in my heart that this is where my path with Francis Hoyt would finally intersect.

As it turned out, I was right.

Francis Hoyt

I bore easy. That's why as a kid I hated school. Boring teachers. Boring subjects. Boring students. Boring. Boring. Boring. Hour after hour with nothing much happening. Just a lot of bullshit. I like to get up and move around. School? That was just a bunch of sitting around on your ass listening to some moronic teacher who didn't know shit about what life was really like.

I cut school all the time. Only got caught once or twice. I think the teachers were happy to get me the hell out of there. When he found out, my old man whipped my ass good, even though he couldn't have cared less about my cutting school. Any excuse to beat the shit out of me worked for him. He certainly wasn't any role model, if that's what fathers are supposed to be. He dropped out of school by the tenth grade. That's because he was dumb as shit. Me, I did well even in the classes I missed. I liked books. I liked reading. I just didn't like what they were giving us to read in school. Silas Fucking Marner? Ivanhoe? Tess of the Fucking D'Urbervilles? You gotta be kidding.

I liked knowing more than anyone else, especially the teachers. So why did I have to waste my time listening to a bunch of boring shit taught by a bunch of boring old maids? I kept myself busy with other shit, shit that would put money in my pocket.

By the time the bus pulled into Charleston, South Carolina I'd had about enough. My legs ached and the old lady who got on in Savannah and sat next to me wouldn't shut the fuck up. So, I waved goodbye to Greyhound and looked for a half-decent motel to check into. It took a while, but I finally found one with the help of Yelp. I like Yelp. Only I think they ought to rate guys like me. No secret the kind of reviews I'd get when it comes to breaking into houses and stealing shit.

The motel was on the fringe of the city, which is perfect for me. Not too expensive, but not a fleabag dump either. The idea is to be as invisible as you can, always flying under the radar. It's not so much that I was afraid of someone finding me here in Charleston, but it's so easy to fall into bad habits.

When I was in the joint I read anything and everything I could get my hands on. There wasn't much else to do. A lot of stupid people say you learn how to be a better criminal when you're locked up. Think about that. Pretty ridiculous, right? I mean, what the hell can you possibly learn from some dude in the cell next to you? *He's in the cell next to you, for Chrissakes*, which means he got fucking pinched. Probably more than once. You're in the joint with fuckin' losers. If they were geniuses they wouldn't be there in the first place. Even me, I did a stupid thing by letting myself be talked into taking assholes along with me on a job. At least I learn from my mistakes. Not these dudes. Most of them are repeat offenders and they'll keep coming back because they *don't* fucking learn. They love to talk about all the shit they've done, but how far do you think I'd get listening to them?

When I was a kid my mom used to make me go to church with her. That lasted until I was maybe eight or nine. Same with Sunday school, which I didn't like any better than regular school. We had to read a whole bunch of stuff by a whole bunch of saints. I didn't pay much attention to any of it, except something this guy Thomas Aquinas once wrote. I never forgot it. I even memorized it because I figured it was an important lesson. "If a man indulges himself in murder, very soon he comes to think of robbing, and from robbing he comes to drinking and

Sabbath breaking; and from that to incivility and procrastination."

That's exactly what I mean. It's a slippery slope, man. One thing leads to another. And there are always consequences to what we do, so you have to be on your toes all the time. You gotta always be ready for something going wrong. Preparation and anticipation. Those are the keys to success. And I learned that lesson very early on.

Once I checked in, I took a walk to shake off the foul smell of that bus and get a little exercise before finding a place where I could get a decent meal. I need to keep in shape, just like any professional athlete. I let myself go, lose a step, I'm in deep shit. I'm forty-two-years-old now. That's fucking ancient for someone who does what I do the way I do it. But I hate those motherfuckers who say they like working out. I fucking hate it. But it's essential to what I do. Cops, they're rarely in shape. You should see some of them. In a footrace, I'm gonna wear them the fuck down. I can run five, six miles easy, without hardly breaking a sweat. That's because I run at least three times a week. I hate it, but I do it. I figure I keep in shape I can go at least another decade, maybe longer. Only when I can't do what I do at the level I'm doing it now will I think about quitting. Until then, I'm just gonna get better and better.

There was the smell of late spring in the air, as the trees and flowers were beginning to bloom. Honeysuckles? Maybe that was it. I used to hate that smell because it meant summer was getting closer and that meant the old man would be all over me to get a fucking job.

"Get your lazy ass off the couch," he'd yell, and if I didn't get off quick enough I knew what was coming next. The toe of his work boot or the back of his hand. Or, if he was really pissed, the belt would come off. By the time I was a teenager I was quicker than he was, especially if he'd been drinking, so he rarely landed one of those blows. But it wasn't because he wasn't trying. And if he did connect he'd start laughing, like it was funny. Like it was some kind of big joke. I fucking hated that damn laugh. It made me want to punch him right in the fucking face. Let him fucking laugh about that.

Didn't take long to realize the last place I ought to be was home, so I did what he taught me to do. I lied. I told him I had a job. It was always something he couldn't check, not that he would've ever taken the time. All he was interested in was how much money I made. He wanted all of it. "It's about fucking time you paid your way, Francis. The free fucking ride is over, kid." That's what he'd say, like I was living in some fancy hotel and we had a butler and a maid. Hotel from hell was more like it.

Every week I made sure to give him a little something just to keep him off my back, just something to keep his hand away from his belt. But the dough wasn't from the kind of work he thought I was doing. It was what I made stealing shit and selling it for whatever I could get.

At first, it was easy shit, like stealing bikes, or shoplifting from stores. But after a while I graduated to breaking into houses. At first, I didn't know what the hell I was doing and a couple times I nearly got caught. But somehow, I got it done. Maybe that's because the neighborhoods near where I grew up, nobody could afford security alarms. It's not like they had all that much to protect. And maybe that's because I did it during the day, when no one was home. I never took anything big. Maybe I'd find some cash lying around the house. Or a radio. Or some cheap costume jewelry—I wasn't going to find much of real value. I took anything that looked like it had some resale value. I didn't care how much.

I could always find someone to buy what I grabbed. I'd go to neighborhoods across town where no one knew me and try to sell it. I could get as much as fifty bucks for a good bike, one of those racing jobs with the thin tires. No one asked any questions. They didn't care if it was stolen. If they said anything about it being hot, I just told them to throw a coat of paint on the damn thing and no one would ever know the difference. I never told them my real name or where I lived, just in case the cops tracked the stolen goods down and tried to find out who sold it. I didn't really think there was much chance of that, since it was all penny ante stuff. Besides, people in my neighborhood usually didn't make it a practice of going to the cops.

Even back then I was pretty good at covering my tracks. I always wore a baseball cap pulled down over my forehead, so no one could get a good look at my face. I never took anything I didn't think I could turn into cash easily. I always thought ahead, thought about ways to cover myself. I knew the mistakes that got people pinched. That wasn't going to be me.

It wasn't long before I was bringing in a few hundred a week. I was smart about it. I didn't go around spending it like I was some kind of pint-sized Rockefeller. I knew that would only bring attention to myself. I'd give my old man his cut, maybe ten, twenty percent, just to keep him off my back, then I'd stash most of the rest. What I didn't put away I used on cigarettes—I smoked then, but gave it up when I got serious about what I was doing—and maybe a little weed, every once in a while. Or I spent it trying to impress girls by taking them to the movies *and* dinner. I loved the movies, especially the gangster films. My favorite was *Goodfellas* and yeah, I liked the *Godfather* movies, too. But *Goodfellas*, I just couldn't get enough of that flick, what with that brilliant Lufthansa heist. I must've seen that flick a dozen times, taking mental notes on how they pulled it off, and the mistakes they made after. They still don't know exactly who has the take from that. And if they didn't start spending the dough and knocking each other off they probably never would've been pinched.

Once a thief always a thief, I guess, and before long, as I strolled through the quiet, tree-lined streets of Charleston, I started thinking about getting in a little practice session. After all, I hadn't broken into anything in almost a month and I was afraid I might be getting a little rusty, you know, losing that edge. Breaking into houses is like a muscle. You don't use a muscle, it gets flabby and after a while it doesn't work very well. But there was more to it. I missed the excitement, the high. It's like a fuckin' drug. You don't do it for a while and you start to crave it. The only way you're going to get over that craving is to either start planning another job or do one.

After a half hour or so of aimless walking, I wound up spotting what looked like the perfect house. It was on the outskirts of the city, set back far enough from the sidewalk so I'd be out of the line of sight of passing cars or anyone who happened to be walking by. Surrounded by hedges, it was one of the many two-tiered historic houses I saw all over town. I was immediately taken back to the old days, when I hit at dinnertime, looting valuables from the upstairs master bedroom. This one would be a piece of cake, using the column to climb up to the second-tiered porch, which I was pretty sure opened onto the master bedroom. It was tempting to go back to the old days, when I busted in when people were awake, but those days were behind me. I was the new and improved Francis Hoyt. I was the Francis Hoyt who went in and out on the ground floor. No more climbing trellises and shimmying down drainpipes.

I walked past the house slowly then stopped to make it look like I'd forgotten something. Then I continued a few feet before I turned and retraced my path back to the other end of the house. I did this a couple times till I seared a mental picture of the lay of the grounds and house into my mind. It was now almost seven-thirty and darkness had begun to fall. It was close to dinnertime so the upstairs of the house was dark while the downstairs was all lit up. I stopped in front again and checked my watch, as if I was waiting for someone. I could see into one of the large windows at the front of the house. There was a partial view of a dining room table. I could make out a man seated at the head of it. He was in shirtsleeves. He had a fork in his hand. He was waving it around. Like he was lecturing someone at the table. A kid, maybe. Or his wife.

Most burglars get caught because they're stupid. They do

dumb things. They're just asking to get caught. One guy I met in the joint told me he brought his dog along with him and tied him outside while he broke into the house. Someone saw the dog there, got suspicious, and called the cops. How stupid can you be?

Truth is, burglary is one of those crimes where the odds are with the house. I once heard a cop admit that the clearance rate on burglaries is maybe fifteen percent. I'll take those odds any time. Cops hate investigating burglaries because the clearance rate is so low. It's a waste of their time. My jobs are in a different category, not only because of the high value of the goods I steal, but also because of who I steal from. You steal from someone poor or even middle-class, no one gives a shit. You steal from someone rich, suddenly you're Public Enemy Number One. Do I mind that? No way. I like it, man, I like it. They talk about the dude who steals several hundred thousands of dollars' worth of swag, not the one who steals something worth a few thousand dollars. That don't even make one of those fillers on page eighteen.

Even from as far away as thirty feet, I could tell what the alarm system was. And giving me a little help was one of those ridiculous decals on the window announcing the alarm system company that protected the house. Thanks for the helping hand, guys.

Sometimes, people put these things up thinking they're going to scare off burglars. Maybe it works with amateurs but no real thief gives a shit about a fucking decal. Any pro worth his salt can tell whether there's a system installed just by just checking the house out. Sticking on one of those things on the window just tells me and every other thief, "look, we've got plenty of stuff worth stealing but we're just too goddamn cheap to put in a real system."

Wireless is one of the best things that ever happened to us because it gives us two shots at disabling the system. One way is that we can walk right up to the front door and suppress the alarm. The other way depends on the system being used. Certain wireless alarm systems rely on radio frequency signals sent between the door and the window sensors to a control system that then triggers an alarm when these entryways are breached. The signals either deploy any time a tagged window or door is opened, whether the alarm system is enable or not. When the system is enabled, the alarm will be tripped and send a silent alert to the monitoring company, which contacts the house's occupants and the cops. But the system can fail to encrypt or authenticate the signals sent from the sensors to the control panels, making it easy for someone like me, with the right equipment, to intercept the data, decipher the commands, and play them back to the control panels whenever I want.

The signals can also be jammed to stop them from tripping an alarm by sending radio noise to keep the signal from getting through from the sensors to the control panel. Once you jam the home communications you can suppress the alarm to both the occupants of the house and the monitoring company.

The alarm this house was using was an old one, from the mid-nineties, which meant it was very susceptible to manipulation. I had the little gizmo in my pocket that could accomplish that, so there'd be no problem disarming the system.

If it had been an electrical hookup, I could find the box on the side of the house and instead of fooling around with the alarm, I could just shut down the electricity to the house. If I came back late enough, when everyone was asleep, they wouldn't even notice the electricity went down until they woke up in the morning and found that their clocks were an hour or so slow.

Once I knew what I was in for, I headed back to my motel to find something to eat. After dinner, I'd hang out in my room for a while, doing a little prep work and then, when it was late enough, I'd head back out to the house.

I didn't have my work clothes with me, so I had to improvise. A pair of black jeans and black turtleneck sweater would do. I was already wearing a pair of black Chuck hi-tops, size seven and a half. When I work, I always wear a pair of sneakers a couple sizes too large. I put on three pairs of socks to fill the shoes. I learned this little trick after I broke into a place early on and stupidly left a footprint on one of the kitchen cabinets after climbing in through a window. Fortunately, the cops couldn't match it to my sneaker because I got rid of that pair as soon as I read about the footprint, a detail printed in a newspaper story. Stupid cops let some reporter know what they had and he printed it. If he hadn't and I was picked up for the heist they would have had me dead to rights. That wasn't going to happen again. I always have multiple pairs of sneakers in lots of different sizes. After every job, I get rid of the pair I wore. Today, there was no time to buy another, larger pair. But the ground was dry and I'd just have to be extra careful about leaving any impressions.

I didn't have a screwdriver, a tool that does most everything I need it to do, so I copped a couple knives from the joint where I had dinner. The knives, one butter knife and one dinner knife, neither of them sharp enough to slice open an apple, would serve me well enough to pry open a window. No point in carrying anything sharper because if, on the unlikely chance I'd get pinched, something I didn't see happening in this rinky-dink town, I didn't want to be charged with armed robbery. Not that it matters much because not only do cops lie all the time but they can also be very creative in what they charge you with. Let's face it. If they want to nail you they'll nail you. Nothing you can do about it. That's where a good lawyer comes in. And that's where the money goes out. I've got several all over the country I can call if I get into trouble, but the only time I ever had to use one was that mob fiasco thing.

I found one of those all-purpose drugstores on my way back to the motel and bought a pair of surgical gloves, a couple candy bars and a package of condoms. Anyone asked, all the kid at the checkout would remember would be the condoms, not what I looked like. Just some dude who bought condoms and candy bars. And, knowing all these stores have surveillance cameras now, I made sure I wore my baseball cap and kept my head down. The only other thing I needed was a flashlight but I had one of those small ones attached to my keychain and that would do.

I was ready to rock and roll.

Most jobs I spend days, sometimes weeks, studying, observing, not only the house but the neighborhood. I like to know where I'm going and where I can go if I have to. But this was different. This was strictly for fun. It didn't count. I didn't give a shit who lived in the house or if they had anything of value.

I found one of those internet cafes, went online, and found a street map of the neighborhood. I studied it until I knew every block, every street, every intersection, every cul de sac, every dead end. I came up with at least four different escape routes. I never write anything down. Don't have to. I've got one of those near photographic memories. I see it once, I've got it forever.

That time of night I'd be too conspicuous walking alone on the streets, a likely target for any passing patrol car, so I checked for the local bus line on the internet and found a stop not far from the motel where I was staying, and another only a couple blocks away from the house. According to the online schedule the last bus arrived at the stop nearest the motel at eleven-twenty-six and the buses stopped running at midnight. No problem. I'd be dressed like a jogger, so I'd jog back to the motel, which was only two, three miles away. An easy run for me. And if I was stopped, I'd tell a sanitized version of the truth: I was stopping over for one night, couldn't sleep, so I decided a little run might help.

I got to the stop ten minutes early. The bus, practically empty, was on time. Only a couple old black ladies with shopping bags on the seat next to them, probably coming from work; a homeless dude nodding off; and a couple Goth teenagers making out in the back of the bus.

There wasn't much traffic so the bus moved quickly, even skipping several stops. By the time the bus finally reached my destination only the two horny kids, still going at it, were left onboard, and they'd have no way of recognizing me if it came to that.

I checked my watch. It was a few minutes past midnight. I was alone on the sidewalk. It was so damn quiet I could hear my slow and steady heartbeat. I walked the couple blocks to the house. The lights were out. Everyone was asleep. All I heard was the sound of crickets and the faint sound of a TV. I needed to know where that sound was coming from before I got started. I glanced at the neighboring house on my right and saw a flickering light coming from an otherwise dark upstairs window. It was either a kid playing video games or someone having a tough time falling asleep.

I was in full work mode. I was totally focused as I silently went over my plan in my head. I could see every step I'd make. I was in a familiar zone. I could hear better. I could see better. I could move better. I was better. I flattened myself against the hedge in front of the house then suddenly leaned my body into it, pushing myself through carefully so I didn't make a sound.

Crouching low, I moved quickly toward the side of the house. I pulled out the little gizmo I'd use to deactivate the alarm. But at the last second, when I noticed the electrical box, I changed my mind. I wanted a challenge. Instead of using technology, I'd disconnect the power. People are so stupid. They pay thousands of dollars for fancy, high-tech alarm systems and don't give a thought to protecting the electrical box. The alarm installers couldn't care less. All they care about is that their stupid system works and the monthly fees roll in. As if any system could ever keep me out. This box had such a dinky little lock on it a child could have opened it. I slipped on the surgical gloves, pulled a wad of tissues out of my pocket, wrapped it around the lock, then I used one of the knives from the restaurant to bust it open. I unhooked a couple connections. The house was now totally without electricity. Even if they had a motion detector inside the house, it would be useless. From this point on it was like cracking open a piggy bank, only easier.

I hugged the side of the house and slowly made my way toward the back, always on the lookout for the best place to make entry. A window. A back door. A storm cellar door. The best are glass doors that open up onto a pool area or the backyard. They're easiest to pick, and lots of times people forget to lock them at all. People with alarm systems get lazy. They rely on technology to keep them safe. Big mistake.

As I slowly edged my way back around the house, keeping one hand on the house as I felt my way in the dark, I spotted a small window by the back, chest-high, that had been left partially open. No more than an inch or two, but that was enough. Could they have made it any easier for me? I wouldn't even have to break a sweat prying my way in or risk someone hearing when I broke a pane of glass. I stood on my tiptoes and peered inside, using my small flashlight to see what was in what looked like a small room. Coats hanging from a rack on the wall and a washer/dryer tucked against the back wall gave it away. It was the mudroom, a perfect place to land. If I did leave any residue from outside it would mix with what was already there. It was far enough from the upstairs bedrooms that I wouldn't have to worry about any noise I might make. If there was a downstairs bedroom that was occupied, it wouldn't be anywhere near the mudroom.

I wrapped my keychain in the wad of toilet paper so they wouldn't jingle and give me away, then jammed them into the front pocket of my jeans. I pulled out a couple pats of tinfoil wrapped butter squares from my back pocket. They were soft, almost liquid, from my body heat. I squeezed them out on either side of the middle of the window frame so the window would slide open easily, without making noise. I carefully pushed up the window until there was an opening of about twelve inches, more than enough for me to squeeze through. I hoisted myself up on the windowsill, then went in head first. When my waist was resting on the windowsill I shimmied the rest of the way down until my hands touched the floor, then I pulled in the rest of my body until I was practically standing on my hands. Slowly, I leaned forward so my legs were touching the closest wall, then carefully walked them down the side of the wall until I was standing upright.

I was in. A jolt of electricity shoot through my body ending up in my brain. It was a familiar feeling, a feeling I live for. I was Frankenstein's monster suddenly given the gift of life.

I was now *in* someone else's space, an uninvited guest. I was a ghost who could walk through that house with no one knowing I'm there.

For that brief moment I am part of someone else's family. I am the eccentric uncle. The prodigal son. The perfect father. The trusted family friend. I am whoever and whatever I want to be. I am taking something from them, something they will never get back. Not their most treasured valuables. Their privacy. They have been violated and their lives will never be the same.

I had no idea what the layout of the inside of the house was, but I could pretty much guess. After all, I've been inside enough of them. The mudroom is usually off the kitchen and this house was no different.

The house was fifty, maybe sixty years old. I knew that from outside, by the thickness of the paint on the wood, the architectture. But the kitchen is new. The refrigerator was one of those sub-zero jobs. I opened it. It was filled with food. Leftovers from dinner. Roast beef. Broccoli. Roasted potatoes. All in blue dishes wrapped tight with Saran wrap.

I'm wasn't hungry but still I grabbed a potato and popped it in my mouth. It was good. I took another. They probably wouldn't even notice they were gone. But I will know there are fewer of them than there were an hour ago. That made me smile. I took out a container of orange juice from the side of the refrigerator. It was the fresh squeezed kind, not from concentrate. I opened the cap and took a swig, then put it back, not in its place on the side of the door, but in the front of the refrigerator. I wondered how long it would take for someone to realize it's been moved. By rearranging a carton of orange juice I have rearranged lives, without them even knowing it.

I'm finished in the kitchen. The next room should be the dining room. If I was there for silver, this would be where I would find it. But I'm not. What would I do with it? Where would I put it? How would I explain it if I were caught? No, tonight is just for kicks. Just to prove how good I am.

In the dining room, I spotted the breakfront. That's where the silver would be stored. Most of it would probably be the cheap, plated stuff. Not worth the trouble. I was curious enough to see for myself, so I opened one of the drawers. I was right. Cheap crap. I opened the glass door and took out a pitcher. This was more like it. Not antique, but real silver. I put it back. I smiled. *They'll never know how lucky they were.*

I didn't want to linger long, so I moved into the living room. That's where I really wanted to be. Although there might be a playroom downstairs for the kids, and a den where the man of the house can go to drink his beer and watch his football game in peace, this is the heart of the house. This is where the family meets. This is where guests are entertained.

I stood in front of the plush, cream-colored sofa and listened. There was complete silence except for the faint, harsh sound of snoring coming from upstairs. Every once in a while. There was a burst of noise, like the sound of a small cannon, then it settled down into a monotonous monotonal drum beat.

I sat down on the sofa. So plush I sunk into it, as the cushion molded itself to the shape of my ass. It was more comfortable than any sofa I'd ever sat on. The couch I grew up with was hard and frayed and smelled of cat urine. I'd never been in a house this long, long enough to sit and enjoy the comfort of another man's home.

I didn't want to get up. I wanted to stay there forever. But I knew I couldn't. I looked at my watch. Twelve-thirty. I needed to get back to the motel. I would leave this burg in the morning, back on the Greyhound headed north for New York City.

I stood up but before I headed back into the dining room, on my way to the kitchen and then the mudroom, I did something I've never done before. I don't know why I did it, but I did.

There was a dish of nuts on the coffee table. I picked it up, and dropped it on the carpeted floor. It made a dull thud, and the nuts scattered all over the carpet.

I heard noise coming from upstairs. The sound of feet hitting the floor. Like someone was getting out of bed. Slower than I should have, I headed back the way I came, a smile on my face. I wished I could have been there when the dad came downstairs and found nuts all over his floor. What the hell would he think?

But I had no time to wonder because I could hear bare footsteps coming down the stairs. I made it to the mudroom. I opened the window I came in a little wider. I stood back several feet, then took a perfect dive through the window. I tumbled through the air until I landed outside on my feet. A fucking circus acrobat couldn't have done better.

I looked at my watch. I had been in the house for less than half an hour. I was there, but I'm not there any longer.

In the blink of an eye I'm someplace else.

Charlie Floyd

My boy, Georgie Porgie, came through. By the time I got back home, managing to just beat the rush-hour traffic, there was an email from him.

Here's a start, Charlie, and I'm working on some other leads for you. Good to see you back in the saddle, my friend.
Porgie

It was a lot more than a start. He listed a New Jersey cop, Theodore Sullivan, the one who'd set up that unsuccessful stakeout for Hoyt; a New York City fence named Tommy Pfister; and a Hartford pimp named Ricky B.

Sullivan would be easy to locate. Porgie included the city in New Jersey, Westfield, where he worked. I was sure he'd be cooperative. The fence, well, that might be a problem. Porgie was going to try and get an address for him but I knew that wouldn't be easy. Pimps don't like talking to cops. They move around and don't leave forwarding addresses. Since Ricky B worked mostly around Hartford, I figured I could track him down with the help of some friends I still had on the force, guys I'd made cases with. Once I found him I had plenty of ways to make him cooperate. As for Pfister, well fences don't like to talk to cops either but I was pretty sure between Manny and me we could convince him it was in his best interest to help us out.

When Manny got back from the city I'd sit down with him and we'd figure out how to split up the workload. Time was important because we didn't want it leaking out to Hoyt we were on his trail. So long as he didn't know we were after him, there was a better chance he'd get complacent and make mistakes. The longer we could keep it quiet that we were after him the better our chances of nailing him.

A little after seven Manny texted me from the train, saying he'd be back around eight and would grab a cab back to my place.

I texted, back, *You're my guest and that includes pickups and drop-offs.*

It was almost nine, long after the last of the commuters had arrived home, when Manny's train pulled in. As I watched from the parking lot I could tell it was him walking down the platform by his familiar gait. He has this bounce in his step, almost as if he's dancing the cha-cha or the rhumba instead of walking. I wondered if maybe he was humming some popular salsa tune in his head as he walked.

"Long day?" I said, as I met him at the ramp and we started walking toward my car.

"Yes, Charlie Floyd. It has been a very long day but it has also been a very satisfying day."

"You're just dying to tell me about it, aren't you?"

He smiled broadly. I loved seeing those perfect white teeth.

"Tell you what, there's a pub on the way home. Why don't we stop there, grab something to eat, and you can unburden yourself."

"I believe that will work out just fine, Charlie Floyd."

While we waited for our burgers to arrive, Manny filled me in on his day. A blow by blow description, leaving nothing out. Did I mention how much Manny likes to talk? Fortunately, the man knows how to tell a tale.

"I visited two libraries, the main branch and the Annex, but there was no sign of Francis Hoyt. It was only when I made a visit to the Society Library that I was rewarded. It is a wonderful place. Have you ever visited the Society Library?"

"Don't believe I have. But then I'm not much for libraries. They kind of give me the willies. All those books, all those ideas, all those words, all that silence. As you probably know by now I'm not exactly the silent type. But then, neither are you."

"Oh, but you are missing so much, Charlie Floyd. Libraries are such wonderful places. The entire world is at your fingertips."

"That's what they've got the internet for."

He shook his head. "I am afraid you are missing the point, my friend. Have you never held a book in your hands and felt like you were transported to another time, another place? It is the cheapest, most efficient way to travel."

"Honestly, Manny, it's been a while since I was transported anywhere, by a book or anything else. I'm pretty much a here and now kind of guy. And to tell you the truth, I'm much better at getting information from people than from books. But that's a discussion for another day. Tell me what happened, and then I'll fill you in on my day."

"Of course. The Society Library was my last stop of the day. No one else at any of the other libraries recognized the man in my photograph. But when I showed the photograph to a woman at the Society Library, her eyes lit up. She said it looked very much like a man who had been in earlier in the week. She said that he inquired as to where the magazine room was and she gave him directions. She said he was there a little over an hour."

"She's sure it was him?" I asked, as the waitress plopped our burgers, surrounded by heaps of fries, in front of us.

"As sure as she could be. You know how these things are, Charlie Floyd. Witness identification from photographs is not very reliable. However, she also described him physically as on the small side, slim, with a very muscular build. She said he reminded her of a gymnast named Bart Conner. I looked him up on the internet and she is right. Francis Hoyt does bear a remarkable resemblance to the former American gymnast. I am certain that was our man."

"So now we know for sure he's up here."

Manny nodded as he bit into his burger, the juice spilling onto his plate. "It is only a first step, but it is a step in the right direction," he said, wiping his face and hands with a napkin.

"Did you find anyone in the magazine room who recognized him?"

"I am afraid I did not. But this means that Francis Hoyt is already researching his potential targets. I am afraid there is no way of knowing precisely what magazines he read, but I made a list of all the relevant magazines in the room. Now I will find a local library and read through all of them to see if I can discern some kind of pattern which will tell us where he plans to target his criminal activity."

Manny popped a couple of fries, dipped in ketchup, into his mouth, as if rewarding himself. He'd been successful and he was proud of himself. There was something almost cute about that. He was taking all this so personally that I couldn't help but start to make it personal myself. And the more personal it became, the more excited I became. What was it Sherlock Holmes used to say? The game's afoot, right? Well, now this definitely felt like it had legs.

As we finished our burgers and fries I told him about my day. We agreed we'd made pretty good progress for the first day out. As I drove us home I couldn't help wondering what Hoyt was doing and where he was at that very minute. Had he already pulled his first job up north? Or was it still in the planning stage?

When we got back to my place we sat at the dining room table figuring out our next moves. And I don't think that smile ever left Manny's face.

Manny Perez

Criminals are creatures of habit. Criminals adhere to patterns. Some patterns are quite simple, as is often the case with the criminal himself. Other patterns are far more complex and therefore more difficult to ascertain. The patterns of Francis Hoyt were difficult because he, having a very brilliant criminal mind, is aware that he has patterns and that if those patterns are discovered, his criminal career might well be brought to an abrupt end. And so he is very aware that his best defense is to be unpredictable. And yet he is human and therefore he cannot help himself from developing distinct patterns of behavior. To function successfully he must find methods that work to his advantage, methods that end in his reaching his goal: to take from people what is rightfully theirs. By taking from others he enhances himself, not just financially but emotionally. As a result, his patterns, and he does have them, are more difficult to expose. Sometimes, with a man like Francis Hoyt, it is his un-predictability that becomes predictable. Unfortunately, unpre-dictability is impossible to anticipate but it can and should always be factored into the equation.

The job of a detective is to uncover these patterns, make sense of them, and somehow disrupt them so the criminal is ap-prehended or forced to improvise. With improvisation comes the distinct possibility of error.

Francis Hoyt is as nimble in his thinking as he is on his feet. Nevertheless, he is human and to be human is to err. It was up to Charlie Floyd and me to get to know Francis Hoyt better than he knows himself. In effect, we would *become* Francis Hoyt and by *becoming* him we could perhaps anticipate his next move. And if we could not anticipate, perhaps we could, as the Americans say, "throw him off his game." As Charlie Floyd would say, "shake his world up a little bit." We would turn his world upside down and he would fall out.

To that end, as Charlie Floyd and I sat across from each other at his kitchen table, having just returned from dinner, I asked my new partner if he could get the states of Connecticut, New York, and New Jersey to provide us with a list of the high-end break-ins in the past two years that could possibly have been the work of Francis Hoyt.

"That's not going to be so easy, Manny. Remember, I'm no longer one of the boys. I'm just a regular civilian. Any help I get would be totally unofficial. What Georgie did for me was out of friendship. Something like this would mean a lot of man hours, and I'm not sure I could ask him or anyone else to go that far to help us out. But how about you? You could probably make an official request to the attorney generals of all three states through the Miami Police Department."

This was a question I was hoping Charlie Floyd would not ask. There was a problem, a problem I had not informed him about. Was this the time? Would he understand? Or might it lead to the end of our collaboration?

"Is there something wrong with that?" he asked, cocking his head to one side, an indication to me he very well knew that something was amiss.

Charlie Floyd is a good investigator. Good investigators know when someone is lying, or holding something back. It might be a slight change in the tone of voice, an unexpected silence, a shift of the eyes downward, telltale body language. I suspect at that moment it was quite possible I was guilty of all those telltale signs.

"You're not telling me something, Manny. I've done this long enough to know."

He had me. I knew he would. I would have been disappointed if he had not. He reached out and touched my arm. I saw the same thing in his eyes that I saw in my father's eyes when as a child I had done something wrong and my mother expected him to punish me. It was something he did not wish to do because he hated even the idea of inflicting pain, but knew he had to. That is the same look I saw in Charlie Floyd's eyes. Compassion. Understanding. Resistance.

"Give," he said and so that is exactly what I did.

Charlie Floyd

You want to know our dirty little secret? Cops lie. They lie to perps. They lie to their superiors. They lie to their wives. They lie to their kids. They lie to other cops. They lie to themselves.

In other words, they're no different from anyone else.

You work in law enforcement long enough you become cynical. That's not a maybe that's a certainty. You believe nothing. You trust no one. Everyone is guilty till proven innocent, not the other way around. You have to think that way. Otherwise you could never do your job. I know it's not the way it's supposed to be, but when you get down to it, our job is to prove you innocent. If we can't, then chances are you're the one we're looking for. This attitude can't help but spill over to the rest of your life. Your family becomes the enemy. If no one's innocent until proven innocent, then the default setting is that everyone is guilty, which means everyone is lying to you. That mindset might make you a good cop, but it sure doesn't make you a good family man. You look at your wife and kids as liars and probable wrongdoers. Believe me, no good can come of that. I don't think about it much, but it's probably what did in my marriage and resulted in an estrangement from my kid.

At that moment, sitting across the kitchen table from Manny, I knew something was off. I didn't know exactly what it was, but I knew it was something. Either Manny was holding something from me or he'd lied about something. It was so many things. His eyes, for instance. He's someone who looks you right in the eye when he's talking to you. It's his way of forcing you to interact with him. But at that moment his eyes were cast down. He was staring at a spot on the table. And at one point he picked up a napkin and started trying to wipe the spot clean. Not only was he avoiding my eyes but he was trying, unconsciously I'm sure, to take my attention away from the direction the conversation was headed.

These are the tip-offs. They're there. You just have to pick up on them.

I figured I should put him out of his misery.

"You might as well come clean, Manny, because you know sooner or later you're going to have to spill the beans."

He looked up from that spot and made eye contact again. I had him. I knew I was about to get the truth.

"You remember, Charlie Floyd, how I did not answer when you mentioned something about the Miami Police Department paying my expenses."

"I do."

"For that, my friend, there is a good reason."

"And that would be?"

He hesitated. He bowed his head. I could see this wouldn't be easy for him. He was ashamed. Of what, I was about to find out. But first I had to reassure him. Not because I thought of him as a suspect I was interrogating. Not because I was trying to break him down to get to the truth. But because he was a friend. I don't have that many but I now considered Manny to be one of them. And more than that, we were now partners, which in a sense made us as close as two human beings can be. That's not something you want to admit to your wife or your lover or your kids, but it's true. When you're in law enforcement, a partner is someone you must trust with your life. It doesn't get any closer than that.

"Manny, whatever it is, believe me, I'm not going to think any less of you. Unless, of course, you've murdered someone. And maybe even then, depending on who…"

He laughed, but it was one of those forced laughs. A laugh to break the tension. A socially obligatory laugh, because he was obviously not in a jovial mood.

"No, Charlie Floyd, I have not murdered anyone. Not today, at least." He forced another laugh.

"Then what is it?"

He cleared his throat. He tapped his fingers on the table. Finally, digging deep inside his psyche, his head bowed, the words came tumbling out.

"I am on suspension."

He said it so quickly that it came out as one word. "Iamon-suspension," is what it sounded like. Nevertheless, I got it.

"You. Suspension?" I couldn't help myself. I laughed. I laughed because the thought of Manny doing something that would result in a suspension was indeed a joke. Now if it had been me, well that would have been something else. But Manny Perez? It just didn't make sense. So, I laughed.

Manny, his eyes still cast downward, shook his head back and forth.

"I am afraid it is not a laughing matter, Charlie Floyd."

"I know. And I'm sorry. It's just that the idea of you doing anything that would get you suspended is really kind of laughable. What the hell was it?"

"I am very much embarrassed, Charlie Floyd."

"I can't imagine there'd be anything you should be embarrassed about. Hey, you're talking to Charlie Floyd, the man who's probably broken every rule there is and probably a few there aren't."

He lifted his head and stared at my face, his deep brown eyes boring through me, fixing me solidly in place. It was as if I couldn't move even if I'd wanted to. Manny was about to confide in me. With his eyes, he was bonding me to him. I would know his secret and it would be a secret I would keep. It would be our secret. Why? Because for this moment in time I was Manny and he was me. Before this we were two professionals working on a case. But now we were something a lot more. We were partners.

"But I do not believe, Charlie Floyd, that you have ever been suspended."

"True, but only because I've been damn lucky. And because I've been smart enough to avoid anyone finding out what I've done. Give," I said, offering him no choice. He couldn't go back now. The toothpaste was well out of the tube.

"I was assigned to the burglary division and so it was my job to investigate high-end robberies. As I'm sure you are aware, we have many, many wealthy people in Miami Beach and Fort Lauderdale. As a result, men like Francis Hoyt, men who take what does not belong to them, are attracted to the homes of these people. Several of these mansions had been burglarized within in the same two-week period and I knew it was the work of Francis Hoyt. But I could neither prove it nor could I find him. And then one day an anonymous tip came in. From whom, I still do not know. Most likely, it was from someone who held a grudge against Francis Hoyt. A former business associate, perhaps. Someone who felt aggrieved and wished to get back at him. The tipster told me that I could find Francis Hoyt at a motel in West Hollywood, just off Collins Avenue. And so, I traveled up there to find him and bring him back to Miami for questioning."

I knew what was coming and it wasn't pretty.

"Let me guess. You didn't inform the local cops and you probably didn't inform your bosses either, which means you didn't have a warrant or probable cause."

He nodded.

"There's more, though, isn't there?"

"Yes, Charlie Floyd, I am afraid there is more. You must remember, Francis Hoyt was my white whale. I became obsessed with him. Even my wife, Esther, could see that I was not the same man I was before Francis Hoyt entered my life. He was all I talked about, all I thought about. I could not let him get away with what he was doing. And I knew he was not finished. It was much too early in the season. There were too many other people to steal from, too many other houses to break into. When I received the tip that he had checked into that motel in West Hollywood, I went up there on my own, with no backup, with no official authority.

"I arrived at the motel, a rundown horseshoe-shaped building across the street from ocean. It was a wreck, but it was just the kind of anonymous place Francis Hoyt would most likely choose. I confronted the desk clerk and asked if a man named Francis Hoyt had checked in, knowing full well that he would not have been foolish enough to use his own name. But much to my surprise he had used a variation of it, registering as F. Harold Hoyt. A fiction, of course, since Francis Hoyt has no middle name.

"I showed the desk clerk my badge. He did not realize I was not with the West Hollywood Police Department and I did not enlighten him otherwise. I asked for the room number. I lied and told him I had the authority to enter the room. He gave it to me, of course, along with a passkey I had requested."

Manny hesitated a moment. He cleared his throat. He was getting to the hard part.

"Excuse me, Charlie Floyd, but would it be possible for me to obtain a glass of water?"

"Of course." I got up, went to the cabinet, grabbed a glass, opened the refrigerator, took out a pitcher of water and poured him a glass. It was only when I got back to the table and handed it to him that I noted the ironic circumstance of how many times I'd done the very same thing for a suspect I was interrogating.

He took a large gulp, then a couple of sips before he put down the glass. "My mouth was very dry."

"This isn't easy for you, is it, Manny?"

He shook his head.

"We don't have to talk about this now if you don't want to."

He shook his head again. "No, Charlie Floyd. If we are to

work together to find Francis Hoyt we must be honest with each other. I would expect nothing less from you therefore I expect nothing less from myself."

He took another sip of water.

"I made a choice, Charlie Floyd. It was not the correct choice nor was it the proper choice, but I am afraid that if I had it to do over again, if the circumstances were the same, I would most likely do it again. That is how much I wanted Francis Hoyt in prison and out of my life."

I noticed beads of sweat forming on Manny's brow.

"Manny, let me turn on the AC. It's probably a little warm in here."

He shook his head, picked out a napkin from the holder, wiped his forehead and said. "No need for that, Charlie Floyd. The temperature is fine. It is me who is a little overheated. I shall continue. I went to the room, knocked on the door and waited. There was no answer. I knocked again. Still no answer. And then I did something I should not have done. I used the passkey that I had been given by the desk clerk and I entered the room."

"Without a warrant."

"Yes, without a warrant. I proceeded to search the room."

"You must have known that anything you'd have found would have been inadmissible as evidence."

He nodded.

"I was not thinking about any of the right things, Charlie Floyd. I was only thinking about finding something that would help me to trap Francis Hoyt. I wanted to confront him, to face him man to man. The room, unfortunately, did not have much in it of value to me. It was small. It smelled of antiseptic and insect spray and yet I still saw cockroaches scampering into the bathroom. There was a bed that looked as if it had not been slept in, a night table with nothing on it, and a small dresser. I opened the drawers and found nothing of interest. I entered the closet and found a small bag. Excited, thinking I might have found where Francis Floyd carried the tools of the trade he used to commit his crimes, I was disappointed. I found only common, household items. A flashlight. A screwdriver. A small vial of some kind of clear solution. Drugs, I hoped, but when I sniffed it there was an alkali-like odor. I put it in my pocket. Later, when it was tested, we found it was simply a solution used for verifying silver content. I was hoping to find maps, perhaps notes pertaining to the next place Francis Hoyt intended to burgle. But there was nothing of the sort. It was as if the room had been inhabited by a ghost. Perhaps, I thought, he would soon be returning from a job and have with him the spoils of his labor. If that were to occur, I could arrest him for being in possession of stolen property. And so, I made what would become a fateful decision."

"Which was?"

"I decided to lay in wait until Francis Hoyt returned and..."

I knew what was coming next. I knew because, although I might not admit it to Manny or anyone else, it would be exactly what I would do. But from what I knew about Manny, a cop who always went by the book, every single word of the book, right down to the punctuation, it was totally against the grain.

"...I turned off the lights waited almost two hours before he returned. I heard him come up to the door, but he did not open it. I have told you many times, Charlie Floyd, that Francis Hoyt is a brilliant man. But more than mere brilliance I believe he must be in possession of a heightened survival instinct. I believe either he attached something to the door so that he could see if someone had entered, or he intuited that something was amiss, and that is why he hesitated before entering."

"So, did he enter?"

"No."

"You went out after him, didn't you? That's what I would have done."

"Yes."

"What happened?"

"By the time I reached the door he had started to run. I ran after him. I would never have caught him, he was much too quick, but a car drove into the parking area at that very moment and Francis Hoyt had to veer out of the way. When he stumbled slightly, I caught him. There was a struggle. He is surprisingly strong for such a small man. Even I am bigger than he is yet I could not hold onto him. It was as if his body was greased with oil. He twisted my arm and wriggled away from me. Someone watching from the motel or perhaps it was the driver of the vehicle that almost hit Francis Hoyt, had called nine-one-one. Within moments a police cruiser arrived on the scene, only to find me chasing Francis Hoyt down Collins Avenue. Since I was the closest one, and since they had no idea who I was, it was I who they stopped. By this time, Francis Hoyt had disappeared into the night. I was questioned and when they found I had no jurisdiction and that I had entered Francis Hoyt's room without permission, well, I am sure you can imagine what happened next."

"The proverbial shit hit the fan."

"I am much ashamed, Charlie Floyd. I failed to live up to my own code of conduct."

"I don't know what to say. It's ironic that you're the one who got suspended while I somehow always managed to escape any kind of official reprimand. And believe me, I've done lot worse. How long?"

"Three months."

"Three months. Hell, Manny, that's a vacation not a suspension."

"Not for me, Charlie Floyd. For me it is a grave embarrassment. My heart is heavy. It is something that will go on my permanent record. It is something I will carry around with me for the rest of my life. Perhaps now you can understand my need to find Francis Hoyt and put him where he belongs. It is the only way I can make things right."

"I get that. He's the cause of you screwing up and getting suspended."

"No, Charlie Floyd. Only I am responsible for, as you say, 'screwing up.' I am the only one responsible for my suspension. Francis Hoyt was simply the flame that ignited the fuse. I wanted him too badly and because of that I allowed myself to go beyond the purview of the law I swore to uphold. As a result of my own foolish obsession and the behavior that emanated from that obsession, I have brought shame on me and on my family."

"No offense, but that's a lot of BS. I think you're taking this way too seriously. I'd wear it as a badge of honor. We do what we do for personal reasons. My white whale was a guy named John Hartman, who killed his entire family then disappeared. It took me years to find him and in the end, it was he who found himself. You and I are very different people, Manny. But there are ways we're the same. We both want to do our jobs better than anyone else. We both share a hatred of failure. I failed to find that murderer. I won't fail this time. Hoyt will not remain a free man. I don't care how good he is, he's going down. And it's going to be because of us."

Manny smiled.

"Thank you, Charlie Floyd. From the bottom of my heart, I thank you."

He took my hand and shook it.

"If we can do this together I can hold my head up high again and I will gladly serve out the rest of my suspension. But I do not see it as a vacation, Charlie Floyd. Instead, I see it as an opportunity to do something good and right."

I don't know why, but at that moment I wanted to hug Manny and believe me, I am not a hugging sort of guy.

Francis Hoyt

I go too long without a woman, I get horny.

Lucky for me, I've never had a problem getting chicks. It's probably the "bad boy" vibe I've got going and believe me, I don't have to fake it.

The first thing I did when I hit the city was give Melinda a call. She likes to be called Mel. Melinda, Mel, makes no fucking difference to me.

She's a good-looking chick, late thirties, brunette, an inch or two taller than me, more when she wears those ridiculous elevator-to-the-penthouse, fuck-me platform heels. How the hell she can walk on those is beyond me. Looks like she's going to topple over any second. She's always complaining about her weight, but she looks plenty okay to me. No matter how skinny chicks are they still think they need to lose weight. Nice boobs. Nice ass. Nice legs. Most of her money goes into clothes and makeup and shit like that. She lives on the Upper West Side in a tiny studio she pays a fortune for. She doesn't care. That's where she wants to be, "in the middle of the action," she says, so she's willing to pay for it. I like to joke that if I sat in a chair in the middle of the room I could touch all four walls. I was exaggerating, but not by much. She laughed when I said it, but I could see it bothered her. Like I was criticizing her lifestyle choices, which I wasn't. If I did, that would mean I gave a shit.

She's been divorced from her husband for a couple years now. No kids. He was a cheapskate and she didn't get much in the divorce. She claims she got screwed in the divorce settlement because she was stepping out with me while she was still with him and he found out about it. I think maybe he hired some private dick to follow her. But I didn't twist her arm. I didn't hold a gun to her head. I'm no pied piper. She wanted to be with me, that's her business. Don't blame me.

I met her in a bar, asked her out, and she said yes. It took me two dates to get her into bed but since then it's been pretty easy sledding. The way I see it, that makes her a lot guiltier in this scenario than me. Still, I try to help her out when I can. A little dough toward the rent. A little dough for "maintenance." And I did buy her that car and I pay for the garage, since she was always bitching about finding parking on the street.

"I have to get up so much earlier, Francis. And sometimes I have to drive around for half an hour before I find something."

That was enough for me to open up my wallet. What the fuck, I can afford it and forking out the dough was a lot better than hearing her complaining all the fucking time. Besides, I don't mind. I've got enough dough to last me a couple lifetimes, even spending it the way I do. She's happy, I'm happy. That's the way it works. Just so she doesn't crowd me, if you know what I mean.

She's got a regular job. I think she's somebody's private secretary or something like that. We don't talk much about work. Mine or hers.

She likes to party. I don't kid myself, that's why she likes hearing from me. I stay away from drugs. I've seen too many guys ruined by snorting stuff up their nose or shooting it into their veins. Far as I'm concerned, it's a one-way ticket to hell.

We've got an understanding. She sees me when I'm in town, but only when I feel like it. Let's face it, chicks are pretty much interchangeable. And nothing is forever. Everything fades and one of the first things to fade is love, if there really is such a thing. Don't go by me because I'm not much acquainted with the feeling. I don't know what it is or how it feels. There wasn't any of it in my house growing up. Unless you call what my old man had for a bottle love. My old man showed love by smacking my mother around. By cheating on her. By verbally abusing her. By putting her down. But no matter what he did, either to her or me and my sister, she never stood up to him. It wasn't because she loved him, that's for sure. Standing up to him would have taken guts and guts is something my mother lacked. My old man, too. Doesn't take much guts to wail on an eight-year-old kid and a woman half your size, does it?

My sister favors my mother. Passive. Classic case. She lets things happen to her. Somehow, she always manages wind up with the wrong guy. The guy who treats her just like our mother was treated by the old man. A while ago she was with this asshole who used to knock her around when he got drunk—sound familiar? One time, I had to go all Sonny Corleone on him. Sent him to the hospital for almost a week. He was half a foot taller than me and had me by fifty, sixty pounds, but if you surprise a guy, get in the first shot—the nose is best, it breaks easy and once they're in pain they're vulnerable—the fight is pretty much yours. I beat the crap out of him. I almost couldn't stop. Someone had to pull me off him. Maybe I would have killed him if they hadn't. I came out of it without a scratch. He was going to press charges because he was embarrassed, a little guy like me kicking his ass. My sister talked him out of it. Said I'd kill him if he did go to the cops. I probably wouldn't have gone that far but who knows, maybe I would have had someone take care of it. Plenty of guys owe me favors. Whatever. It worked. He never laid a finger on her again and a couple months later he took off and she never heard from him again. But people don't change and it didn't take her long to hook up with another fucking loser who was maybe even worse than the one I just got rid of for her. Now, I stay out of it. She gets in trouble, she's on her own.

She's married now, second time, and this one seems to be the pick of the litter. She's got one kid from her first husband and one kid from this one. She lives close to our old lady, just outside Minneapolis. Every so often I send her some dough. She doesn't ask for it but I know she could use it. We used to be close when we were kids—probably a Stockholm syndrome kind of thing—but we kinda drifted apart once we were both out of the house. Every so often, when I get out there and visit my old lady, I stop by Brenda's to pay my respects. You can't count on many people in this life, but if there's anyone I could count on it would probably be Brenda. We got that brother-sister bond thing of growing up in a train wreck of a household.

I guess my mom loves my sister and me. She just don't know how to show it. Maybe now she feels bad she didn't protect us. I don't worry about things like that. The past is the past. She says she worries about me so maybe that's her way of showing she loves me. Especially 'cause I send her dough every month. That's the kind of love everybody understands.

I don't call these chicks girlfriends because that implies there's more to it than there is, than there can ever be. Of course, that's not the way they see it. But women and men think different. I mean there are chicks who think like a man and men who think like chicks, but that's only up to a point. They create this whole story in their head and you're supposed to know what it is and say, "Yeah, I'm down with that." How are you supposed to know anything if they don't tell you? As far as I'm concerned, it's a draw. They can't figure us out and we can't figure them out.

Mel seemed happy to hear from me.

"You're in town, Francis?"

Of course, I was in town. There'd be absolutely no reason for me to call her if I wasn't in town. But she doesn't know that. Like I said, these women make more out of it than there is. She thinks she's my girlfriend. Fine. Let her think whatever the hell she wants to think.

"Just pulled in. You're the first person I called."

That happened to be the truth, but it could have been a lie. This is one of those cases where the truth is really a lie. Just shows how blurred the lines can be.

"You're very sweet, Francis."

"Don't I know it. And I come bearing gifts."

She screeched so loud I had to hold the phone away from my ear.

"You're the best. The absolute best. When am I going to see you?"

"I'm free tonight. You wouldn't happen to be available, would you?"

I knew she would be. But it would have been bad if I assumed she was. This is just part of the game men and women play. We lie to each other all the time and we usually assume the other one buys the lie. Not me. I don't believe anything anyone says. And that goes for me. That's why I've survived as long as I have.

"Of course, I'm available, sweetie. Do you want to go out or do you want to come over here?"

Truth is, I was beat. I just wanted to go over there, fuck her brains out then get the hell out and go to sleep. But that's not the way it works with chicks. You've got to play the game.

"Why don't I take you out to a nice dinner and we'll see where we go from there."

"That would be very nice. Should I dress up?"

"Dress any way you like, baby. You look good no matter what you're wearing."

She laughed. Chicks love that shit. They eat up compliments like Godiva chocolates. Now I'd either have to go out and actually buy her something or just score some good drugs. Probably both.

By the time we finished dinner she was a little tipsy. Okay, more than a little. Three glasses of wine and an after-dinner aperitif. Like I said, I don't drink at all anymore. You drink, you lose control. You lose control, you make mistakes. You make mistakes, there are consequences. I don't believe in consequences, therefore I don't like to lose control. Ever. The joint is filled with assholes who can't control themselves.

We went back to her place, that small studio off Amsterdam and 71st. I have a place I keep in the East Village. But no one knows about that, except me. Ditto the studio apartment I keep in Westport and the one I have in Miami. They're places to crash between jobs. There's a bed, clothes, a few books. Stuff like that. Nothing that'll give the cops anything to chew on in case they somehow track me down. Every time I leave I give the place a thorough cleaning. By the time I'm outta there it smells like a combination of Mr. Clean and Pledge. I pay the rent a year in advance by bank check and the utilities are under one of my aliases, a different one for each of the three apartments. Sounds like I've thought of everything, but I know there are always ways I can improve.

I wasn't in the city long enough to score any coke, but I had a pocketful of Percocets and a few 'ludes I'd brought up with me from Miami, and that was good enough to keep the party going. But I got a line and I watch that no one goes over it. She gets too fucked up, that's not good. I don't want an overdose happening on my watch. That means complications. The cops, EMTs get involved. Moderation isn't one of Mel's strong points. She's got an incredible capacity. She'd swallow fucking everything I had if I gave her the chance. But I don't give her that chance. I know what her capacity is, even if she don't. Look, I am kinda fond of her and I don't want her to get hurt. Bottom line: You're with me, I take care of you. That's the way I am. But don't get the wrong idea. I don't feel anything special for her. I'm just all about protecting my interests, and right now, she's one of my interests.

Once we were back in her apartment I pulled a little box out of my pocket and waved it in the air.

"Francis, is that for me?"

"Have you been a good girl?" I said, offering it to her then pulling it back.

"A very good girl."

"Are you going to be an even better girl tonight?"

"No. Tonight I'm going to be a very bad girl. The box is blue, Francis," she said.

"Yeah. It's blue."

"Is it from where I think it's from?"

"Take it and find out for yourself." I smiled and handed her the box. No time to get it wrapped, but it didn't seem to matter. She opened it and squealed. She took the earrings out of the box and held them up to her ears.

"They're beautiful. Do you like the way they look on me?"

"Like they were made for you, baby."

"Tiffany's!" she could hardly contain herself.

She took off the earrings she was wearing and put on the new ones. She looked at the full length attached to the door of the apartment. I stood behind her.

"You like the way they look, baby?"

"Yes, yes, yes!"

She threw her arms around me and kissed me.

"And I think you've got something else for me, haven't you?" she said, pulling away.

"Greedy little bitch, aren't you?"

"Yes," she purred, "I certainly am."

I put my hand back in my pocket and pulled out a baggie of pills and waved them in front of her. She grabbed the baggie then me. Let the games being!

I tried not to wake her when I got up early the next morning, but when I came out of the bathroom, she was sitting up in bed, the sheet pulled up to her chin.

"Francis," she started, and I knew by the way she said my name we were headed into territory where I did not want to go.

"You know, honey, you never like to talk about yourself. How am I going to get to know you better if you never talk about yourself?"

I don't like to talk much in the morning and I certainly didn't want to get into any kind of personal discussion.

"I'm not a very interesting guy, Mel."

"That's not true, honey. Everyone's interesting if you get to know them. For instance, I don't have any idea where you are when you're not in New York, and that's only for a few months of the year. I don't even know what you do for a living."

"I have to travel a lot, Mel. It's as simple as that."

"For what?"

"What do you mean, 'for what'?"

"I mean what's your job?"

"Does it matter?"

"Of course, it matters."

"What if I said I was a hitman?"

She laughed. "I wouldn't believe you."

"How about sales."

"I'd believe that. What do you sell?"

This was a conversation I didn't want to have. It wouldn't end well. I could just say "None of your business," but that would only lead to hurt feelings which would escalate to pouting and after that, who knows what. I knew what this was all about. She wanted to get to know me better. She wanted to bond with me. She wanted me to fucking *share* with her. She wanted us to be closer than we could ever be. I could have made shit up, but that would have taken way too much energy. What energy I had I wanted to use to get the hell out of there. But I figured I'd be nice about it. After all, she was a good kid and she wasn't doing anything wrong, other than pissing me the hell off.

"Mel, honey, it's a boring job and the only thing more boring than actually doing it is talking about it."

She leaned forward. "You sell drugs, right?"

Shit! That's all I needed. Her thinking I was a low-life drug dealer. Like if I was, knowing that would give her power over me. Something to hold over my head, if I got out of line.

"Huh?" I said, trying to stall for time, time to figure out how to get out of this conversation that had no good end.

93

"Like you're in the pharmaceutical industry, right? That's why you always have drugs with you. They're like samples you get."

I picked up my shirt from the chair, put it on, and started buttoning it.

"That's right. But I really can't talk about it, baby, because using it for my own purposes, well, that's not only against company policy but it's also against the law. I could get fired for it and I could go to jail. You wouldn't want me to get fired and wind up in jail, would you?"

"Of course not."

"So, the less you know the better. For both of us."

She got out of bed. She was bare-ass naked. In the light of day, she didn't look half as good as she did last night, in the dim light of her apartment. But maybe that was just me. Maybe I was so horny anyone would look better than they actually were. Not that she was a dog or anything. She was pretty, but her body was beginning to soften. Not like mine. I probably look better now than I did twenty years ago. It kinda pissed me off that she didn't take better care of herself.

I finished buttoning my shirt and sat down on the edge of the bed to put on my shoes. She sat down next to me and put her arm around my neck and rested her head on my shoulder.

"It's Saturday morning. Where are you going?"

"I've got meetings to go to."

"On Saturday?"

"In this business, you work seven days a week."

"Then I don't like this business you're in, Francis."

"See those earrings over there on the dresser?"

"Yes."

"My working seven days a week pays for those suckers."

She took her head off my shoulder and sighed.

"When am I going to see you again?"

"Soon."

"That's so vague."

I turned, put one hand on her shoulder, and the other behind her neck, so she had to look me right in the eye. "Look, Mel, this is the way it is. This is the life I live. Maybe one day it'll change, but right now this is what it is. If you can't handle it I understand. We can just call it a day."

Her eyes opened wide. She licked her lips. She was weighing what she was going to say, how far she could push it. Not very far.

"You're not breaking up with me, are you?"

I didn't say anything.

"Please, Francis. I won't ask any more questions. I promise."

"It's the way it has to be."

"Then it's fine. It's fine. Really. It's fine. But you will call me, won't you?"

"Of course, I will, Mel," I said, and I probably meant it. I just didn't know when.

Charlie Floyd

Manny and I took the train down to the city. I thought about driving but the idea of fighting New York City traffic, trying to find a place to park then dealing with the tunnel traffic to Jersey didn't seem like a good idea. I'm much too restless to sit in traffic. I need to move around. Sitting in one place gives me too much time to think. And the things I think about are usually bad. My broken marriage. My estranged son. Worst of all, what I'm going to do with the rest of my life. Fortunately, I had something else to think about now: Francis Hoyt.

The plan was to pay a visit to the fence, Tommy Pfister, then head out to Jersey to speak to Theodore Walsh, the Westfield cop.

"Pack a bag, Manny. We'll stay overnight in Jersey and come back Thursday."

"That sounds like a fine plan, Charlie Floyd, but I insist upon paying all expenses, including meals," he said, as we sat at the breakfast table, finishing our coffee.

"Listen, I'm pretty much a ward of the state, what with my pension and all and you being on suspension with a family to..."

Manny shook his head vigorously.

"I have budgeted funds for this trip, Charlie Floyd, and thus far you have paid for everything as well as being so gracious to allow me to stay in your beautiful home. It is now time for Manny Perez to carry his own weight."

I wasn't going to get into a fight over it. Manny was a proud man and I'm sure the idea of me taking care of everything rankled him. "Okay, suit yourself. But that deal about the reward. That's null and void. We'll split it fifty-fifty."

He started to object but when I held up my hand he saw it would do no good, that my decision was final. He was right.

We got an early start, leaving my place a few minutes before seven. Manny was impeccably dressed in a suit and tie, me in a pair of faded blue jeans, my cowboy boots, a pale blue oxford button-shirt and a black blazer. It was a little too hot to wear the hat, but it was a crucial part of the look so I wore it anyway. Manny carried a briefcase I assumed was filled with a change of shirt, underwear and toiletries, plus his files on Hoyt. I stuffed everything I might need in an old gym bag I appropriated from my kid when he was still in high school.

I parked the car in the lot by the station and we headed to the platform. We were early but not early enough to avoid the throng of commuters headed down to the city. I led Manny to the back end of the platform where we waited for the commuter train to arrive.

"Here's the trick, Manny. Everyone waits for the train in the middle of the platform. Some people think they're smart and they plant themselves at the front of the platform. Bad choice. That's the car that fills first. I wait back here because there's a better chance of finding a seat in the last car than in the front or middle. Sometimes it pays to be last rather than first."

"It is most certainly counter-intuitive, Charlie Floyd," Manny said, as he turned on his phone and stuck it in his inside jacket pocket. "But I trust in your judgment which comes from your many years of experience."

I smiled. I knew Manny was pulling my chain. I didn't mind it at all. In fact, I kind of liked it.

We caught an express, which meant we didn't stop at every goddamn half-assed town along the route. I removed my hat and carefully placed it on the overhead rack along with my gym bag. Manny preferred to keep his briefcase near, keeping it on his lap. I'd picked up a copy of the *New York Times* at the station and offered Manny a section.

"No thank you, Charlie Floyd. I prefer to listen to this." He pulled out an iPod.

"What kind of music you like, Manny?" I asked. Me, I favor Dylan, the Band, Muddy Waters, Tom Waits, the Stones, music I guessed was not high on Manny's list.

"It is not music. I much prefer to listen to audio books."

"You don't like to waste even a minute, do you, Manny?"

"There are so few minutes in one's life why waste any of them?"

"Can't argue with that. What's the book?"

"Last year I made a vow to read every American Pulitzer Prize-winning novel since 1948 when Mr. James Michener won the prize for his wonderful novel, *Tales of the South Pacific*. I am up to 1967, and I shall be listening to *The Fixer* by Mr. Bernard Malamud. It is my small way of connecting with the American experience."

"Jeez, you're already more American than I am. Any good?"

"It is superb, Charlie Floyd. Did you know that Mr. Bernard Malamud also wrote a novel called *The Natural,* a book about baseball, the American pastime, which was made into a movie of the same name starring Mr. Robert Redford?"

"Saw the movie. Didn't know it was based on a book. What's this one about?"

"It is about a Jewish man in Russia who is arrested on suspicion of the murder of a small Christian boy. He is imprisoned, interrogated, and treated poorly. It is a novel of forgiveness."

I shook my head.

"You do not believe in forgiveness, Charlie Floyd?"

"We're in a business where the notions of forgiveness just gets in the way of the job we have to do. I'll leave forgiveness to the theologians and writers like Malamud. What I do believe in is justice."

"What about redemption?"

I thought a moment. Did I believe in redemption? Of course, I did. That's what I was seeking now, wasn't it? At one time or another don't we all seek some kind of redemption?

"Yeah. Redemption is possible, I suppose. You're a Catholic, aren't you?"

"I am."

"So, I guess you believe redemption is possible."

"Of course, I do." He smiled. "That is the road upon we are traveling on at this very time."

"Speaking of which, I've been meaning to ask you, what was it like getting your hands on that little pissant?"

Manny tipped his head back and closed his eyes, as if trying to recreate the scene in his head. After a moment or two his eyes opened, he leaned forward and turned to me.

"It was not at all what I expected it to be like. I thought I would be staring into the face of pure evil but instead I saw only cunning, intelligence, and determination. There was no fear or panic. Quite the contrary, in fact. As we struggled I saw he was smiling, as if he knew what the ultimate outcome of our struggle would be. He did not attempt to hurt me. He did not throw a punch. He did not pull a weapon from his pocket. Instead, he was skilled enough to slip out of my grasp, as if he were a trained wrestler, which as I learned later, is exactly what he was."

"How do you know something like that?"

"After our encounter, I went to the trouble of learning as much about his past as I could which included retrieving his high school transcripts. I even spoke to his high school wrestling coach and one of his teachers."

"Jesus, Manny, you're fucking serious about this guy, aren't you?"

"Yes, Charlie Floyd, I am very serious." He raised one hand and put the other on a section of the newspaper that sat between us. "I swear I will not rest until Francis Hoyt is behind bars, where he belongs."

I smiled. "I'm not sure if swearing on *The New York Times* counts as a solemn oath, Manny. But I get your point. How long has it been now that you're after Hoyt?"

"It has been more than a year since I was assigned to a string of high-end robberies in and around Miami. Eventually, we linked them to other robberies in Fort Lauderdale and Palm Beach. The pattern fit the work of only one man. Francis Hoyt. The more I learned about him the more I wanted to know. His criminal career fascinated me and I knew that I was the one who would put an end to it."

"Sounds like you're taking this very personal. That's not always such a good thing. Believe me, I know."

"My father used to say that nothing was personal, Charlie Floyd, and my father was a very wise man. But in this case, I believe he was both right and wrong. Nothing is personal and yet, in the end, everything is personal."

"Well, I guess if you put it that way, I see what you mean."

"But knowing who committed the crimes and then catching him and proving it in a court of law, well that is a very different matter."

"That's right."

"Of course, I do not expect you to be as informed about the life of Francis Hoyt as I am." He stopped and smiled again. "Perhaps one day soon it will become as personal to you as it is for me."

"You know as well as I do the best way to nab someone is to get inside their head, to try to think like they do then hope you can anticipate their next move. It's a game of chess."

Manny nodded solemnly then plugged the earphones into his ears. I leaned back and began to read the *Times*. Not another word passed between us during the rest of the ride into the city.

I'd checked back with Porgie before we left for the city and he provided me with a little more background information on the fence, Tommy Pfister. He worked out of a small office in the Diamond District of Manhattan, one block running between

Fifth and Sixth avenues and 47th Street. Pfister passed himself off as a jewelry dealer, buying and selling whatever came his way legitimately, but it was only a cover for his real business—handling hot goods. New York cops believed Pfister had ties to the mob, but he was a very careful man and they'd never been able to pin anything on him. It didn't surprise me. You do this kind of business in a city like New York there's no way the mob doesn't stick its fat finger into the pot. Pfister was most likely the link between the mob and Hoyt, which ended poorly for Hoyt when he found himself involved in that shooting incident.

Manny and I walked the six or seven blocks from Grand Central to the Diamond District. We discussed our strategy and Manny asked me to take the lead in questioning Pfister, while he played the "silent partner" role.

Pfister's office was on the fourth floor of a small building squeezed between two larger buildings. The elevator was so small that Manny and I had a tough time squeezing into it together, and if it wasn't the slowest elevator in the world it was certainly close.

The name on the door was Global Jewelry Exchange, an attempt, no doubt, to add a touch of legitimacy to an illegitimate fencing operation. I didn't bother to knock. I just opened the door and walked in, with Manny trailing close behind.

The office was tiny, maybe fifteen feet wide and eighteen feet deep. The room was split in half by a long glass counter filled with all kinds of cheap looking jewelry and watches. Straight ahead was a window that looked as if it hadn't been opened or washed in years. It didn't matter much since the view appeared to be the back of another building. There was a three-drawer steel gray filing cabinet in one corner and above it hung a monthly pinup calendar. Behind the counter, facing the entrance to the office, was a desk covered with papers, a computer screen, a gooseneck lamp, and the detritus of what could have been this morning's breakfast or last night's dinner. Sitting behind that desk was the man I presumed to be Tommy Pfister.

He reminded me of the actor, Peter Boyle. He was fat, bald, and wore a white button-down shirt rolled up at the sleeves, open at the neck. A pair of eyeglasses were perched atop his bald head. He was leaning back in one of those old tilting, slatted wooden chairs, reading the sports section of the *Daily News.*

Only after I rapped on the counter a couple times did he bother to look up and acknowledge our presence. "Yeah? Can I help youse?" he asked, lowering the paper but making no move to get out of his seat.

"I think so," I said, as Manny stood beside me, examining the items under the glass counter. "We're looking for a friend of yours."

"Who'd that be?" he said, dropping the newspaper to the desk.

"Mr. Francis Hoyt," I said.

"Never heard of him," said Pfister.

He picked up the paper again as if that was going to shield him from what was coming next.

"Maybe you didn't hear the name right," I said.

"I heard yiz okay. Nothing wrong with my hearing. It's my eyes been giving me some trouble."

I leaned over the counter. "I don't care about your fucking eyes, Tommy."

I nodded to Manny. As I moved to the left side of the counter, Manny moved to the right, so that we were blocking Pfister from getting away. We stood there a moment, until I made a move toward Pfister. Manny, picking up my lead, did the same. We kept closing in on him until we were standing on either side of Pfister's desk.

The office was air conditioned but I could see beads of sweat on Pfister's heavily creased forehead.

"Hey, no one's supposed to be back here but me. Get the hell back on the other side of the counter, will ya?"

"I don't think you heard me very well, Tommy. You don't mind if I call you Tommy, do you?" I slowly moved my hand so that it was at my belt, then I pushed back my jacket so he could see I was carrying. Manny unbuttoned his jacket and did the same.

"Who the hell are youse guys?"

I sat on one the edge of his desk and Manny on the other.

"Manny, show him who we are."

Manny went into his back pocket, took out his wallet, flicked it open and flashed his badge, snapping the wallet shut before Pfister could get too close a look.

"Cops, huh?"

Neither Manny nor I said anything.

Pfister looked at Manny, then back to me.

"What the hell you want from me?"

"I already told you what we want, Tommy. We want to know about Francis Hoyt."

"I already tole ya I don't know the guy. So, fuck off."

"You kiss your mother with that mouth?" I said.

"Fuck you."

Manny, tossing me a wink, got up from the side of the desk and moved toward the door, where he stood, his arms folded in front of him.

"Hey, whatchoo doing?"

"This is a private conversation, Tommy."

"If you don't mind my asking, Mr. Pfister," Manny said, speaking for the first time, "how much of this inventory is stolen property?"

Pfister's face turned red and he roared, "What the hell you talking about? I'm a legitimate dealer in jewelry and precious metals. You come here to sell me something, I don't ask where it come from."

"Any of this stuff come from Francis Hoyt?" I asked.

"I already tole ya—"

I grabbed Pfister by the arm and spun him around in his chair so that he was facing me. I got my face as close to him as I could, no more than an inch or two away.

"You smell my breath, Tommy?"

"What?"

"You heard me. You smell my breath?"

"Yeah. I smell it."

"That's how close I am to you. Close enough for you to smell my breath. You're a lucky man. I brushed my teeth this morning, used a little mouthwash, too, but maybe it doesn't smell so good after lunch. Maybe it's even worse after I eat dinner at some Italian joint. You can't imagine how much I love garlic. You don't want me this close then, Tommy. But this is how close I'm gonna stay until we get the answers we came here for."

I smacked him across the cheek. Not too hard, just hard enough so I could see the slight imprint of a couple of my fingers it left on his face.

"Hey! You can't—" He started to get up but I pushed him back down.

"Sure, I can. You want me to do it again?"

I turned to Manny.

"Maybe you ought to lock the door. Until we finish our business with Tommy here. We wouldn't want to disturb the neighbors."

Manny flipped the lock.

"Listen, you guys can't..." Pfister whined, like a baby.

Pfister's bravado disappeared. He was beginning to believe we could and would hurt him. He slumped back in his chair. This would be the beginning of the end.

"I guess we can, Tommy. Because we're doing it."

Manny, came back to the desk and fiddled with some papers.

Pfister's hand shot forward to try and stop him. But Manny pulled his hand away with a fistful of papers.

"Hey, that's private stuff."

"That's funny, I thought I heard you give us permission to search your office," I said. "Didn't he give us permission?"

Manny nodded.

"I didn't give no one no damn permission. I'm gonna report yiz guys. That's what I'm gonna do. This is an illegal search and seizure."

I picked up a cell phone from his desk and handed it to him.

"Which police department you wanna call, Tommy?"

"Whaddya mean?"

"We didn't say we were from here, so who you gonna call? NYPD? You think they're gonna show up on their white horses and save your ass?"

"Where the hell are you from?"

"Somewhere else."

"You got no right..."

Manny, who'd been thumbing through the papers he'd removed from Pfister's desk, moved to the file cabinet near the window. He went to pull open a drawer, but it was locked.

"Mr. Pfister, I am going to need the key to this file cabinet, if you please."

"I don't please. I don't fucking please at all. You fucking guys don't have a warrant. You can't—"

I got up in his face again and grabbed his shirt collar.

"Read my lips, Tommy. We. Don't. Need. A. Fucking. Warrant. And you know what? We're not interested in what's in those files. But someone else might be. What do you think about the idea of cops nosing around the stuff you've got in that file cabinet?"

"You ain't got no right," he sputtered, his face turning bright red.

"You want us to leave you alone all you have to do is tell us what you know about Francis Hoyt."

Beads of sweat began to roll down Tommy's cheeks. I let go of his shirt. I could tell we'd broken him. Now, it was just a matter of time.

"I already tole ya, I don't know no Francis Hoyt."

"These drawers would be very easy to open," Manny said, as he removed a pocket knife from his pants pocket.

"Come on, guys," Pfister whined.

"Look at me."

He turned his face back to me.

"In the eye, Tommy."

"Okay, so I'm looking at you. It don't matter where I look, you guys ain't got no right coming in here and—"

"You've got this all wrong, Tommy. This isn't about rights. And even if it was, right now you haven't got any. You want us to leave, all you have to do is tell us what you know about Francis Hoyt."

"I tole ya like a hundred times, I don't know who you're talking about."

I grabbed him again, twisting his shirt around his neck.

"Hey, you're hurting me."

"That slap was just to get your attention, Tommy. It could get worse. A lot worse. Just be glad it was me and not my partner here. See, he's got impulse control problems. You know what that means? It means he's got some very interesting ways of making people talk. Especially when he's frustrated. See, he's not from around here. He grew up not far from Guantanamo in Cuba and you know where that is and what they did there, right?"

There was fear in Tommy's eyes. He was a trapped, panicked animal. He had no idea what we were capable of doing and that frightened the hell out of him. I let go of his shirt and stood up. Manny took his cue. He backed away from the file cabinet and took off his jacket, exposing his holstered pistol.

"You guys ain't gonna do nothing...right?"

I shrugged.

"I have to be honest with you, Tommy. My partner's kinda hard to control. It's not his fault. It's his culture. You know what that's like, right? It's hard to break old habits. I've seen him pistol whip guys until they'd confess killing Jack Kennedy and Jimmy Hoffa." I threw up my hands. "I'm out of it now. You had your chance with me. Now you have to deal with my partner."

"Okay, okay. I really don't know where he is. Honest, I don't."

"But you know he's up here, right?" I said, sitting back down on his desk as Manny put his jacket back on.

Pfister hesitated. I saw fear in his eyes again, but I couldn't swear it was us he was most afraid of.

"You know, Tommy, speaking as a new friend, I think you ought to do something about this condition you have," I said.

"What condition? I ain't got no condition."

"Sure, you do. It's the sweating, man. It's kind of gross. I've never seen a man sweat so much. How about you, Manny? You ever see a man sweat this much?"

Manny, his hands akimbo, holding his jacket apart enough so Tommy could still see he was packing, shook his head, no.

Tommy opened his desk drawer and took out a handkerchief. He had a pistol in there but he made no move to reach for it. He wiped his brow with the handkerchief then shoved it back into the drawer so that it covered the pistol.

"Day like this I bet you go through at least half dozen handkerchiefs. If I were you, I'd probably get myself a box of Kleenex, that way you'd have one handy all the time and you'd save plenty on laundry bills."

"You guys, you guys are stepping over...the line. Way over—"

"What line, Tommy? Manny, you see any lines around here? 'Cause I don't see any lines."

Manny shook his head, no.

"Okay, yeah. Maybe he's up here. I don't know for sure. But yeah, he's probably up here."

"Which one is it? Is he up here, or isn't he?"

"Yeah. For sure. He's up here."

"Have you seen him?"

"No, I ain't seen him. That's just what I hear."

"You fence for him, right?"

"Not anymore."

"Why not?"

"We had a falling out, that's why."

"What kind of falling out?"

"Just a falling out, okay. Things happen."

"Did you see him when he was up here last year," asked Manny, who was now back sitting on the other side of Pfister's desk.

Pfister swung his head in Manny's direction. "I don't remember."

I looked at my watch then tapped the face of it. "You think we've got all day to sit around playing patty-cake with you, Tommy? My partner and I have more important things to do than sit here listening to you lie about things we know you're lying about. You're wasting our time. We don't have a lot of time to waste, Tommy. My partner here has to get back home. So why not answer the questions truthfully so we can be on our way?"

Pfister opened the drawer, pulled out the handkerchief and wiped his brow again.

"Who told you he's up here?"

"Someone."

"Who?"

"People."

"What people?"

"Just people. You know, word gets around. I don't remember what people. I see people all the time, you think I remember all of them? What the hell's the difference?"

"There is a difference, Tommy. But let's move on to a more important question. Where is he?"

"How should I know?"

"The same way you know he's up here."

"Look, this guy doesn't take out an ad in the newspaper giving out his address and itinerary. He just shows up when he wants to show up."

"When was the last time Francis Hoyt showed up, Mr. Pfister?" asked Manny.

"It's been a couple years. Like I said, we had a kind of falling out. We don't do business no more."

"Was it because of that thing that put him in jail?" I asked.

"You know about that?"

"We know everything, Tommy."

"That wasn't my fault. Guys I work for set that deal up. I had nothing to do with it. But yeah, Hoyt blamed me for it. Said he wasn't going to deal with me anymore. Said he'd find somewhere else to take his business to."

"Who might that be?"

He shrugged. "Beats me. There's lotsa guys like me around. A lot of 'em don't work out of an office like me. You guys probably know who they are better than me."

"So, he has nothing to do with the mob anymore?" I said.

"Mob? What would I know about any mob?"

I smiled. So did Manny. This had been fun but it was getting a little old. I could see we weren't going to get anything else out of Tommy Pfister, probably because he had nothing else to tell.

I got up, reached into my wallet, pulled out one of my old business cards and tossed it on Pfister's desk. I'd blacked out the old information and written in my phone number and email address. It was sloppy and I knew if Manny got a look at it he'd wince, but it would do the job.

"You find out anything, Tommy, you'll let me know, right?"

"Yeah, sure," he said, picking up the card and squinting at it.

"Charlie Floyd, huh?"

"That's right."

"Why's this stuff blacked out?"

"That doesn't concern you."

He held the card up to the light.

"Says here something about Connecticut."

"It doesn't mean anything. That's why I blacked it out."

"Why would I call someone I don't know who he is?"

"You do know who it is, Tommy. It's me. Or would you

rather deal with my partner? You know who he is, right?"

Manny, his face turned hard, just stared at Pfister. Even I was a little unsettled by the menacing look on his face.

Pfister hesitated a moment. "Nah, I'm okay," he said as he opened a drawer and tossed in the card. "So, you're a private cop working with a real cop?"

"Did I say that?"

"What's your friend's name?"

"I don't think it's necessary for you to know that, Tommy. Just so long as you don't forget mine."

We moved toward the door. Manny unlocked. I turned back to Pfister.

"Remember, you're gonna let us know if you find out anything about Hoyt." I pointed to his glass case filled with jewelry. "You've got some nice merchandise here. It would be a shame if someone got the cops to come up here and check it out. You know, like to see if it might not belong to you. Like that."

"I tole you guys what you wanted," he whined.

"I'm just saying, Tommy."

Rather than waiting for the slowest elevator in New York, we took the stairs down.

"You know that we will never hear from Tommy Pfister," said Manny.

"I'm not so sure about that. He was practically pissing in his pants. I'm not sure who he was more afraid of. Us or Hoyt? If it's us, we might just hear from him."

"You know, of course, that the first thing Tommy Pfister will do is contact Francis Hoyt to tell him that we are looking for him."

"I do. In fact, I'm counting on it. I want Hoyt to know some-one's on his trail. And you know why."

"Francis Hoyt is not the kind of man who will panic or go underground. Instead, he will most likely take it as a personal challenge that someone is looking for him."

"Exactly. That's the only way we're going to catch him—by letting him know we're after him. His ego makes him as good as he is but it can also work against him. Who knows, maybe he'll come looking for us instead of the other way around."

Manny patted me on my back. "You see, Charlie Floyd, I made a very wise decision enlisting you to help my find Francis Hoyt."

"I hope so, Manny. I really do."

Francis Hoyt

"You fat little fuck."

"Francis, what're you getting all bent out of shape about? I'm your friend, aren't I? I mean I call you as soon as these two guys leave. I figure you'd want to know everything."

"I want to know what the fuck you told them."

"Nothing. I told them nothing. What the hell am I going to tell them? What the hell do I even know? I didn't even know you were here for sure. I just called that old answering machine number you got somewhere, left a message then you call back. I swear, Francis. Nothing. I told them nothing. I don't know nothin'. What could I possibly tell them?"

"Who the hell were they?"

The fat little worm dipped into his pocket and pulled out a scrunched-up card and handed it to me. It was filthy, like he'd used it to wipe his mouth after a meal.

"What the fuck you do to this card? It looks like shit. You know, everything you touch turns to shit, Tommy?"

He looked at me with these sad little beady brown eyes. He's the reason I spent two years in the can. He had to open his big fat mouth to those mob guys. If he hadn't I never would've had to take those two clowns along with me and I never would have been caught. I guess I was just as much to blame. I knew it would end in disaster, but I didn't have much of a choice. Not if I ever wanted to work again. You don't say no to *the boys*. But I thought, hey, it's only one time, maybe nothing will go wrong.

I would have slapped Tommy upside his head, just to scare

the shit out of him, but that wasn't going to happen sitting in an uptown West Side diner, filled with fucking millennials and gen Xers, or whatever the hell they're called. Besides, it wasn't worth the effort. But the more I verbally knocked him around the better I'd feel and the better the chance I'd get the fucking truth out of the little weasel.

My veggie burger was sitting in front of me, untouched, while he was halfway through his cheeseburger, which oozed ketchup over the sides of the bun.

"And you're fuckin' sure they didn't follow you?"

"Give me some credit. I ain't no amateur. After I spoke to you I did just like you said. I waited a couple hours until I come up here, just like you said. I took the subway, just like you said. I got off at Columbus Circle and waited on the track for the next train. Just like you said. I kept my eyes wide open. Those guys weren't within ten miles of me. I swear."

"You better be right, Tommy." I looked at the card he'd handed me. It was a name I didn't recognize. Charles Floyd. There was stuff blacked out in heavy ink so I couldn't quite read where he was from in the dim light of our booth. He was trying to hide something, that's for sure. I had to ask myself, how professional could this guy be he couldn't even afford new business cards?

"Who the hell is Charles Floyd?"

"I don't know. I figure he's just another cop."

"Cops don't give out cards with information scratched out. Cops want you to know they're cops, unless they're undercover. These guys weren't undercover."

"Yeah. Yeah. You're right, Francis. He wasn't a cop. I can smell cops a mile away. Maybe he's a private dick."

"Maybe," I said, running through all the possibilities in my mind.

Tommy took another bite of his cheeseburger and a piece of onion fell on his plate. He grinned, picked it up and stuffed it back under the roll.

"You ain't hungry?"

"I lost my appetite the minute I sat down across from you, you little fat fuck."

"That ain't very nice. I'm just trying to do a solid for you. You know, trying to make good on what happened to you, though I swear it wasn't my fault. How was I gonna know they would contact you and ask you to work with some of their guys? You gotta understand. I work with them all's the time. They're my best customers. And those guys don't fuck around. What was I gonna do they ask me to hook them up with you?"

"You could've kept your big, fat mouth shut in the first place."

"I'm sorry, Francis. I really am. You know, they showed up and we just got to talking and I was just kind of proud of you, you know, how good you are and all, and I just got to bragging a little—"

"Would you just shut the fuck up? That's in the past. I don't deal in the past, Tommy. I deal in the future. Describe the two guys to me."

"Sure. The dude that gave me the card was a big guy, maybe six-two, six-three. I couldn't really tell 'cause I was sitting down the whole time. Maybe fifty. Maybe a little older. He looked like some kind of dime-store cowboy. Cowboy hat, jeans, boots. But he didn't have one of those accents, you know, the western thing. So, I think he's from like around here."

"What about the other guy?"

"He was a cop for sure."

"How do you know?"

"He flashed a badge."

"From where? New York? New Jersey? There are some cops out there that got a real hard-on for me."

"I don't know. He flashed it so fast, you know. And he was too far away from me to get a real, good look at it. But it was the genuine article. I know real badges when I see 'em and I know fake badges when I see 'em. This one was the real thing."

"Describe him."

"He was shorter, much shorter than the other guy, maybe just a few inches taller than you. Not that you're short. That's not what I mean. He was very well dressed. You know, a suit and tie. Oh, yeah, and he was kinda dark-skinned, black hair, Latino, maybe. He had and accent and he spoke funny."

"Funny how?"

"Funny like in full sentences. Big words. I think maybe he's Puerto Rican or Dominican. Wait, I just remembered something. The other guy said something about him being from Guantanamo. Where's that?"

"Cuba, you idiot."

"Yeah. Right. He's the one showed me a badge. Oh, yeah, I already said that. They were both packing. They made sure I saw that. Maybe he wasn't even a cop, the little one, I mean. The way they acted, I don't think they were cops. But they coulda been."

Once you got this idiot talking, there was no way to shut him up. He was like one of those Energizer bunnies that just keeps on going and going and going. The only way to shut him up was to either stick the rest of that cheeseburger in his big, fat mouth or say something.

"I know the second guy. Name's Manny Perez and he's a Miami cop. But he's on suspension. Fuckin' didn't think he'd follow me all the way up here."

"They followed you?"

"Not literally, asshole. I mean he came up here looking for me. He knew where I'd be."

"I don't think the other guy was from Miami. Maybe Texas, 'cause of the way he was dressed, only like I said he didn't have the accent."

I shook my head. "He's not from Texas. There'd be no reason for anyone from Texas to be looking for me. He's either from Florida or he's from up around here, and he's private."

"Wait a minute. I remember something else. I looked at the

card real close and I could kinda make out the word, Connecticut. Maybe he's from there. Look at the card, Francis. You'll see what I mean."

"Later. It doesn't matter anyway. They probably teamed up to bring me down."

"You mean back to Florida?"

"No, asshole. Not that kind of down. I mean pinching me. Catching me doing something up here."

"Maybe you oughtta lay low."

I laughed.

"Yeah, right. I'm going to let two dumb dicks stop me from doing what I do. No way. I'm going to do exactly the opposite. I'm going to make fools out of those clowns. You know something, you just made my day."

"I did?" he said, his eyes open so wide I thought his eyeballs were going to fall into his plate of half-eaten, ketchup-soaked fries.

"Yes, Tommy, you did. And to show my appreciation, lunch is on me."

"That's great of you, Francis. I don't mean just buying me lunch. That's nice, very nice, and I appreciate it. But I think this is a step in the right direction in rebuilding our relationship, don't you?"

The little twerp had no clue. Did he really think I was going to go back to using him as my fence? Did he really think I was going to forgive him for him being reason I did time? But I wasn't going to let him know that. I needed him on my side. I needed him to keep feeding me information. I needed to make sure he didn't shoot his mouth off and let anyone else know I was back in town. Not that it would matter. They had no idea where I was going to hit. I also needed him to keep his mouth shut and not let the boys know I was back in town. They tried once and there was nothing to stop them from trying again to jump on the bandwagon. No way that was going to happen.

"It's possible. Only I need you to do a couple things for me."

"Sure, Francis, anything. What do you need me to do?"

"I need you to let me know if you hear from those guys again…"

"That goes without saying—"

"I'm not finished."

"Sorry. I'm just a little excited, that's all."

"Well, calm the fuck down. Have another bite of that cheeseburger."

"What else?"

"I don't want anyone else to know I'm back up here, Tommy. You understand?"

He nodded his head.

"I want you to say it. I want you to say that no one else is going to hear from you that I'm up here."

"No one else is going to hear from me that you're up here. I swear."

"That means the boys, the cops, the fucking guy who serves you your coffee in the morning. No one."

He put up his hand. "I swear, Francis."

"Okay, Tommy. I think I get it. And when I tell you to, you're gonna call this Floyd guy."

"Why would I do that?"

"Because you're going to be my double-agent. You're gonna tell them what I want them to know and then you're gonna report back to me."

"That's great. Because I know I have to work myself back into your good graces. But I'm hoping someday, whenever day is, that we can do business together again. That you'll come to me, not as a favor but because you know I'm the best and I can do the best for you. So, until that happens I'll do anything you want me to do. Anything. Just so we can patch things up between us. You know, get things back to the way they were."

Fat chance, I thought. But that's not what I led him to believe.

Manny Perez

Detective Theodore "Teddy" Sullivan of the Westfield Police Department was well-acquainted with the man we were after. It was Detective Sullivan who attempted to catch Francis Hoyt in the act by saturating one of the wealthiest neighborhoods in his town with police officers.

"It was the damnedest thing," Detective Sullivan said as Charlie Floyd and I sat in his Westfield, New Jersey office. He sat at his desk behind which was a large map of the area. "I still don't know how the hell he did it. We thought the plan was foolproof. I mean, he'd hit one of our houses for three straight Thursdays, so we knew that was his day of choice, though we never figured out why. Anyway, we knew which neighborhood he'd most likely hit, it's the area where the most wealth is situated, and so I had over a dozen officers scattered strategically throughout the neighborhood. It was costing us a pretty penny but we figured it would be worth it if we snagged the sonuvabitch. We had all kinds of surveillance, electronic and human. But we didn't even pick up a hint of him."

Detective Sullivan shook his head in disbelief.

"We were out there all night and didn't see anything out of the ordinary, so as soon as it got light we just packed it in and came back home. We figured we'd missed the boat, that he'd moved on to another town, another state even. Or maybe he just took the night off. But we were wrong. The first call came in at eight o'clock in the morning—"

I looked over at Charlie Floyd. He was focusing on every

118

word that came out of the mouth of Detective Theodore Sullivan. It was easy to see why he was such a good investigator. His eyes were like lasers. He never took them off Detective Sullivan. I felt like I could see the inside the brain of Charlie Floyd. It was working, working, working. Taking in everything Detective Sullivan was saying without taking a single note. Later, I asked Charlie Floyd why he did not find it necessary to take notes and he replied, "Manny, I've been blessed with a photographic memory for the spoken word. You ask me what I had for dinner last night I might not remember. But if you ask me about a conversation we had three years ago I can give it to you pretty much word for word. My wife and kid hated that because they could never get anything by me. You know, like 'you said.' Or, 'you never said.' They couldn't win an argument with me. I'm not saying that's necessarily a good thing you want to have in your personal life, but in our line of work it sure comes in handy."

As for me, I had a notebook and I took copious notes, copying down everything Detective Sullivan said. I also had a small tape recorder that I had switched on when the interview began. You never know what small detail, something you might never have thought was important, might lead you to solving the case. Many investigators prefer to rely on an audio or videotape tape, but over the years I have found that if I rely solely on that I will not focus on what is being said. Writing things down forces me to concentrate. And watching the subject for a tic, or an expression, can often tell me if he or she is telling the truth. Later, I will use the tape to see if there is something I missed.

"—from the owner of a house on Lambert's Mill Road," Detective Sullivan continued. "The house had been entered that night and all the good silver had been taken. And that's all that was taken. They had some plated stuff, but he left that untouched. No jewelry was taken and he didn't even take some cash that was lying around. That's how we knew it was Hoyt. Then, ten minutes later, we get another call from a homeowner on Westfield Road. Same deal. The good silver. Nothing else. We couldn't believe it."

"Jesus," said Charlie Floyd.

"Wait. You haven't heard everything. Fifteen, twenty minutes later we get another call. This time from a homeowner on Martine Avenue. Same deal. He'd never hit more than one home in our area before and now, suddenly, with us on the lookout he'd hit three! It was like he was taunting us. Letting us know he was smarter than we are."

"I believe, Detective Sullivan, that that is precisely what Francis Hoyt was doing," I said.

"This guy's some piece of work, all right," said Charlie Floyd. "And you're sure it was him and him alone?"

"It was him, all right. Couldn't have been anyone else," said Detective Sullivan, who had the same tone of awe in his voice as everyone does who comes across Francis Hoyt. "Can't imagine he had any help. That would have been way too risky. The spooky thing is not only did he do it right in front of our eyes, but there wasn't a sign of his ever having been there. We dusted those houses like we were Felix Unger's housekeepers. I mean everywhere. Outside, inside, all around the town and absolutely nothing. Not a fingerprint. Not a footprint. Not even a stray hair. It was downright uncanny. Like the homes were burgled by a ghost."

"I believe he covers himself remarkably well, Detective Sullivan," I said. "I would not be surprised if he shaves his body and wears a hairnet."

"Sonuvabitch thinks of everything," Charlie Floyd said.

"Well, he is human and he's got to screw up some time," said Detective Sullivan. "Just not that time."

"I am afraid that is a hope more than it is a prediction," I said. "But one way or another Charlie Floyd and I will catch Francis Hoyt. Of that you can be sure."

Detective Sullivan shook his head. "I admire your confidence, Detective Perez. But I gotta tell ya, I don't think anyone's ever going to catch that sonuvabitch in the act. I get the feeling that even if we knew the precise home he was going to break into and the precise time he was going to do it, he'd still figure out some way to get it done without getting pinched. He's like Houdini or who's that other guy? The one who makes the Statue of Liberty disappear..."

"David Copperfield," Charlie Floyd said.

"That's the guy. And remember, these houses had top of the line alarm systems. One of them even had a motion sensor. Somehow, this guy's figured out how to disarm them or get around them. One of the houses even had a dog and they didn't hear a peep out of it. It's really kind of spooky. And that's exactly what some of my officers were calling him: a ghost. And you know, I understand what they mean."

"What we need to do is figure out where he's going to work next," said Charlie Floyd. "If we figure that out then we'll figure out how to nail him. Maybe we can even pinpoint the exact house or houses he plans to rob."

"How're you gonna do that, if you don't mind my asking?"

"He studies magazines very carefully," I explained. "That is how he finds his target. If we can learn which magazines he has studied recently, that will point us in the right direction."

"You gonna find out what magazines he subscribes to?" said Sullivan.

"We don't need to. Manny here found the library he used and from that we're hoping to figure out what magazines he likely used for research."

"Smart. But finding him ain't enough. You need to find proof you can use to send him away. I wish I could help you guys more other than to tell you I'm sure it was Francis Hoyt. But we're yesterday's news. It's unlikely he'll hit here again."

"We believe that for Francis Hoyt it is not just about the money. He requires a challenge."

"He's trying to prove something to himself," said Charlie Floyd.

121

"What's that?" asked Detective Sullivan.

"That he keeps getting better," said Charlie Floyd. "He's got to constantly push that envelope because that's how he stokes his ego. He's a narcissist. Not only does he need to impress us, but he needs to impress himself. He ups the ante whenever he can. The bigger the hit, the bigger the splash he makes. The more impossible it appears to be, the more important he is. He believes he's the best and when you're the best you have to keep proving it not so much to others but to yourself. He has to prove to himself that he's not a fraud. I don't care what anybody says, this guy is never going to stop until we stop him."

I nodded in agreement. Charlie Floyd was absolutely correct in his analysis. We were looking for a man who like so many of us is defined by what he does, not who he is, and a man like that, a man as good as Francis Hoyt is, rarely makes mistakes. But he will make one. That, I believe, is inevitable.

There was little else Detective Sullivan could tell us and so we thanked him and asked if he could suggest a motel where we might stay the night.

"There's the Best Western Inn over on North Avenue. I'll give 'em a call and let 'em know you're checking in. That way you'll get the best room. And I'll be happy to get one of my guys to drive you over there."

While we waited in Detective Sullivan's office as he went to find someone who could give us a ride Charlie Floyd turned to me and said, "What do you think, Manny?"

"I think precisely what you think, Charlie Floyd. That we will have to concentrate on trying to find out where Francis Hoyt intends to next ply his trade. And then I am afraid that we will have to find some other way to ensnare him as opposed to catching him in the act. That, I think, as history has shown us, is an impossibility. And I believe you are correct about another thing, Charlie Floyd."

"What's that?"

"That Francis Hoyt knows we are on his trail. We must

make him think of us as his audience and that he is performing only for us. If he does that, he is bound to fail. You said it before. From now on we are not going to go after him as much as he is going to come after us."

Charlie Floyd

I dropped Manny off at the local library where he was planning to spend a few hours going over the list of magazines he'd received from the Society Library librarian. I knew it was a longshot, like finding that proverbial needle and that it wouldn't be fun poring through all those magazines. But police work isn't glamorous. It's not fun. It can be mind-numbing, but it is necessary. And the best investigators, and in my experience Manny was in that category, approach tasks like this eagerly. If successful, it would add one more piece to the puzzle and bring us that much closer to Hoyt.

Meanwhile, I was on my way back to Hartford to try to find the pimp, Ricky B who, according to what Porgie told me, had had some dealings with Hoyt in the not-too distant past.

I put in a call to Joe Stagione, a Hartford cop I'd known for years, and asked him if he'd ever heard of Ricky B and, if so, where I might get a bead on him.

"Unfortunately, the answer's yes, Charlie. Real piece of work, that one is."

"Is he still working Hartford?"

"Far as I know. But roaches like him move around and they don't leave forwarding addresses. He could be in Stamford, he could be in Norwalk, he could be in Fairfield, he could be in Timbuktu. Guys like him go where the action is and the heat isn't. What's up with him, Charlie? Didn't I hear you retired a ways back?"

"That I did."

"You working private now?"

"It's complicated."

"Meaning you don't want to talk about it."

"Now's not the time, Joe. But we'll grab dinner some night and all will be revealed."

"So why are you looking for Ricky?"

"He might have some information about someone I'm looking for."

"Who's that?"

"Francis Hoyt."

He whistled into the phone.

"You're kidding. You're on the hunt for Hoyt. Well, good luck to you, man, because you're going to need it."

"Why the hell does everyone in the world know who Hoyt is when I didn't?"

"Not everyone, Charlie. Just anyone who's ever worked robbery in this state or in the vicinity. He's a goddamn legend. What makes you think Ricky B knows anything about him?"

"I got a tip."

"Tell you what, why don't you come on down and you and me will hook up and go snark hunting for this asshole."

"How about this afternoon?"

"You don't let grass grow, do you? Okay. How's two p.m. I'll meet you at Dino's."

I got to Dino's a little early. I took my old table in the back, the same one where Georgie and I had eaten a few days earlier, and opened up the folder on Hoyt Manny had so painstakingly put together. Most of it was a series of police reports about various burglaries around the country, all of which seemed to be the work of Hoyt. He did have a particular footprint, but that didn't seem to make any difference in terms of catching him in the act. There were reports from New York, Florida, Connecticut, New Jersey, and Massachusetts, but there were also similar reports Manny had culled from Illinois, a couple of suburban towns outside Chicago, and even a few break-ins in the Dallas and Houston suburbs.

The timeline was pretty obvious. For the first six or seven years, Hoyt was stealing jewelry, breaking in exclusively during the dinnertime hours. Then there was that gap of close to two and a half years when he was incarcerated. The past three years he had switched things up and was stealing very high-end, antique silver from wealthy homes up and down the East Coast. Each home held treasure troves of silver, ranging anywhere from a hundred fifty thousand dollars' worth of antique candlesticks pilfered from the home of the former wife of a famous industrialist, to close to half a million dollars' worth of silver, some of which could be traced back to Paul Revere whose vocation, many seem to forget, was as a silversmith.

During the past three years Hoyt had been amazingly productive. He rarely took a week off once he started his "season." Reading the reports from those five or six states and knowing he probably only got from ten to maybe, if he was lucky, fifty cents on the dollar, I figured he still took in close to a million bucks a year. Tax-free income.

Even more amazing, was his work ethic. During the season, whether it be winter down south or spring/summer/fall up north, it seemed there was never more than a week between jobs.

According to a report from one of the insurance companies, most of the antique silver was most likely fenced abroad, where its sale wouldn't gain as much attention as it would here. The rest of it was probably melted down and sold at the prevailing price for silver. At today's price of about sixteen dollars an ounce, a pound of silver was worth at least a couple hundred bucks.

There were a number of photographs in the file. Most of them crime scene photos, but there were a couple mug shots of Hoyt. I turned them over to see if they were dated and found none of them had been taken within the last couple of years. Somehow, Manny also had gotten his hands of surveillance photos of Hoyt with various women. One showed Hoyt holding hands with a pretty blonde in a tight mini-skirt and tank top. Another was of Hoyt and the same woman standing outside a restaurant. There was also a photo of him with an attractive brunette. They were holding hands. In another shot they were kissing. I wondered who'd taken them and how wound up in Manny's folder. I turned them over to see if there was any information.

On the back of the photo of Hoyt and the brunette Manny had written in a script so perfect it looked as if it had been typed, "Melinda Shaw, New York City, suspected girlfriend of Francis Hoyt." The date was last August. On the other photos of Hoyt holding hands with and kissing the blonde, Manny had written "Evelyn Kerns, Fort Lauderdale, suspected girlfriend of Francis Hoyt." It was dated this past December.

I spread the photos out on the table and stared at them. I wasn't quite sure how, but I sensed this might be a way to get at Hoyt. I was just closing the file when Joe showed up.

"Man, I'm sorry, Charlie. I couldn't get out of the office. Damn paperwork. It never ends."

"No problem, Joe. I made good use of the time."

"That's my Charlie. What say we get started? I've only got a couple hours."

We cruised the city for close to forty-five minutes until we found a couple of hookers who Joe thought might lead us to Ricky. He was right. After I parted with a little cash, they mentioned a place called The Pigs Eye Pub over on Asylum Street. When we got there, it was pretty empty, just a few guys at the bar watching a ball game and a few tables filled with the late lunch crowd.

We sat at the bar. The bartender, bearded, stocky, wearing a plaid shirt with the sleeves rolled up, exposing a sleeve of tattoos kept his distance.

"He's made us," said Joe.

"Must be you," I said.

127

"Really? You think you don't have the look anymore?"

"I'm a chameleon, man. Now that I'm retired I'm just another every man."

Joe snorted. "Yeah, right. Once a cop always a cop, and these dudes can smell one a mile away."

Joe turned his attention to the bartender. "Hey, you, you gonna do your job, or what?"

He didn't break any speed records moving down the bar toward us.

"Yeah, what can I do you two for?"

Joe flashed his badge. The bartender didn't look surprised.

"You see any minors in here, dude?"

"From what I see, business isn't that good. But that's not why we're here. We're looking for a dude named Ricky B."

"Don't know no rappers."

"Wrong profession." Joe pulled out his phone and called up a mug shot. "He's a pimp, one of Hartford's finest."

The bartender shook his head, grabbed a rag out from under the bar and started wiping down nonexistent wet spots. "This ain't that kinda place."

"Let's cut the song and dance, pal. I just want to know if you know this dude. I'm told he hangs here. Take another look." Joe shoved the phone in his face.

The bartender's eyes dilated slightly, his head tilted to the left. You do interrogations long enough you recognize that look on a man's face. He was concocting a lie.

"You're working too hard, man," I said. "Just tell us the damn truth and we'll be out of your hair. It's so much easier than telling us something we know is a lie."

I opened my wallet and slipped a twenty across the bar. He stared at it a moment, then pocketed it.

"We don't allow that kind of stuff in here. We're on the level. No gambling other than when the Pats are playing. And no solicitation."

"But you know him, right?" I said.

"Yeah. He comes in here sometimes. Has a drink. Shoots some pool. But he don't do business in here. Like I said, we don't allow that kinda thing. We'd lose our license."

"We just want to talk to him," said Joe.

"I wouldn't know how to reach him if his fucking house was on fire."

I took one of my revised business cards out of my pocket and handed it to him.

"How about you just let me know when he's in here again?"

He turned it over in his hand. "Charlie Floyd. Name's familiar. Don't you work for the state?"

"Not anymore."

"No more?"

"Not since last year."

"You're the one looking for this dude?"

"I am."

"What for?"

"Parking tickets."

"Very fucking funny."

He shoved the card in his breast pocket. "Like I said he only comes once in a while and he don't stay long. Unless you live nearby, he'll be gone before you pick up the phone."

"Let's say we forget the phone call. Just give him this, when he comes in." I opened my wallet and counted out five twenties. "You got a paperclip?"

"Yeah, sure, in the office."

"Go get one."

"Why?"

"Because I asked you to."

A moment later the bartender dropped several paper clips onto the bar. I took the twenties and tore them neatly in half. I clipped one of my cards to the half twenties and handed them to the bartender.

"You tell him he gets in touch with me I'll have the other halves for him."

129

"Ain't this against the law, tearing money up like this?"

"Tell you what," said Joe, "you turn him in and we'll split the reward. How's that sound?"

When we got back outside Joe was shaking his head. "You really think you're ever going to hear from Ricky? I'm mean come on, Charlie. It's only a hundred bucks."

"I'll hear from him. A hundred bucks is a hundred bucks, Joe." I took the half twenties out and waved them in front of him.

"He'll be wanting these."

Francis Hoyt

I am the Muhammad Ali of the criminal world. Ali knew how good he was and he didn't fake that humble shit. Neither do I.

Having two lawmen hot on my tail doesn't bother me. I love it. It makes me work harder. It makes me focus. I can't afford to be sloppy. I can't afford to make mistakes. I can't sleepwalk through the process, doing things strictly by the numbers. I have to be creative. I have to take charge. I have to be the one calling the shots. I have to be what I am. The best.

I'll just rope-a-dope them till they're dizzy and drop to the ground.

I keep a small studio apartment in Westport, Connecticut, one of the wealthiest suburbs in the Northeast. It's where Paul Newman lived with wife, Joanne Woodward. A couple years before he died I saw them walking around town, holding hands, if you can fucking believe it. I wanted to go up to him and tell him how much I loved his performance in movies like *Cool Hand Luke, The Hustler,* and *Hud.* He was a lot smaller than I thought he'd be. Bigger than me, but not by much. It's that silver screen thing. Makes them much bigger than they are. But he still had that thing about him, the charisma thing that let you know he was someone important, someone to be respected, someone not to be messed with, someone you don't just go up to on the street and say hello to. That kinda charisma is rare. People envy and hate you for it. I want to be like that. I want to be feared. I want to be respected. I want to be hated. Do I give a fuck? No, I don't.

The plan was to work north of Westport, up the coast a bit,

into Fairfield and Litchfield counties. No sense hopping the train every morning from the city, like a fucking commuter. I leave that to the suckers who do an honest day's work for an honest day's pay. When I pick the houses to hit, I'll check into local motels and work from there.

I did some research on Floyd and Perez. There was plenty out there on Floyd. He made the papers when he led a manhunt for a killer named John Hartman. He was on that case for years and still wasn't able to bring him in. The dude just up and turned himself in. Floyd must have been pretty pissed about that. I mean, come on. You spend two years of your life on something like that and the guy just walks in one day and gives himself up? Man, that's gotta suck.

He was also involved in a bunch of other high-profile cases and according to newspaper reports he fancied himself quite the cowboy. Except for the Hartman thing, he was damn successful. His retirement as chief investigator for the state of Connecticut, not long after Hartman turned himself in, was front-page news. That meant he was important. If he was after me that made me important. I liked that. I don't want just any asshole on my tail. The better he is, the better I'd have to be.

Perez, that roly-poly Cubano asshole that tried to take me down last fall in West Hollywood, well, I already knew more than enough about it him. He was another so-called star of law enforcement. He'd risen pretty quick in the Miami department. Probably because he knew how to deal with all those Cubanos down there who think they're fucking Tony Montana. I gotta give it to him. He's a gutsy little guy, coming after me like that. But he fucked up. Went rogue. Didn't have a warrant so anything he found, which wasn't going to be much, wouldn't have been admissible in court. And if he thought he was going to get anything out of me even if he brought me in, he was going to be one disappointed spic. I remember looking back at him chasing me, huffing and fucking puffing, like he ever had a chance of catching me.

They probably think they've assembled some kind of Dream Team to bring down Francis Hoyt. Too bad they're going to be disappointed.

Bring it on, Charlie Floyd and Manny Perez. Bring. It. Fucking. On.

I got the car keys from Mel. Told her I had some calls to make upstate. She knows better than to question me. She knows it would piss me off. I don't lose my temper much but when I do it isn't pretty. I get that from my old man. I'm not proud of it. I'm not proud of anything I might have gotten from him. But I know how to make it work to my advantage. Plant it in people's mind that you're dangerous, that you have a hair trigger, that you aren't one to be messed with, and you never will be. This is something I learned in the joint. You act the part good enough you don't have to be the part. Besides, Mel knows any answer I gave her would be a lie. These broads create a picture of who you are and what they can make you into. Let her think whatever the fuck she wants to think, just so she doesn't get in my fucking way.

It was one of those beautiful spring days. Not a cloud in the sky and the temperature clocked in at a perfect seventy-two degrees. I've always loved May and June because it means the end of something bad—winter, school, being stuck in the house—and makes the promise of something better—freedom. That meant getting away from my old man. Every spring and then again in fall, the slate is wiped clean. I get to start all over again. Every spring brings the hope of something better. When I was a kid it meant one month closer to freedom. Let's face it, I was lucky to graduate high school, and that was mostly because my teachers couldn't wait to get rid of me. I was an asshole with a chip on my shoulder. If there was trouble I was usually in the middle of it. That's the way I liked it. I got the reputation of being a badass and that wasn't by accident. No one messed with Francis Hoyt, not even teachers. People kept their distance, which was exactly what I wanted. When no one is anywhere near you, you can get away with murder.

I found a parking spot on the street, maybe half a mile or so from my place. Before I got out I wiped the steering wheel clean of my prints. I did the same thing with the rearview and side-view mirror. I took a Dustbuster I keep out of the trunk and vacuumed the floors and seats. I made sure there was nothing in the car that might be traced back to me. Like I said, I'm a fucking ghost when I want to be.

I retrieved my oversized backpack from the trunk and flung it over my shoulder. In it were my essentials:

A pair of black jeans
Black, hooded sweatshirt
Black sweatpants
A couple pairs of brand new black Chucks
Six brand new pairs of athletic socks, three pairs my size, three pairs two sizes larger
Two ski masks, both black
A black watch cap
A package of latex gloves
An electric shaver and razor
A bottle of silver testing solution and two small empty vials
A roll of duct tape
Three screwdrivers, various sizes
Wire cutter
A dozen burner phones
A loose-leaf folder filled with pages of notes and diagrams of various alarm systems
A pair of night vision goggles
An electronic device used to deactivate alarm systems
A brand-new Mac Air
Assorted magazines: *House Beautiful, Architectural Digest, House and Garden,* the *Smithsonian, Vanity Fair, New York, Entertainment Weekly, People, The New Yorker*

An up-to-date copy of *Who's Who in America*
Current copies of several local country club newsletters. I subscribed to these under various pseudonyms and had them sent to a P.O. Box I kept down in Miami. I kept another one, under a different alias, in the FDR branch of the post office on Third Avenue and 54th Street and switch deliveries to up there for the spring and summer months.

I opened the apartment windows to let in some fresh air then unpacked, laying everything out neatly on the sleeper couch. I picked up all the furniture either at a yard sale or from a thrift shop. And if I can't get it back myself, it stays where it is. I'm not totally off the grid but I'm damn sure on the edge of it.

I'd hang out in the apartment a couple days, researching various houses and the people who lived in them. Rich people think they're invulnerable. They're so fucking arrogant and full of their damn selves. It's like they never heard of the word *privacy.* Some of them even go out and hire fucking publicists to make sure they get into the media. They invite the press into their homes and let them take photographs of every fucking room. When I've finished researching, I know their lifestyles, their habits, and the layout of their houses. Thanks, assholes. Why not mail me a fucking blueprint while you're at it? Maybe I ought to send them a fucking thank you note.

Some of them brag about their alarm systems, about how state-of-the-fucking-art and impenetrable they are. The more impenetrable they claim they are the more of a challenge they are to me. I haven't found one yet I can't beat. I don't think I ever will.

After I finished researching I'd make a few field trips to the houses. I'd find a cheap motel a town or two away, then check in under an alias. I'd case the houses a couple days to see what kind of security they have, and how many people go in and out and at what times. If the house is open for a tour, and yes, that's what these assholes sometimes do for charity events, I sign up for it. It's like being invited in for a preview before the main event. I'll find a good spot to watch the house deep into the night, just to get a feel for what I can expect. Once, I even activated an alarm just to see the response time. I was not impressed.

When I've collected enough information, I'll come back to Westport for a day or two till I feel the time is right. I'll check into a motel at least twenty miles from the area I'm going to work. I'll decide on how many houses I'm going to hit, in what order, and over what period of time. I've even done two or three in one night. Other times, I've spaced them out over a period of several days or even weeks. There's no particular rhyme or reason to it. I figure if I'm not sure what pattern I'm following, how will the cops figure it out?

Once I settled into the apartment, I called Pfister.

"Francis, you are not going to fucking believe this but I was just ready to get in touch with you."

"It's like we share a brain, Tommy."

"No. Really. I was. Honest to God."

"Why's that?"

"Why what?"

"Why were you going to call me?"

Asshole. It was like talking to a fucking retard.

"Oh, yeah. Well, I figured a few days have passed and I thought maybe you wanted me to give that Charlie Floyd guy a call. You know, to tell him what you want me to tell him. I'm right, aren't I, Francis?"

"Yeah, Tommy, you're right."

"See, we're on the same wavelength. What do you want me to tell him? I mean, I don't want to tell him nothing you don't want me to tell him. I want to get this right. I know it's important. This is a first step in rebuilding our relationship. It's very important to me."

"What's important?"

"Our relationship. It means a lot to me."

"You told the boys I was back in town, didn't you?"

There was silence. It was the kind of silence you know is really the answer to a question that wasn't really a question.

"It's all right, Tommy."

"You mean it?"

"Yeah. I mean it."

"I couldn't help it. I swear. I mean a couple of them came by to drop off some stuff and they asked about you—"

"They asked about me?"

"Yeah. I swear. They did. They asked if you were back in town yet. And, well, it kind of just came out of my mouth. I mean, they were talking about the job and how tough it was with all this new digital alarm system shit and when they asked about you, it just kinda spilled out. You know, how it didn't seem to bother you, the new systems, I mean. And then one thing led to another..."

"I said it's okay."

"You mean it? I mean, you're not pissed at me or nothing."

"You are who you are, Tommy."

"Yeah. I am. But I want to do right by you, Francis. I want to make up for that other thing."

"You think you can make up for it?"

"You know what I mean. I know I can never get back those two years you spent in the joint. I mean that's over and done, right?"

"Yeah, it's over...and done."

"So, what do you want me to do? Anything you want. I'll do it."

He was really beginning to get on my nerves. I don't like worms and that's what Tommy Pfister was. A fucking worm. A worm that crawled out of the dirt and primordial slime and landed in front of me. Lucky me, right? But he was a worm that might be come in handy.

"I haven't given it much thought."

"You can call me back. It's not like I have to know now. It's not like I ever have to call him. I don't want it to sound like I'm being pushy. I want you to trust me again. I mean I like you and all, but I'd really like your business back. You bring in some high-class shit. I mean most of the stuff I get is crap. I can't make a living on that. You bring me stuff I can actually make something on. That's why I want to get back into your good graces."

"So that's why."

I was playing with him. I didn't trust the little prick. He'd sell me out in a New York minute. All this bullshit about helping me out might mean be a setup for dropping a dime on me. I wouldn't put it past the little prick. I know there's a price on my head and I wouldn't be surprised if Tommy was already counting the dough.

"Well, that's not the only reason why. The big reason is because I owe you."

I was getting bored. I could think of a million other things to do other than waste my time talking to him. Time to cut the cord.

"All right, Tommy. Here's what I want you to do. I want you to call up this Charlie Floyd and I want you to tell him you heard I was back in town."

"They already know that."

"I know they know it. I wasn't finished..."

"Sorry."

"I want you to tell them I'm back in town and you heard, through the grapevine, I was on my way up to the Boston area."

"Is that where you're headed?"

"Why don't you just the shut the fuck up. You really think I'm going to tell you where I'm headed and where I'm not headed?"

"No, I just thought—"

"Don't think, Tommy. It'll just wind up in disaster. I'm telling you what I want you to tell Floyd. You tell him you heard I'm headed up that way. You don't know if it's true or not, but that's what you heard. And you also heard I been talking about using you as my fence again."

"You are?"

"What the fuck you think?"

"Oh, I get it. You want them to think you'll be using me because then they'll keep an eye on me."

"You ever think about joining Mensa, Tommy?"

"Huh?"

"Never mind."

"So, all's you want me to do is tell him you're definitely in town but you're headed up to Boston and that you're seriously thinking about using me as a fence again."

"Bingo!"

"I can do that, Francis. I really can. You can count on me and you know what, as soon as I do it I'm going to get back to you and I'll let you know exactly how it went down."

"You're aces, Tommy."

"I really appreciate this opportunity to make things right."

"That's okay. You pull this off and you're well on your way to getting back into my good graces."

"That's all I want. Really. That's all I want."

After I hung up the phone I couldn't stop laughing.

Francis Hoyt

"Do you want me to take my clothes off?"

"What do you think?"

"It's up to you. You're the one paying, honey."

Her name was Eileen Kim. She wasn't particularly pretty, more like exotic, with long black hair and dark skin. Asian. Korean. Chinese. Vietnamese. Maybe a mixture. Didn't really matter what she looked like. I was horny and when I'm horny I don't think straight, so I have to do something about it. That's what whores are good for. Helping me think straight. And then, after, I can just walk away.

"Look, just take off your fucking clothes, lie down on the fucking bed, and let's get going."

She made a face.

"You don't have to be so...crude."

"Let's get this straight. This isn't a relationship. This is a business deal. I pay, you fuck. It's as simple as that."

I opened my wallet, peeled off five one-hundred-dollar bills and threw them on the table opposite the bed. "I'm paying for the room by the hour, so let's get started."

She shrugged and started taking off her clothes. She was small. Even smaller than me. Maybe a hundred pounds soaking wet, maybe less. She had a nice body. Not perfect, a little too skinny for my taste, but good enough. At least her tits didn't sag. I hate that. They looked out of proportion with the rest of her body. Probably because they were fake. I'd find out soon enough.

"Sometimes guys like to talk," she said, taking a step closer to me. She had beautiful brown, almond-shaped eyes.

"Not me."

"Why are you so unhospitable?"

"That's inhospitable."

She was still standing there, wearing only her panties, with this stupid look on her face.

"That's what I said."

"No. That's not what you said. The word's inhospitable, not unhospitable."

She shrugged. "What are you, some kind of professor? You got what I meant, didn't you?"

"Yeah, I got it," I said, as I stripped down to my underwear.

"What do you do, if you don't mind my asking?"

"I mind."

"You're not very nice."

"You're right. I'm not nice. You ever done this before?" I said, as I moved toward the bed in only my undershorts.

"Why would you ask me something like that?" she said, as she slipped out of her panties and flung them on the chair along with the rest of her clothes. Now that I saw everything up close and personal I started to get kind of excited. I told Ricky B I didn't want one of his skanky street whores and for once he came through with what he promised.

"Because you don't seem to know how this works."

"I know how it works," she said, giving me a disapproving look, the kind of look I used to get all the time when I did something wrong as a kid. "You want a blow job, or a hand job, or what?"

"I'm paying for two hours, so we can start there."

I lay down on the bed and she sat beside me, her legs dangling over the side. I could see her tits much better now and I could see from the way they stuck straight out that they weren't real. I reached out and touched one just to see for sure. I was right.

"How long you had these?"

"That's a pretty personal question," she said, as she started caressing my thigh.

"You don't want to answer it, don't answer it."

"A year. Pretty good, huh?"

"Not bad," I said, fondling one and then the other.

"They feel like the real thing, right?"

She ran her hand down my leg.

"You have nice skin. Soft. And you're not too hairy. I don't like hairy men."

I pulled her down and kissed her on the mouth.

"Hey, there's not supposed to be any kissing. Remember?"

"Yeah, right. There's another hundred for you."

She smiled then bent over to kiss me this time. Whores. They'll do anything you want you pay them enough.

She slipped off my shorts and started stroking my cock, then licked it until it was hard, which didn't take long.

The rest of it went the way it was supposed to. Two hours passed, I got my rocks off, and Eileen Kim was seven hundred bucks richer. I tipped her real good. Part of that tip was to keep her mouth shut.

"I don't even know who you are," she said when I slipped her the extra money, "so how could I tell anyone anything?"

"Just keep it that way."

"Whaddya got to hide?"

"Think about that, Eileen."

"About what?"

"About asking what I've got to hide."

"Yeah. What about it?"

"I tell you what I've got to hide then there's nothing to hide anymore."

She started to giggle. "You're right. I guess that's pretty funny, isn't it?"

"Yeah. It's a riot. Now why don't you get the hell out of here?"

"Jeez, you don't have to be so mean. By the way, I wouldn't mind doing this again sometime," she said, as she finished putting on her clothes.

"I'm sure."

"It ain't just about the money, you know. You're in terrific shape."

"I got news for you, honey, it's always about the fucking money. And you know why?"

"No. Why?"

"Because money is nothing more than a measurement. The more you pay, the better it is. That's how we measure things in this country. By the price. I paid top dollar for you and I got what I paid for."

She thought for a moment then a smiled curled over her mouth.

"I guess you're right."

"Of course, I'm right."

"Well, I kinda enjoyed myself. Hey, I just realized something. I don't even know your name."

"That's right."

"Aren't you going to tell me?"

"You think if I gave you a name it would be the real one?"

"I guess not. But why don't you throw out something just so when I think about you I'll have a name to connect you with."

"Mike."

"Mike," she rolled it over in her mind. "Mike. I don't like that name."

"Why not?"

"It's kinda harsh, you know? And it doesn't really fit you."

"What name do you think would fit me?"

"Anthony. Yeah, I think you're an Anthony. Or maybe a Christopher."

"Tony, it is."

"No. Not Tony. That's as bad as Mike. Christopher. That's it. And Chris for short. That's what I'm gonna call you. Christopher."

I smiled. I kinda liked Eileen Kim. Maybe I would see her again. You never know.

Charlie Floyd

"Where'd you get these photos?" I asked Manny as I flashed him one of the glossies of Melinda Shaw and one of Evelyn Kerns that sat on the car seat between us.

We were headed over to Westport where we were supposed to meet up with Ricky B. "Don't forget to bring those other halfsies," he rasped into the phone when he called. I knew he would. Money is a very powerful aphrodisiac.

"The Miami Police Department had those photographs of Evelyn Kerns on file, Charlie Floyd. Our confidential informers provided us with information that she is one of Francis Hoyt's paramours," said Manny as he took the photos from me so I could concentrate on the road ahead.

I laughed. "Only you could use the word 'paramour' in a sentence and not make it sound ridiculous. Where'd they get them?"

"The ones of Melinda Shaw were obtained from her husband. He had hired a private investigator to follow his wife, whom he believed was cheating on him."

"With Hoyt?"

"That is correct."

"And Kerns?"

"The Miami Police Department was investigating a club on the strip and these were among several photographs taken while under surveillance."

"Kerns is the one in Miami, right?"

He nodded.

"But you've never actually met or interviewed her?"

"No, Charlie Floyd, I have not. I did not even know of her existence until I searched the files for Francis Hoyt's known associates. The photograph you have in your hand was there among several others. I had planned to interview her, of course, but I was suspended before I could locate her."

"Speaking about known associates, are there any others up here beside Pfister?"

Manny nodded his head, no.

"Francis Hoyt is a loner. We know he has had relationships with several women in various parts of the country, but never for too long. Evelyn Kerns and Melinda Shaw are the latest, but they will not be the last. It is very possible that there are others, but we have not identified them, as yet. He also had ties to an organized crime family in this area, but those are solely for business purposes and after he spent that time in prison he appears to have avoided them."

"What about his family? I mean the guy wasn't brought up by wolves, was he?"

Manny laughed. "No, Charlie Floyd, no wolves were involved in the raising of Francis Hoyt. His father is deceased but his mother and sister are still very much alive."

"You've questioned them?"

"I went to his mother's home, she resides in a small town outside Minneapolis, but she would not come to the door. In some ways, Francis Hoyt is a dutiful son. He makes sure she is well taken care of. I learned from the real estate agent who facilitated the purchase that that the house in which she resides was paid for in cash, presumably cash provided by Francis Hoyt. She also informed me that although she never met Francis Hoyt, she did speak to him over the phone. She was surprised when the entire purchase price of the house, one hundred ten thousand dollars, was delivered in a shoebox filled with one-hundred-dollar bills."

"Didn't she think this was strange enough to report it to someone?"

"She said she thought about it but could not think of a reason why this was illegal. And that, as she said, 'people keep money in strange places.'"

"What she really meant is that she didn't want to think of a reason. This way, she takes her commission in cash and hides some of it. Money talks, Manny. Don't let anyone tell you otherwise. What about the sister?"

"She, too, would not talk to me. Using a common vulgarity, she told me what I could do with myself."

"Ha. I've been told that plenty of times. I'm still trying to work out the logistics. What about the other one?" I asked, picking up another photo. "This Melinda Shaw chick?"

"So as far as we know, Evelyn Kerns is his current Miami girlfriend and Melinda Shaw is his current New York girlfriend. But things change very quickly with Francis Hoyt."

We were only a few minutes away from Westport. Our meeting with Ricky B was scheduled for 2:00 p.m. in, of all places, the playground of an elementary school. Not the best place for a pimp to be hanging out but he was adamant about having the meeting there.

"Meet me by the jungle gym, man," he said.

"Are you kidding?"

"No, man. It brings me back to my childhood. I used to love swinging from them bars."

I checked myself from saying he was probably far more familiar with being behind bars. I didn't want to alienate him before we even started.

"There'll be kids around, Ricky. Why don't you choose another venue?"

"It's Saturday, man. There ain't gonna be no kids around there. It's the jungle gym, or you can forget about it."

"You know," I said, as I pulled off the highway. "I think we may want to work this girlfriend angle."

Manny nodded.

"All we have to do is find both chicks and see if we can get them to cooperate. Why don't I try tracking down the Shaw woman and you go back to Miami and see if you can find Kerns?"

"I would be very happy to do that, Charlie Floyd. I miss my family."

"Before you leave can you get some information on the PI who took these shots of Shaw with Hoyt?"

"That should not be a problem."

I parked across the street from the school. Ricky was right. The playground, part of a sports complex, was empty. To the left, there was an empty baseball diamond. To the right, a soccer field where there were a few girls kicking the ball around. Behind the playground were two tennis courts. One was empty the other was being used by a couple of older women, dressed all in white, wearing white hats turned down at the brim. They were whacking the ball back and forth at a pretty good clip. I'd played a little tennis in high school. I was even good enough to make the team but my temper did me in. If I missed a shot I'd as often as not slam my racquet on the ground in disgust. This did not endear me to the coach who claimed it got in the way of my effectiveness as a player. I pointed out that it didn't seem to hurt John McEnroe. He pointed out I was no John McEnroe. He was right. I missed enough shots so that my racquet took a pretty good beating. Instead of replacing it, I quit the team and joined the baseball squad instead. I was a pretty good hitter and a more than adequate outfielder. If I did mess up I figured I couldn't do much damage to my glove when I slammed it to the ground. But I lost interest in that after a season when I realized I wasn't much of a team player.

We spotted Ricky B on the jungle gym, swinging from one bar to another.

"You want to take this, Manny, or should I?" I asked as we closed in on our target.

"You have the other halves of those bills, Charlie Floyd, so I believe you are the one he would prefer to converse with."

"Okay. But feel free to jump in any time."

As soon as we reached the jungle gym, Ricky B had a sweet face that reminded me of Little Richard. He was wearing a light blue jump suit, with a gaudy gold chain hanging from his neck. His skin was caramel colored, so it was hard to know if he was black or Hispanic. Most likely a touch of both. It didn't matter. He was just another pimp living off the backs of vulnerable women.

When he saw us approaching, he dropped to the ground.

"You Floyd?" he asked.

"I am."

"You bring those halfsies, man?"

"I did."

"So, whatchoo want with me?"

In the background, I could hear the rhythmic *thwap-thwap* of the tennis ball traveling from one court to the other. The sound was soothing, like a mantra.

I looked Ricky up and down and shook my head.

"Anyone ever tell you you're a walking cliché, Ricky?"

"Cliché? What's that, man?"

"It means over-worn, trite, expected."

"I might be a lot of things but I ain't none of those, especially expected. Why you call me that?"

"The way you're dressed might have something to do with it."

"You don't like the way Ricky B dresses? Ricky B don't give a shit. The only thing Ricky B cares about at this particular moment is hos and halfsies. Speaking of which..."

"First you talk, then we'll see about the halfsies."

"Who's this dude? What's he, like your bodyguard?" he asked, jerking a thumb toward Manny.

"This is Manny Perez. He's my partner. And yes, he does watch my back and I watch his."

Manny didn't offer his hand. His arms were folded across his chest and he had a solemn expression on his face.

"I smell cop."

"Manny's not from around here, so he can't pinch you. This is strictly unofficial."

"Whatchoo wanna know then?"

"I'm looking for Francis Hoyt."

"Don't ring no bells." He stuck his hand out. "Now where's them halfsies?"

"Not so fast."

I pulled out my phone and showed him Hoyt's mug shot.

He stroked his chin as the *thwap-thwap* of the tennis ball hitting a racquet punctuated the air.

"You ain't gonna give me them halfsies till I tell you something, right?"

"Right."

"Something about this dude?"

"Right again."

He took the phone from me and stared at the photo of Hoyt.

"Maybe he looks like someone I maybe mighta known sometime in the past."

"That's an awful lot of qualifiers, Ricky."

"What dat mean, man?"

"It means you're getting closer to those halfsies, Ricky, but you're not quite there yet."

"Ricky B can do the math, man. Those halfsies only add up to a C-note. Ricky B don't get outta bed for less than five."

"Good thing Ricky B's already out of bed."

"You a funny dude. Ricky B likes you, man. In spite of who you be."

"You'll never know how happy that makes me. Now let's get back to Francis Hoyt."

I went into my pocket and dug out the five half twenties. I handed two of them to Ricky.

"You're halfway home, my friend."

He stared at them, as if to make sure they were real, then jammed them into his pocket.

"Hey, man, I tape these halfsies together they gonna take 'em anywheres? I mean they kinda look like they be destroyed. And ain't it against the law to what you call, deface, yeah that's it, deface US money."

"Money's money, Ricky. Bring them to a bank. Tell them you accidentally cut them in half when you were opening a letter. They'll make good on them."

"Dat for true?"

"Yes, dat's for true."

Manny, his arms still crossed over his chest, a solemn expression still on his face, took a step closer to Ricky. It was a smart, subtle move announcing to Ricky that we wanted to get down to business, that we wanted answers and we wanted them quick.

I showed him the photo again.

"Yeah, that be the man, all right. Francis Hoyt."

"We know who it is, Ricky. We just want to know what you know about his whereabouts. I take it he's used your services in the past."

"Yeah. Lotsa people gots my number, man. Now you gots my number, too. So, what?"

"When was the last time he used it?"

"It be a while."

"How much of a while?"

He scratched his head. He was stalling. Manny took a step closer.

"Hey, man, whatchoo doin'? You be crowding me."

"We'll both get out of your way as soon as you tell us what we need to know."

"I gets lotsa calls. That's what my business is all about. I'm in the people business, y'understand?"

"I'm glad you brought up business, Ricky, and I'm glad it seems to be going well for you. But you know, with one phone call to the right people I can change all that."

"What you mean?" he asked defiantly, sticking his jaw out.

"Even though I'm not working for the state anymore I've still got plenty of friends in law enforcement. You don't work a job for twenty-five years without being owed a few favors. I don't ask for favors very often but when I do people seem to want to honor them. You see where I'm going with this?"

He nervously stroked his chin. "Maybe."

"I'm gonna ask you one more time and if I don't get the kind of answer I think I ought to get, me and my partner are going to turn around and walk away. And you know what I'm gonna do after that?"

"What?"

"I'm gonna get on my cell and I'm gonna make a call. And that call is going to be life altering, Ricky. Not for me but for you."

"I think I sees what you mean."

"I thought you would."

"I mighta got a call from him maybe a week or so ago."

"And what might have transpired as a result of that call?"

"You mean what did we talk about?"

"Yeah, Ricky, that's what I mean. What did you talk about?"

"You know, things."

"What kind of things?"

"Like the weather and like that shit."

"Did you introduce him to a new friend, by any chance?"

"I mighta done that."

"She from around here?"

"It mighta been around here."

"You mean like around where this playground is?"

"Not exactly around here, but kinda like in the vicinity."

"Let's get a little more specific," I said, pulling out the remaining three halfsies.

"I think maybe it was like Norwalk."

"Now when you send him a new friend you have to give that friend an address, don't you?"

"How else they gonna get together?"

"So, what was the address?"

"You expect me to remember something like that, the busy man that I be?"

"You're a businessman. Either you write it down or you keep it up here," I tapped my temple.

"It was maybe some motel up around there. I don't remember exactly which one. There be a lot of 'em up that ways."

"Maybe your friend remembers."

"She might, only she not be my friend anymore. Friends come and go in the line of work I'm in, if you know what I mean."

"I do know what you mean, Ricky."

Manny was shifting his weight back and forth. He knew we'd come to the end of the line.

I handed Ricky B the rest of the halfsies. I took out my wallet, pulled out a fifty and waved it in front of him.

"This is a retainer, an advance on future services. I'm gonna give this to you, Ricky, and because I do you're going to be beholden to me to call me if you hear anything at all about Francis Hoyt or about this friend you sent him. You hear what I'm saying, Ricky?"

He reached for it. I pulled it away.

"I want to hear you say it because when you do in the eyes of the law we have a contract. Manny is a witness to this transaction. And if I find out you've breached this contract, Ricky, I'm going to bring down the wrath of Charlie Floyd on you. That's not something you want to experience."

I handed him the fifty and he quickly stuffed it in his pocket.

"You just signed the contract, Ricky, so I'm counting on you to keep your end of it."

"I am very impressed, Charlie Floyd," Manny said as we got back into the car.

"Well, thank you, Manny. I'm sure if you did it you'd get the same result."

"Perhaps, but I do not think I would have been half as

amusing. So now we know that Francis Hoyt is most likely in Connecticut, or at least he has been recently."

"It's a start. But until we get something solid, he could be anywhere."

Francis Hoyt

If you're looking for a fight, the best place, other than prison where the trick is to avoid them as much as you can, is a bar. Low-class, blue-collar bars are best, but any bar will do.

I don't drink anymore but I been around drunks long enough to know how they act. I had a pretty good role model in my old man. It didn't take much to get him started and once he did the only way he stopped was when he fucking passed out. First my mom then me, when I got old enough, had to collect him from whatever bar he was at, which meant any bar he hadn't already been thrown out of and banned from coming back. I dreaded those calls but when they came I did what I was supposed to do: I got my ass over there and dragged the sonuvabitch back home where, if he had anything left in him, he'd whack me around for pulling him away before he drank enough to pass out again.

He got into plenty of fights and most of them he lost. He'd come home, his face all bloodied, his eyes half-closed, and he'd tell us he fell down. He fell down a lot. Maybe he shoulda been a little more careful.

I vowed that would never happen to me. Get drunk or lose a fight.

Newark, New Jersey seemed to be as good a place as any. I picked one of those anonymous working-class, Irish bars figuring it wouldn't be too hard to find the right patsy there.

It was the middle of the week, Wednesday, late, maybe a little after eleven, when only the serious drinkers were left. There were maybe ten, fifteen people in the joint, mostly guys.

Most of them paying attention to the glass in front of them. When it got close to empty, they motioned the bartender for another.

I sat at the end of the bar and ordered vodka and a glass of water. Like I said, I don't drink, but this time I kinda made an exception. I nursed the vodka, every so often adding a little water so the drink always appeared to be full. When the water glass was empty enough and when I was sure no one was look-ing, I'd pour the vodka into the water glass and order another vodka. By the time it appeared as if I'd had three or four drinks under my belt I forced myself into a conversation with a burly dude who had a tough time reaching over his enormous belly to grab his beer. He had me by about a hundred pounds and six or seven inches, but that made him perfect for what I had in mind.

When someone's already three sheets to the wind it don't take much to get him into an argument. If he's the right kind of drunk, the guy who's having trouble at his job, or his wife don't understand him, or his kids are the devil's spawn, or he's just plain pissed at the world, he's got so much anger welling up inside he's looking for an excuse, any excuse, to blow.

He didn't know it, but I was about to give this sucker that chance.

I know exactly what to say to and how far to go to provoke someone into hauling off and throwing a punch. And I'm quick enough to see it coming, dodge it, then throw my own punch so I'm the one who makes first contact. Not that I can't take a punch. Just back away from it, while at the same time moving slightly to one side or the other. Even if he connects, it'll be a glancing blow and he'll be off-balance and he'll fall forward. Once that punch is thrown the other guy leaves himself wide open and you give it to him. *Pop. Pop. Pop.*

"What the hell did you say?" he slurred.

"Are you fucking deaf, you moron?" in a voice close to a whisper. "You want me to say it again, asshole? Okay. Try to read my lips, if you can fuckin' read. This fuckin' state sucks.

Your governor sucks. Your football team sucks. Your state stinks like an outhouse. Did you fucking hear that? Or maybe you'd like it in sign language?"

He telegraphed his punch and I let his fist graze the side of my cheek. Then, while he was still off-balance, my right connected with his nose. I heard the crunch and felt bone when I quick hit him with another shot flush on the upper cheek. Surprisingly, he didn't go down, but he did sag heavily against the bar. One more punch and he would have kissed the floor, but I wanted him to throw another before I did. It took him a couple seconds to get over the shock of being slugged by someone small as me, but I had plenty of time. Finally, he threw another and this one was wilder than the first. I shifted to my left and watched as it passed by me. I could have done some serious damage, but I didn't want to hurt the guy too bad. I didn't have anything against him. I just wanted him to go down. One more blow should do it, this one to his kidney. I heard a whooshing sound, like when the air is let out of a balloon. He grunted then went down. You could hear the thump when he hit the floor.

It was all over in less than a minute. Next thing I knew, someone was pulling me away and the bartender, waving a baseball bat he'd gotten from under the bar, was yelling something. I looked up to the end of the bar where I knew the surveillance camera would be and smiled, then let myself go limp.

I heard someone yell, "I called the cops."

"You saw it," I said to the bartender. "He threw the first punch. I was just defending myself."

The bartender, a panicky look on his face—probably worried that any trouble with the cops might get him closed down—nodded. "Yeah, yeah. I don't know what the hell happened but yeah, he threw the first punch, all right."

Mission accomplished.

Manny Perez

The day I was suspended from the Miami Police Department I became a hero in the eyes of my fellow police officers many of whom silently and not so silently cheered what I had done. I was both honored and embarrassed by this show of support from my brothers in blue, and yet it only magnified the shame I felt.

I had done the wrong thing, even if it was for the right reason, and I deserved to be punished for it. And so, I did not object to what I believed was the harshness of my punishment nor did I request the union to appeal my case.

And yet, I was forced to listen to several of my less sensitive colleagues mock me.

"Hey, Perez, I hear you let some hundred-pound punk get the best of you. Maybe we ought to assign you to the kindergarten beat where you can kick some serious ass."

I know that it was all meant in the spirit of good fun, and yet I would be lying if I did not admit that the words of some of my colleagues stung deeply. I am a proud man and I was deeply ashamed of what I had done. I knew that by engaging in foolish and selfish behavior I might have seriously compromised a case against this master criminal. It was possible that my irresponsible action might have resulted in prolonging Francis Hoyt's reign of terror.

It was at that moment I swore to myself I would hunt down Francis Hoyt, no matter how long it might take me. I would do what no other law enforcement member has ever done: produce evidence of his crimes that would result in sending him to prison for a very long time.

I told only one of my fellow officers what I had planned. This was my former partner, David Chung, a first-generation Chinese police detective who feels the same way about America as I do. He promised to help me all he could by keeping me abreast of any information that might come in. And so, when I received a phone call from him, I knew it had to mean that he had some important information about Francis Hoyt.

"Something came in over the wire this morning I thought might interest you, Manny. It's from the Newark, New Jersey police department and it's about your boy, Francis Hoyt."

"What is it?" I asked eagerly, as I sat on the back porch of the house owned by Charlie Floyd. He was inside preparing dinner, and I was reading the notes I had taken on the likely periodicals Francis Hoyt had access to when he visited the Society Library. Looking for some kind of pattern in terms of location, I catalogued every article in terms of wealth and geography.

"Just an alert that Hoyt had been detained as a result of a little fracas in a Newark bar the other night. It went out to departments across the country that have expressed interest in our boy."

"Did you, by chance, get any details?"

"Sure did. Soon as Hoyt's name popped up, I gave them a call. Seems he was in a local dive and somewhere around midnight he got into an altercation with another patron. It didn't last long. A few punches and it was over. When it was, Hoyt was the one standing, the other guy wasn't. Broken cheekbone, broken nose. Someone called the cops, but no arrests. The whole thing was on video. I had them email me a copy of the video and it showed your boy Hoyt didn't throw the first punch. So, it was self-defense. But, man, he sure as hell messed up the other guy who, by the way, looked like he was twice Hoyt's size."

"He remained at the bar until the police arrived?"

"Yup. He even mugged for the camera, like he was in some

kind of stupid reality show. And the odd thing, Manny, is that he gave his real name. That's what set off the alert. They fed it into the computer and his sheet came up. But there are no outstanding warrants on him so they let him go. I'm guessing the other guy was probably too embarrassed to press charges. It was one of those David and Goliath things."

"Thank you so much, David Chung. I truly appreciate your taking the time to relay this information to me. Would it be possible for you to email me the video file?"

"So long as no one catches me. You know how they are down here. Everything by the book. I'm not about to go through all that red tape. You know what that's like."

"I do not wish to see you get into any trouble, my friend."

"Don't worry about me. You, me, we gotta stick together to get the bad guys. I'll keep my eyes and ears open in case something else comes in. And Manny, one more thing. We miss you down here. Like I told you, we all know you were just doing your job and we think you got a raw deal."

"No, I was not doing my job. If I had been doing my job I would have obtained the proper warrant. I made a mistake and I accept my punishment. But I will be back and I will, as they say, 'take care of business.'"

"I'm sure you will. If I hear anything else I'll let you know. Oh, and I'm still working on that other stuff for you. I'm hoping to have an address on Evelyn Kerns by tomorrow. Oh, and I stopped by to check on Esther yesterday. She's fine. She and the kids miss you, of course, but I'm sure I'm not telling you anything you don't already know."

"Thank you, David Chung. You are a prince among men. I am hoping I will not be here that much longer."

As soon as I got off the phone I went into the kitchen to share the news with Charlie Floyd.

"He wanted us to know he was there," said Charlie Floyd.

"Yes," I said, "that is exactly what I thought."

"The question is, why?"

Charlie Floyd

Manny's news put an interesting spin on the search for Francis Hoyt. I was sure it was all staged so Hoyt would lead us to believe he was in New Jersey and that's where we should be targeting our search. But this didn't fit with the information from Ricky B that put Hoyt in Connecticut with one of Ricky's whores. I believed he was targeting New York or Connecticut.

"He's playing us, Manny," I said to my partner as we ate dinner out on my deck.

"Yes, Charlie Floyd, I am certain you are correct. He would not be so careless as to get into a senseless brawl and risk being arrested unless he wanted us to know where exactly where he is. Francis Hoyt is a meticulous planner. There is no such thing as coincidence when it comes to Francis Hoyt. I asked my friend, David Chung, to send us the video. I want to see it for myself. He informed me that not only did Francis Hoyt stick around for the police to arrive, but he mugged for the camera."

"The fucker's toying with us, Manny, trying to throw us off. It's his way of giving us a big, fat middle finger."

Manny nodded.

"It's a joke to him. He wants us to know he's got his eye on us. I'd bet Ricky B's been in touch with him since we saw him yesterday."

"I would not be surprised either."

"You think he's in New York, New Jersey, Connecticut, or Massachusetts?"

"It is very possible that he is in all those places, just not at the same time."

"You know, Manny, I hate to say this but I wonder if we're ever going to find him."

This wasn't like me. I've never doubted my ability to do the job. But I couldn't help flashing back to my futile search for John Hartman. If he hadn't turned himself in after all those years on the run, it's very possible I'd never had found him. That case was what precipitated thoughts of retirement. I had to shake out of this funk. I had to forget about the past and concentrate on the future. No more negative thoughts.

As if reading my mind, Manny proclaimed, "We will find him, Charlie Floyd. Of that I can assure you. And in answer to your question, I still have work to do but from my examination of the magazines it appears to me that he is targeting homes in Connecticut."

"I hope you're right. But it's possible he's changed course once he realized we were after him. My guess is Pfister talked. Hoyt is smart. He's a master of misdirection. We can't let ourselves be manipulated. Look, dinner's almost ready. Why don't we go over what we have while we eat? I don't know about you but I'm pretty hungry."

Here's what we knew:

Francis Hoyt was definitely in the tri-state area.

Hoyt knew we were after him.

Hoyt was most likely planning a series of jobs.

Tommy Pfister and Ricky B were funneling information to Hoyt.

Evelyn Kerns and Melinda Shaw were two of his most recent girlfriends.

This gave us something to work with. We agreed the next thing we'd do would be to track down Kerns and Shaw, in hopes one of them might lead us directly to Hoyt.

To that end, Manny, who was anxious to see his family, made a reservation to return to Miami Friday morning to look for Kerns, while I would head down to New York City to track down Shaw.

We had ourselves a plan.

Francis Hoyt

"I ain't never thought I'd ever hear from you again, Francis. I'm thinkin' you're the kinda guy holds a grudge. Ain't that so?"

"Sorry, Vito, but you've got me all wrong. There's no percentages in holding a grudge. You never know when you're gonna need someone's help, so why burn bridges? Besides, grudges never quite work out the way you want them to. There are two times in a man's life when he shouldn't act."

"When's those?"

"When he's in love and when he's angry."

"That's very smart thinkin', Francis. But no one ever said you wasn't smart. So, to what do I owe the honor of your presence here?"

We were sitting across from each other in some shit-ass tiny pasta joint in Little Italy. Dark walls. Dark floors. Very low lighting. I guess that's the way wise guys like it. That way they don't have to see exactly what they're eating and they don't have to see each other too good. Me, I had enough darkness in the joint. And since I work at night, I like to spend the daytime hours in the light. Turns out I'd eaten here once before and didn't think the pasta was all that good. But the wise guys seem to like it and they're creatures of habit, so that's where I knew I'd find Vito.

Here's something to chew on. Wise guys aren't that wise. If they were, they wouldn't get pinched so often. Every morning you open up the *Daily News* you see some other wise guy's been caught with his hand in the cookie jar. The last thing you ought to do if you're playing patty-cake with the law is be predictable.

The feds probably got the place wired. Maybe they've even got a camera hidden somewhere. Or one of those drones circling Mulberry Street. And you can be damn sure they've got the joint under constant surveillance. Hell, everything's under constant surveillance these days. There's cameras on every damn corner, in every damn store. There's no such thing as being anonymous anymore. You're on the air wherever you are, wherever you go. My advice: live with it, embrace it, use it, just don't abuse it.

It didn't matter to me. Right now, the more I was seen, the better. Obviously, it didn't matter to Vito, either. You'd think after all these years mob guys would have figured it out, but they haven't. They still get pinched and sent upstate, nailed by their own words.

Let's face it, the Italian mob is pretty much on the way out. Their heyday has come and gone. Today it's the Russians, Chinese, Armenians, Serbs, and Bulgarians you got to look out for. They'll rip your guts out just for fun. They'll shoot you in the head then chop up your body and use it for fertilizer. Nothing frightens them and if a man doesn't have fear in him, he becomes very dangerous, especially to himself. But they just don't give a fuck. I mean, what sense does it make when Arabs and Muslims are blowing themselves up just to get to heaven where they'll be met by a zillion fucking virgins?

"Just thought I'd stop by and pay my respects, Vito."

Vito smiled. "Bullshit," he said, lifting a glass of red wine. He brought it to his lips, held it there a second, swishing it around in the glass, before he drank. It was all a fucking act. Ever since *The Godfather* every two-bit hood thinks he's Marlon Brando. Give me a fucking break.

"Respect is important, Vito. You know that. I don't always see eye to eye with you, but I respect you. You don't get to the position you're in without earning respect from your peers. I respect you and I think you respect me."

If I'd been in a bathroom I'd be vomiting straight into the toilet.

"If you say so, Francis."

He knew it was bullshit and I knew it was bullshit, but I also knew he was lapping up every bit of it. Because even though it was bullshit it was the kind of bullshit he wanted to believe. That's why I said it.

He took another sip of wine while swishing around what was left in his glass, like he knew what the fuck he was doing.

"This is very good wine. You sure you don't want some?"

"You know I don't drink."

"Things change. I thought maybe you took it up again. I don't know if I can trust a guy who don't drink. Especially when he don't drink vino as good as this."

"You shouldn't trust me. You know why?"

"Why's that?"

"Because I'm unpredictable. That makes me unreliable and untrustworthy. I wouldn't trust me if I was you."

"That so?"

"Yeah, I'm afraid it is. I can't help myself. I'm counter-intuitive. Sometimes even I don't know what I'm doing. That's true of all the great ones, Vito. Michael Jordan, he didn't know exactly how he was going to dunk that ball until he was in mid-air. That's me. You don't know which way I'm gonna go. I don't know which way I'm gonna go. It's how I managed to stay out of the joint. That is until I got hooked up with you."

"See, I knew you held a grudge."

"No. You've got that wrong. It's not a grudge. The way I figure it it's more like a debt."

He rolled some spaghetti on his fork, using his spoon to guide it, then shoved it in his mouth. A little red sauce splattered onto the napkin tucked into his shirt.

"You figure I owe you something? That the way you see it?"

"What do you think?"

"It wasn't me that fucked up, Francis."

"It wasn't me, either. It was one of those two doofuses you sent along with me even after I begged you not to."

SECOND STORY MAN

"I made a mistake in judgment. Shit happens," he said as he ripped off a hunk of bread and dabbed it in a dish of pasta sauce.

"It does. But not when I'm in charge. When I'm in charge shit definitely does not happen."

"So whaddya want me to do? What's done is done. I can't change that. I can't give you back those two years you spent in the joint. And I know you well enough to know it's not about money. You got plenty of that. And even if it was, you'd be barking up the wrong tree."

He glared at me. Just to show me he wasn't joking around. I knew that already. Guys like him don't have much of a sense of humor. They don't see the irony of life. If they did, they probably wouldn't be doing what they do.

"You're right, Vito. I don't give a fuck about the money."

"So whaddya want?"

"I want a favor."

Charlie Floyd

The next afternoon I found myself sitting in the waiting room of Matthew G. Cohan, licensed private investigator. I knew that much because that's what he'd inscribed on the door in broken down, faded gold block letters that looked as if they'd been gnawed at by rats. That couldn't be true, of course, because rats can't jump that high, so it had to be simply the ravages of time and neglect.

While I was on my way in to see Cohan, the PI who'd taken the photos of Melinda Shaw, Manny was on a plane back to Miami to find Evelyn Kerns.

I hadn't called to make a proper appointment and as a result his secretary who could have used a class on the fine art of applying makeup—she obviously did not subscribe to the less-is-more theory—had me cooling my heels in the small outer office while Mr. Cohan was supposedly "on a very important call with a very important client." I didn't believe a word of that. The dust that had accumulated on a small table that resided against the well-worn flowered upholstered couch I was seated on indicated that not many clients had recently passed through the hallowed halls of Mr. Matthew Cohan, licensed private investigator.

"I'm sure he won't be too much longer," she said, while cracking her gum and filing her long, bright red painted nails.

"Hope not," I replied. "How long you worked for Mr. Cohan?"

For a moment she looked confused, like it was a trick question.

"Not long."

She was in her thirties, maybe a little older. Not pretty, not ugly, not plain. One of those anonymous faces you see in the subway going to work every morning. She was wearing too much makeup, especially the lavender mascara on her eyelids. It was a warm day so she was wearing a yellow sleeveless blouse and her shoulder-length brown hair was tied in a bun.

"I'm only part-time," she added, as if it just occurred to her to amend her answer.

"You got a name?" I asked.

"Yeah. Everyone's got name, don't they?"

The more words she spoke the more her borough accent seemed to thicken. Whether the accent was the borough we were in, Brooklyn, or the Bronx, or Queens I couldn't tell.

"Everyone I've ever come across so far. So, what's yours?"

"Lauren."

"Nice name. Female version of Laurence."

"Huh?"

She picked up her mobile phone and stared at it a moment, then plopped it into her large purse which was leaning against her desk.

"Jeez, I gotta get going."

She dropped her nail file into the purse then picked the purse up.

"Late lunch?" I asked, since it was already a few minutes after two o'clock.

"Nope. Time to get to my other job."

"Which is?"

"Pretty much the same thing I do here. Answer the phone. Take messages. But it's for the nail salon downstairs."

"Very convenient."

"Yeah."

"Honey, before you take off," I said to her as she dropped her purse on the desk and began to search in it for who knew what, "why don't you stick your head in there and tell Mr.

Cohan that I'm a busy man and if he doesn't see me in the next two minutes I'm gonna take off." I showed her my badge. "And on my way out I'll have just enough time to make a call to some friends I have up in Albany about the validity of his PI license."

I was bluffing, of course, but she didn't know that so she looked concerned. She dropped her purse and quickly disappeared into the inner sanctum. A minute later she came out and Cohan stuck his head out behind her and said, "Come right in."

"Sorry about that," said Cohan, as he led me into an office that looked as if it had been designed by the Collyer brothers. There were papers strewn all over his desk, open boxes on the floor, magazines and newspapers piled on every surface, and a bookcase sagging under the weight of books and private dick gadgets like night goggles and two-way radios. It looked like a grown-up's version of Dick Tracy's office.

"So, I'm Matthew Cohan," he said, as he plopped into his chair. He was at most five-seven, and at least two hundred and twenty pounds. He wore suspenders to keep up his pants but they weren't doing the job they were hired for. He sported one of those comb-overs that does nothing but call attention to the fact that you're going bald. I'm not particularly good with ages, but Mr. Cohan looked like he could be anywhere from forty to sixty-five. He probably fell somewhere in between.

"Any relation to George M.?"

"Only if his real name was Cohen and he was a member of the tribe. I thought it was a better career move for the cops to think I was Irish."

"Did it work?"

He shook his head. "The jury's still out. And hey, call me Mattie. Everyone does. And your name?"

"Charlie Floyd. You can call me Charlie. Everyone does."

He didn't crack a smile. Evidently, Mr. Matthew Cohan no relation to George M. didn't have much of a sense of humor.

"Well, Charlie, pleased to meet you. Have a seat and tell me how I can help you today."

"I'm here in about Melinda Shaw."

"Shaw. Shaw. Melinda Shaw. Name sounds vaguely familiar. I know I should know who you're referring to but…"

"You were hired by her husband a while back, to see if she was having an affair."

"Oh, yeah. Melinda Shaw. Good looking chick. Yeah, yeah, I know who you're talking about now. So, what about her?"

"Tell me about how you found her and where she is now."

"I'm afraid no can do, Charlie. In case you didn't know it we in the private investigating business have something we call client confidentiality. It's like what priests and rabbis have. We owe it to our clients not to discuss their case with anyone without their permission. I assume you don't have Miss Shaw's permission…"

While he was chatting away about whatever the hell he was trying to say to impress me I took out my wallet, opened it to my expired state ID issued by the AG's office, placed it on the desk and pushed it toward him.

"What have we here?"

He picked it up.

"Well, why didn't you say so, Charlie? We're colleagues. This official business?"

I nodded a lie.

"In that case, I'm always ready to help a colleague. One hand washes the other, right?"

"That's how we both stay clean."

"So, it's Melinda Shaw you're interested in?"

"I'd like to know how and where you got this photo of her."

I'd taken a picture of the original with my phone and I showed it to him.

"That's mine, all right. Not bad work, if I don't say so. The important thing is to get as much of the face as possible so there's no mistaking it. The other person, not so important. Unless, of course, the husband wants to take it any further. Sometimes that happens. Not this time. This guy just wanted out of the marriage and he wanted to keep as much of his dough as he could."

"Nice work, Mattie." I was guessing flattery would go a long way with a guy who'd change his name to Cohan from Cohen.

"Thanks. It wasn't easy. I had to follow that broad for almost a week before I hit pay dirt. It was like she knew she was being followed. And if I do say so myself I'm pretty good at what I do."

"I'll bet. How long ago?"

He scratched his bald head. "Seems to me it was last summer. Yeah. August, maybe? You can tell the way she's dressed. Nice legs, right?"

"Know who the guy with her is?"

He shrugged. "Not a clue. It didn't matter to me. All my client wanted was a photo of her with another guy. In New York, you can't shoot through a bedroom windows unless you're Spiderman. Holding hands on the street with him was enough, but I even got them kissing. My client had money and didn't want to part with it, so he figured photos like this would save him a nice piece of change. You looking for her or him?"

"Both."

"Can't help you with him. Last I heard they're divorced and she was living somewhere on the Upper West Side. Shouldn't be too tough for a guy like you to find her."

"How about a guy like you finding her for me?"

He went silent. I knew exactly what he was thinking: *How much can I get from this guy to find her?* That's the way these private dicks think. On a sliding scale of greed.

"Not too hard, but it would take time and I'm up to my ears right now."

"What's your day rate?"

"Seven-fifty."

I laughed. "What's your real rate?"

"You got me there, Charlie-boy. Five hundred."

"What's your rate for a colleague?"

"All's you want me to do is get an address on her?"

"That's all."

"How about two bills?"

"You won't have to leave this office to do it. How about the friends and family rate: one-fifty?"

"You drive a hard bargain, Charlie, but okay, just because we're compadres now. And I know you're a guy who doesn't forget a new friend. You know, in case I should need something somewhere down the line."

Yeah, he was an operator, all right.

I kept my mouth shut.

"How do I reach you with the information?"

I threw him my old card, which reminded me that one of these days I really ought to get around to getting new ones made up.

"Best to reach me at that number I wrote in. It's my cell. And you're sure you don't have any idea who the guy is in the photo with her?"

His eyes moved away from me for just a split second. "Not a clue."

He was lying. I wondered why.

Manny Perez

I had no official standing as a result of my suspension, and so it was necessary that I fly beneath the radar. That is why I did not identify myself as a Miami police detective when I met with Ms. Evelyn Kerns. Only my good friend and former partner, David Chung, knew what I was doing and he had sworn himself to secrecy. He had performed the legwork necessary in locating Ms. Kerns. He also supplied me with some helpful background information about her.

Ms. Evelyn Kerns was working as a cocktail waitress at one of the hipper hotel clubs that have sprouted up all across Miami Beach in the last two decades. Although at one time Miami Beach and its environs used to be associated with elderly retirees, or snowbirds escaping the northern climes for the sunshine and warm ocean breezes, this changed when the TV show *Miami Vice* suddenly turned the area hip. Today, the Collins Avenue area is dotted with condos, posh hotels, and nightspots, providing Miami with a much-needed renaissance.

Ms. Kerns was originally from the Midwest, a small suburb outside Chicago, and she had been residing in Miami Beach for the past two years. Prior to that she was a resident of Hollywood, California, where she went in hopes of making her name in the movies. Unfortunately, she only made it in so far as performing as an extra in several small, eminently forgettable films, as well as one commercial for panty hose. And so, after spending five unfruitful years on the West Coast, she decided she would try her luck in another city with a similar climate as well as a burgeoning film industry.

David Chung learned she was still a registered member of SAG, the Screen Actors Guild, and that is how he obtained a current address for her, an apartment complex on Wiley Street in Hollywood, Florida, just a quarter of a mile north of the Diplomat Hotel.

When I visited her apartment, it was mid-afternoon, and I found her in the pool area. There were two card games, one populated by four men, the other by four women, in an area at one end of the pool where shade was provided by an overhanging roof. There was an elderly woman doing laps in the pool while two younger women were practicing yoga at the other end of the pool. Ms. Evelyn Kerns was one of those women. I recognized her immediately from the photographs. She was a very attractive blonde with an athletic build. She was wearing a yellow bikini. From the data David provided me with, she was in her early forties. But from a distance she looked much younger.

I waited for her to complete the yoga exercises. When she was finished, she dove into the pool. She swam several laps, in perfect form, I might add. When she was finished, she grabbed a towel from her chaise lounge and began to dry herself. I approached her as she was rearranging towels on her chaise lounge. I identified myself simply as Manny Perez and asked her about Francis Hoyt.

"I am very much aware that you are under no obligation to speak with me, Ms. Kerns, but I would very much appreciate your voluntary cooperation in this matter."

"Matter? What matter? Cooperation for what?" she said as she angled the chair so that it was more in line with facing the sun. "Hey, aren't you hot in that outfit? It's eighty-three degrees. See?" she pointed to a large round temperature gauge fastened to the wall of her apartment building.

I was wearing my normal attire: a short-sleeve, white, button-down shirt, black string tie, seersucker suit, and a Panama hat. And although it was quite hot and humid, I was not the least bit uncomfortable.

"I do not mean to contradict you, Ms. Kerns, but I hardly think that a suit that cost me this much qualifies as an 'outfit.'"

"You talk kinda funny, but hey, that's a real cute accent you got there. Where you from, honey?"

"Miami."

"Nah. I know a Miami accent when I hear it and that's not a Miami accent. You're from south of here, that's for sure. Let me guess. Venezuela? Bolivia? Costa Rica? Argentina? Colombia? Wait, the hat's the tip-off. Panama, right?"

"No," I said with a smile. I was quite pleased with how our interview was progressing. That she was engaging with me in conversation was a good sign. If you keep people talking and if you project an image of friendliness, they will more often than not bond with you and, as a result, provide you with the information you are looking to obtain. On the other hand, if you are aggressive, threatening, and hostile with them, chances are they will resist you and in some cases shut down altogether. You must work hard to win them over to the point where they *want* to help you, by making it appear as if you are not working at all.

"I am originally from Havana, Cuba."

"You're shitting me. Wow, I never woulda thought of that one. But I should've, of course. Miami's filled with you people. Wait, I don't mean that in a bad way. Did I just mess up? Did I offend you, honey? Because I sure didn't mean to."

"I do not take offense, Ms. Kerns"

"That's good. How long you been here? In this country, I mean."

"Twenty-two years."

She whistled. "That's a long time. Whaddya think about what's going on now? I mean, soon we'll all be able to visit your country."

"You're in my country, Ms. Keyes. I am an American citizen."

"Oh, yeah. Sure. I didn't mean anything by that. All's I

meant was, well, you probably still have family there and soon you can visit them. I mean, legally. That's what I meant."

"All my family is here now. Everyone in Cuba who was my family has regretfully passed away."

"Oh, sorry. Look, like I said, I didn't mean to offend you."

"You are not offending me, Ms. Keyes."

"Castro, he's dead now, right?"

"No, I am afraid he is very much alive. Although I don't expect he will live much longer. He will be ninety years old on his next birthday and I understand he is not in the best of health. In fact, he has appointed his brother, Raoul, to his former position as president."

"Yeah? Gee, I really thought he was dead. My bad. Look. It's hot. Maybe you want to take your jacket off and we can get a nice, cold drink. Whaddya say?"

"I think that would be very nice. Thank you for your kind offer, Ms. Keyes."

"Why don't you just call me Evie. That's what everyone calls me."

"Thank you, Evie."

"Why don't you take a seat over there, at that table with an umbrella, in the shade, where it's cooler, and I'll go upstairs and get you a drink. How about a margarita? Or maybe a planter's punch. I love those drinks. I can drink a dozen of them, which is why I never order them. Between you and me, I don't hold my liquor so good. You. Do. Not. Want. To. See. Me. In. That. Condition. Wait a minute. Wait a minute. What the heck am I thinking? A Cuba libre. That's what they call it. Rum and Coke, right? That's what you probably want."

"Yes, that is what they call it. But if it is all the same to you, I prefer to have a simple drink of seltzer with lime."

She shook her head. "I just love the way you talk, honey. Wait, you're not offended because I thought you might like a Cuba libre, are you?"

"I am not offended at all, Ms. Kerns. Rum and Coke is a fine and satisfying drink. It is just that at this particular time I would prefer a seltzer with lime and ice, please."

"Of course. Why didn't I think of that? You're a cop and you're on duty. Of course, you can't drink. What the heck am I thinking? Must be the heat getting to me. I am so sorry."

"What makes you think I am a cop, Ms. Keyes? I did not show you any identification."

She laughed. "Honey, I can smell the fuzz a mile away. I knew you were a cop the minute I laid eyes on you. I don't need a badge or ID to know you're a cop."

I decided to drop the matter there. As long as I did not identify myself as being on the Miami police force, I was not misrepresenting myself. Allowing her to think this was an official visit would make it more likely she would cooperate, assuming she did not have the same disregard that Francis Hoyt has for authority.

I sat at the table under the umbrella while Ms. Evelyn Kerns went upstairs to her apartment. Ten minutes later she was back downstairs. She was now wearing a man's pale blue, button-down shirt over her bikini. She carried a tray that held two drinks, what appeared to be a mojito for her, and for me a seltzer with lime. On the tray she had carefully arrange a plate with a slab of cheese, perhaps it was Jarlsberg, surrounded by a variety of crackers, and a knife.

"I thought you might be hungry," she said, as she placed the tray on the table and sat down across from me.

"Thank you," I said. After she had gone to the trouble of preparing the cheese and crackers it would not have been polite to refuse her hospitality. She was now taking care of me as if I were her guest. I suspected this attitude might change once she learned why I was really there.

I started to reach for the knife to slice off a piece of cheese, but she stopped me by gently placing her hand on mine.

"That's my job, honey," she said. She cut off a couple of slices, placed them each on a cracker, handed one to me and she took the other.

"Thank you," I said.

"So," she said after taking a bite of her cheese and cracker and washing it down with a sip of her mojito, "you're here about Francis."

"Yes, I am. I have information to the effect that you are a good friend of his."

She laughed. "Friend. Gee, I'd hope we were more than that. How do you even know about me and Francis?"

"We have been watching him for some time."

"Why would you be doing that?"

It was at this moment that I realized Evelyn Kerns might not know the kind of man Francis Hoyt was. She might not be aware of the criminal enterprises in which he was involved. She might not know that he was a dangerous, notorious criminal. Or she might be acting as if she did not know anything about his life.

"Would you mind telling me what you know about Francis Hoyt?"

"I'm not quite sure what you're looking for, what'd you say your name was?"

"Manny Perez."

"Of course. Manny. I like that name. It's very...manly." She smiled at her little joke. I smiled with her.

She threw up her hands, as if under arrest. "Okay, Manny, you don't have to use the rubber hose. I'll admit it. Francis Hoyt is my boyfriend. So, what?"

"How long have you two known each other?"

"Jeez, it's gotta be a couple years, at least. Let's see, I met him not long after I moved here, so it must be two and a half years. Yeah. Two and a half years, going on three."

"When was the last time you saw him?"

"Oh, gee, it's been a while. A couple months maybe. But that's not unusual. He does a lot of traveling for business. Besides, he goes up north this time of year, but he always comes back down to visit me a couple, three times. But I don't want you to get the wrong idea. We're not exclusive or anything."

"Are you aware of what business he is in?"

She cocked her head to one side. This was not a good sign. She was getting ready to shut down.

"You know, I'm not so sure Francis would like me talking to a stranger, especially if that stranger is a cop. Especially about his personal affairs."

"You do not have to answer anything you do not wish to answer, Ms. Kerns. And besides, there is no reason you need tell him about this encounter. I repeat, do you know what kind of business he is in?"

"You know, that's something I probably should know the answer to but the truth is he doesn't talk about it and I just haven't thought to ask."

I knew from the way she shifted her eyes away from me that this was not the truth. I had my answer. She knew Francis Hoyt was a criminal. But I could not accuse her of lying. If I did she would become defensive and she would shut down completely.

"Do you not think that is not a little strange? Do you not think that a woman should know what the man she is sleeping with does for a living?"

"Hey, Manny, you're getting a little personal, pal. How'd you like it if I asked personal questions about you and your wife," she said, nodding to my left hand on which I wore my wedding band.

"You are a woman, a very attractive woman, a very intelligent woman." She blushed. "And so you must have become suspicious about what Francis Hoyt does when he is away from Miami, away from you."

"There isn't a woman in the world who isn't curious. We want to know all kinds of stuff and the stuff we don't know we make up. But we also have to know our place. What Francis does is his own business, not mine. Why are you so interested in him? He's not one of those serial killers, is he?"

She laughed but I detected a hint of uncertainty. She knew

Francis Hoyt and whether she admitted it to herself or not, she knew what he was capable of. I would guess that is why she does not ask him too many questions. She is afraid of the answers she might get.

"No, to my knowledge Francis Hoyt has never killed anyone. But that does not mean he is not capable of doing so. The Francis Hoyt I have become acquainted with is capable of anything."

"This is getting a little heavy." She took a sip of her drink. "More cheese?"

"No thank you. I would like to be honest with you, Ms. Kerns."

"I think honesty is the best policy."

"Francis Hoyt is a very bad man. He has done some very bad things. I am sure there are things about him you do not know. Perhaps you would not like to know them."

"You know, Manny, I think we're about finished here. No matter how charming you are, and you are charming, I don't think you're going to get what you came here for. Francis is very important to me and whatever he's done, well, I'm just not interested."

"Would you possibly be interested in what he does with his time when he is not with you?"

Her expression changed to one of anger. "I don't know who you're talking about and even if I did, I don't have to talk to you or anyone else. So, get lost, buster."

She stood. "I just remembered an appointment I've got to get to. I'm already running late. It was a pleasure meeting you." She said with more than a hint of sarcasm in her voice.

"The pleasure was all mine, Ms. Kerns. But perhaps I might leave my card with you?"

"You could leave it, but I wouldn't expect to hear from me if I were you."

I removed a card out of my wallet and handed it to her. "I would hope that is not true, Ms. Kerns. But please do contact me if you would like to know more about Francis Hoyt."

She took the card and stuck it in the bra portion of her bikini. "I don't think that's going to happen, honey."

I could do nothing more and so I left. Although she was not aware of it, I knew I was not finished with Ms. Evelyn Kerns.

Charlie Floyd

"Yeah, this is Charlie Floyd. Who's this?"

"It's Tommy Pfister. Remember me?"

"You're unforgettable, Tommy. What can I do for you?"

It was early evening and I was sitting in my backyard trying to decide if it was worth it to fire up the grill and toss on a steak for one since Manny wouldn't be back for a couple days. He'd called and told me about his episode with Evie Kerns and although he said he didn't get any useful information, he insisted he wasn't quite finished with her. He thought he could break her. I was still waiting to hear from that private dick about Melinda Shaw. I'd bugged him with a couple calls and he swore he'd have the information for me in a day or two. I knew exactly what he was doing. Stringing me along so I wouldn't know how easy it really was for him to get the information. I wouldn't be surprised if he tried to hit me up for some extra dough.

"It's not what you can do for me it's what I can do for you."

"Yeah? What's that?"

"You're looking for Francis Hoyt, ain't you?"

"I am."

"Well, I know where he is."

"Where's that,?"

"You think I'm gonna tell you just because I'm a good fucking citizen? You think I'm just gonna hand over a friend? Just like that?"

"I haven't given it much thought. And with friends like you I figure Hoyt doesn't need any enemies."

"You want I should just hang up and end this conversation?"

"Do whatever suits you, Tommy. Do what you have to do. But remember, you called me, not the other way around."

"Yeah, well, I'm not selling out Hoyt unless there's something in it for me. I know the insurance company's probably got rewards out for him. I know if I help you you're gonna get at least a part of that action, and I want a piece of it, too."

"I'm listening."

"Can you come down here tomorrow morning?"

"I could if I had a reason."

"Is having Hoyt here reason enough?"

"I'd say it was in the ballpark."

"Listen, I want you should be here at nine-thirty sharp. And I want you should bring some kind of contract between you and me, that says when you get Hoyt I get fifty percent of whatever you get."

"That seems a little steep."

"Fifty percent of something is better than fifty percent of nothing. You want Hoyt, I can give him to you. But without that deal we ain't got any business to do. Understand?"

"I understand."

"So, we got us a deal?"

"I'm not going to haggle with you over the phone. I'll be in your office tomorrow at nine-thirty. Okay?"

"And you'll bring the papers? Because if you ain't got no papers then the deal's off. You'll have to find him without me and that ain't gonna be easy. So, you'll bring the papers, right?"

"Sure, Tommy. I'll bring papers."

Francis Hoyt

"I did just like you said, Francis. He'll be here tomorrow, nine-thirty. And I got the feeling this guy's an on-time kinda dude. I did good, right?"

"Yeah, Tommy, you did good."

"Anything else you want me to do? I mean it. Anything?"

Sure, there were other things I'd want him to do, but nothing I was going to tell him now.

"No, we're good."

"You mean it? You really mean we're good? Like in you don't hold that other thing against me?"

"What other thing?"

"Come on, Francis, you know what I'm talking about."

"Yeah, you're right. I do know what other thing you're talking about. I'm just pulling your chain."

He gave me one of those forced, nervous little laughs people give you when they want you to think they've gotten the joke when they haven't a clue.

"I thought so. Look, I just want us to be friends again. And to do business again. You're the best. Ever. And I mean that. There's no one fucking better than you are. No one."

"Okay, I think you've crawled far enough up my ass."

But yeah, he was only telling the truth.

"I mean it. And I'd do anything to get your business back. I've made some new connections since before. And I'd even give you a bigger cut. How does twenty-five on the dollar sound? That's more than double I give anyone else."

"You're right. I'm not anyone else. But I've got things to do, Tommy, and negotiate over the phone with you isn't one of them."

"Sure. Sure. I get that. So anyway, he's going to be down here tomorrow morning. What then? I mean, what do I say, what do I do?"

"You tell him you're expecting me to come in at exactly eleven-thirty. You tell him I'm always on time. You tell him you'll keep me there till he shows up. You tell him he should be there no later than eleven-forty-five. Don't let him hang around till then. Tell him to go out for breakfast or something, and then come back. And, Tommy..."

"Yeah."

"You gotta sell it, man. He's gotta think it's legit and not a setup. He can't think you and me worked anything out. You understand?"

"Yeah, yeah, I can do that. But I got a question?"

"Yes?"

"I don't mean to pry, I mean it's none of my fucking business, but what do you have in mind? I mean, why do you want him to come back? Are you really going to be there at eleven-thirty? You're not going to do something like whack him right here, are you?"

"That's at least three questions."

"Oh, yeah. Well, maybe you could answer one of them?"

"I'm gonna refer to the first part of your statement, Tommy, and that is that it's none of your fucking business."

"Sure, sure, I get that. But this is my place of business. I mean, I wouldn't want anything bad going down here. If that's what you have in mind, I mean."

"Don't worry, you're not going to have to clean up any blood from the floor, if that's what you're worried about. You've got my word on that."

"Not worried. Just a little concerned. But hey, I'm sure you know what you're doing and I'm just happy to oblige."

"If you're happy, I'm happy, Tommy."

Manny Perez

I believed strongly that eventually I could get what I wanted from Ms. Evelyn Kerns, even though she rebuffed me yesterday afternoon. I was confident I had begun the essential bonding process between us and when I sensed that thin filament between us would fray I immediately pulled back.

I had planted the seeds of doubt in her mind about her paramour, Francis Hoyt. I knew that part of her wanted to cooperate with me while the other part needed to remain loyal to him. Rather than push forward I chose to retreat. But only for the moment.

The great author, Ernest Hemingway, who was a hero to all of us growing up in Cuba, once explained that when he was writing he often stopped for the day while he was in the midst of a wonderful sentence, when he was in peak form for the day. He believed that by doing so, when he returned to writing the next day, he could pick up at that point and make it even better. To have quit at a low point, when he was having trouble expressing something the way he wanted to express it, would have had him return to that low point. I have endeavored to apply that theory to the art of interrogation. If you see that someone is getting annoyed or tired or bored, or angry, or indifferent, do not continue. If you do, the target of your interrogation will only become defensive and eventually shut down completely. Some, of course, will say otherwise. They will harangue the subject of their interview. They will spend hours and hours in the interrogation room. They desire the person they are interrogating to break down. That, they believe, is how they will come to the truth. However, I have found that you are not likely to obtain information that is useful or even a confession that you may rely on. In fact, you are more likely to get a false confession than the truth. This is why I do not believe that torture is an effective way to obtain useful and true information. The result of waterboarding or other types of physical and emotional torture, is that the one being interrogated is likely to tell you whatever he or she thinks you want to hear, simply to put an end to whatever torture technique you are using.

I am not out to obtain what I want to hear through torture, but rather the truth, through a process of bonding with the alleged perpetrator.

I was provided the work address for Ms. Evelyn Kerns by David Chung. It was a nightclub within the famed Fontainebleau Hotel. From the manager, I found that Ms. Kerns was working the late shift that evening, which meant that she would arrive for work by 8:00 p.m. and work till the early morning hours.

At 7:30 p.m. I stood by the employee's entrance to the club. At seven-forty-five I saw Ms. Kerns approaching. She was on her cell phone and so she did not see me until I stepped in front of her.

"Hey," she said, obviously not recognizing me. "Watch where you're walking."

"I apologize, Ms. Kerns."

A look of recognition crossed her face.

"It's you."

I tipped my hat. "Yes, I am afraid it is me."

"I've got to get to work," she said brusquely, trying to pass by me.

I got in step with her.

"I regret having to accost you as you are getting to work, Ms. Kerns, but I wanted to show you something."

"What?"

I removed a sheet of paper out of my briefcase and handed it to her.

"What's this supposed to be?"

"This is only one page of Francis Hoyt's arrest record."

"So?"

"Did you know he was a repeat offender, Ms. Kerns?"

"I don't care what he was. I care what he is." She looked down at the paper. "And I don't see anything here that isn't at least five years old. Why don't you leave him alone? Don't you believe a man can be rehabilitated?"

"Do you?"

"Of course I do. Francis has done absolutely nothing to make me believe he's done anything wrong."

There was no point in arguing with her. Once someone has established a narrative in their mind it is almost impossible to shake them from that narrative. Logic is worthless. Facts are worthless. And yet, I was not about to give up on Ms. Evelyn Kerns quite yet.

I opened my briefcase again and this time removed a photograph of Francis Hoyt holding hands with Melinda Shaw. I handed it to Ms. Kerns.

"What's this supposed to be?"

"It is a photograph of Francis Hoyt with another woman."

"So?"

"We have others."

"Why should I care how many you have? If this is supposed to get me to tell you what you want, I'm afraid you've struck out, Manny whatever the hell your last name is."

"It is meant to help you understand what kind of man Francis Hoyt truly is."

"How do I know when this photograph was taken? How do I know you didn't mess with the photograph? I wouldn't put it past you guys. I've heard about these vendettas. I'm sorry you came all the way over here, probably keeping you up way past your bedtime, for nothing. I have nothing to say about Francis.

Now I've got to get to work or else the boss'll dock my pay."
Her tone hardened. "Some of us have to work for a living, you
know? And if you if you keep harassing me I'm going to file a
formal complaint with the Miami PD."

She brushed past me and entered the club.

The bond between Ms. Kerns and Francis Hoyt was far
stronger than I had anticipated. Perhaps she would eventually
change her mind, but for now all I could hope for was that
Charlie Floyd would have had better luck with Melinda Shaw
than I had with Evelyn Kerns.

Charlie Floyd

When I walked through the door Tommy Pfister was in pretty much the same position I'd left him in almost a week earlier: sitting behind his desk, leaning back in his chair, reading the sports pages of the *Daily News.* Only this time he looked up as soon as I entered.

Still holding the paper, he twisted his wrist so he could check his watch. He nodded and smiled.

"Right on time, Floyd."

"So, my friend, what's up?"

I walked around the counter and sat on the edge of his desk.

"You got that paper for us to sign?"

"What paper's that, Tommy?"

"You know, the contract where it says I get fifty percent of the reward you guys are going to collect for bagging Francis Hoyt."

"No, I don't have anything like that."

His face sagged. "You're kidding, right? I mean I told you that's what it's going to take for me to cooperate. I can hand you Hoyt on a platter." He pounded his hand on the table. "That's what you guys are looking for, isn't it? By the way, where's your little partner?"

"That's not your business. And have a little respect, will ya?"

"Cops I know don't deserve no respect. So, what's gonna happen here?"

"That's completely up to you, Tommy."

"How you expect me to cooperate when there's nothing in it

for me? I need incentive, man."

"How about I put you up for the Good Citizen Award?"

"Fuck that. I gotta make a living. And this ain't no joke. I guess you're not serious about nailing Hoyt."

"Oh, I'm serious, all right. So serious I might consider ten percent, but fifty? That would only be in your dreams."

He tucked several of his chins into his chest and thought for a moment. "That don't seem fair for what you're getting out of this. But I guess you got me over a wheel barrel. Hoyt got in touch with me yesterday morning. He's in town."

"You're not telling me anything I don't already know. Please don't fuck with me because I had to get up pretty early this morning to make it down here by nine-thirty and I don't like to get up that early. I need my eight hours' sleep. I don't get it I'm cranky all day."

Tommy flashed one of those smiles that makes you want to wipe it off his face with the back of your hand.

"You might know he's in town, but did you know he's going to be here, in this office, at eleven-thirty this morning?"

"What for?"

"Whaddya mean, what for? Whaddya think what for? To fence some goods, that's what for. I gotta spell things out for you? Since he's going to be holding the swag you can nail him for it. That's still against the law, ain't it? Possession of stolen property. There's your case. All gift-wrapped for you."

"So, you're telling me he's already broken into some homes up here?"

"How should I know? I only know he says he's gonna be here with some stuff he wants me to take off his hands. Maybe he got it from before he came up here. Maybe he did break in a couple places already. He don't confide in me and I don't have his to-do list. You don't think he's coming in just to pay his respects, do you?"

"I only know what you tell me, Tommy."

"Well, that's what I'm telling you. That he's gonna be here

in—" he looked at his watch, "—in about an hour and a half. You want him, you'll be here, too."

"So, you're saying I should leave and come back…"

"Yeah. Come back a little after eleven-thirty. Like eleven-forty, eleven-forty-five. Just to make sure he's here. If you're here already he's gonna see you as soon as he comes in that door and he's gonna bolt. And he's gonna know I gave him up. And then my life ain't gonna be worth shit. So, you gotta leave and come back. Besides, I got other business to conduct and you can't be here when I do. You'll spook my clients."

"If you're fucking with me—"

"I ain't fuckin' with you. I swear. He's got an appointment to be here eleven-thirty. That's what he tole me. Like you, he's always on time. So, you come back and he'll be here. But you gotta make like it was some kind of serendipitous thing or something."

"Serendipitous? Where'd you learn a word like that,?"

"I know plenty of words. Serendipitous is just one of them."

"Okay, Tommy, maybe I've misjudged you and if I have I'm sorry. I'll be back here eleven-forty, eleven-forty-five. But if this is some kind of scam—"

"It ain't no scam. Hoyt told me he'd be here. That's the way he is. He says he'll be somewheres, he'll be somewheres. But if anything changes I got your number."

I told Pfister I'd be back, but my intuition was telling me something wasn't quite right. Hoyt was much too careful, too meticulous, too smart, to trust the likes of Tommy Pfister. Besides, he was most likely the one who tied Hoyt up with the mob and that connection led to his being arrested and sent up. I had the sneaking suspicion Hoyt was behind this and that he was either toying with us or he had some nefarious reason for getting me down here. Maybe I'd come back when Pfister told me to and I'd find that Hoyt wasn't here. Maybe it was just a "fuck you" from Hoyt, a way to make us look like amateurs, like stupid fools.

Nevertheless, I couldn't take the chance Hoyt really would show up, so I planned to be back just like I told Tommy I would be.

I found a nearby coffee shop, took a quiet booth in the back, ordered some breakfast, and gave Manny a call. He was at the Miami airport, on his way back to New York. He didn't have to tell me how he'd fared. I could hear the disappointment in his voice.

"I am very sorry, Charlie Floyd. I just could not make her talk about Francis Hoyt. She is in love with him and so she does not see him for who he really is. If I could have convinced her how evil he is, how he uses people, how he destroys lives, then perhaps things would have turned out in our favor."

"It's okay, Manny—" I looked at my watch, "—in about an hour and a half I'm supposed to be in the same room with Hoyt."

"What did you say, Charlie Floyd?"

Disappointment was replaced by excitement. His voice became so animated that I could feel Manny's energy traveling fifteen hundred miles, surging through my cell phone.

"Pfister got me down here on the promise Hoyt would be in his office around eleven-thirty this morning. All he wants for this act of doing his civil duty is a cut of the insurance dough. I don't think that's going to happen, but something will. The question is, what does Hoyt have in store for us?"

"Do you not believe he will be there, Charlie Floyd?"

"I'd say the odds are heavily against it. Pfister's a rat and I think he'd drop a dime on his mother. As smart as Hoyt is I find it hard to believe he'd trust Pfister and be so careless as to show up at his place when he knows we're on his tail."

"But you will be there anyway?"

"That I will. If Hoyt is just toying with us, jerking us around, and this is his idea of a joke, that's okay. It means he's thinking about us and maybe we can turn it around on him. I'm curious. I want to see where this goes."

"Be careful, Charlie Floyd. Francis Hoyt is a man who is capable of doing anything to further his criminal enterprise."

"I'm not worried, Manny. He doesn't have a history of resorting to physical violence and even if he did I don't think Tommy Pfister's office would be the ideal spot to try something."

"Remember, I saw him up close. I felt him up close. There was evil in those eyes. It is true that he did not harm me, that he just used enough force to escape my grasp, but I could see in his eyes that he would have gone as far as was necessary to obtain his freedom. He is a man without conscience."

"I'll keep that in mind. And I'll see you tonight, right?"

"Yes. I will be renting a car at the airport and I shall most certainly see you tonight, my friend."

"Maybe I'll have some good news for you when you get here."

"That would be lovely, Charlie Floyd. Just lovely."

Charlie Floyd

I recognized the smell as soon as I got within a couple of feet of the door to Tommy Pfister's office. There was no doubt what it was.

Gunpowder.

Trust me, when there's the smell of gunpowder in the air, nothing good follows.

I unhooked my shoulder holster, pulled out a handkerchief from my jacket pocket. From force of habit, I used it to carefully twist open the doorknob, so as to preserve any fingerprints or DNA that might been deposited there. I pushed the door open and entered slowly, my right hand resting gently on the butt of my pistol. I was pretty sure I wouldn't need it, but why take a chance?

The room was empty of anyone except for me and Pfister. One of us was standing, the other was either napping with his head on his desk or dead. I already knew which one it was. His head was resting in a small puddle of blood. As I got closer I saw the puddle had already begun to dry, which meant Tommy had been dead at least a half hour. His eyes were wide open, as if he'd seen it coming and tried to look away. As I moved around to the side of his desk, I could see the bullet hole right in the middle of his forehead. Only one hole, from what I could see, but that was enough.

Tommy Pfister was stone cold dead.

I walked back to the front of the counter to see if there was anything missing. Jewelry and watches were still under glass, all in pretty much the same position I'd seen them in a couple hours earlier. I checked the file cabinet to see if the drawers had been tampered with. Nope. I turned my attention back to Pfister. I knew better than to touch the body, but I did notice his wallet sticking halfway out of his back pocket. Apparently, the only thing amiss was the late Pfister.

One bullet, strategically placed. Nothing taken. Looked to me like a professional hit.

I pulled out my cell and punched in nine-one-one. I told the operator who I was, where I was, and why I was calling. "No hurry," I added. "He's not going anywhere and neither am I."

"Are you sure, sir?" asked the operator.

"Believe me, ma'am, I know a dead man when I see one."

After I hung up I went into the hallway, closed the door behind me, and waited patiently until the cops arrived.

I was impressed by New York's Finest. They showed up in no more than fifteen minutes after I made the call. Two burly, uniformed cops and one plainclothes detective dressed in jeans and an NYPD blue T-shirt, his badge dangling over his chest, emerged from the elevator.

The detective did all the talking. He asked me who I was. I showed him my defunct investigator's ID from the state of Connecticut. He asked me why I was there. I told him I was supposed to meet Francis Hoyt. They'd all heard of Hoyt. It seemed pretty much everyone had, except for me. He asked if I thought Hoyt had done it. I said I didn't know. I said it was possible, but if he had committed murder I couldn't quite figure out why. And besides, I said, it wasn't part of his criminal profile. He was a thief, not a killer. But what I didn't tell him was that I don't believe in coincidences. I'd let them figure that out for themselves.

We're living in a world where everyone and everything is documented, whether it be on video or audiotape. This crime was no different. I waited while one of the cops called downstairs to the building manager to see if there was any video from the lobby and the elevator. There was. While one cop remained stationed in front of Pfister's door until a forensics team arrived, I accompanied the detective and the other uniformed cop to the building manager's office to view those tapes. Since the murder had to take place between the time I left, about nine-forty-five, and the time I arrived back, around eleven-thirty, it didn't take long for the cops to see who got off at Pfister's floor, then got back on the elevator a few minutes later. That's all it would have taken. Not much turnaround time. I didn't figure there was much conversation between killer and victim. No howdy-do, how's your old lady stuff. Just one shot right between the eyes and Pfister was no longer among the living.

It wasn't hard to pick out the killer. He was wearing a dark, slouch hat pulled down over his face and a dark trench coat. Since it wasn't raining and it was well past overcoat weather, the outfit was surely meant to hide the killer's identity. After viewing the tape one thing was certain. It wasn't Francis Hoyt. The killer was at least twice Hoyt's size, both in height and width. So, whoever pulled the trigger and killed Tommy Pfister was not Francis Hoyt.

I don't believe in coincidences. Everything happens for a reason, although it might not always seem reasonable. There is cause and there is effect. That evening, over dinner, Manny and I tried to figure out the cause and effect of Tommy Pfister leaving this mortal coil.

"You think Hoyt found out Pfister was about to roll over on him and had him killed?" I asked Manny, thinking out loud.

"That is certainly possible, Charlie Floyd, but the more intriguing question would be why would Tommy Pfister suddenly decide to turn on Francis Hoyt," asked Manny.

"Money's a pretty good motivator and Tommy knew there was a reward," I said, playing devil's advocate.

"I suppose that is also possible, but that would have meant he was willing to live with the knowledge that everyone knew he was a snitch. It would mean that he could not continue to work as a fence, and in fact it most probably would have meant he was willing to go underground for the rest of his life. Or at least until Francis Hoyt was safely behind bars."

"True. And chances are he wouldn't have lived long. Snitches usually pay the ultimate price, just like Tommy did. Besides, he couldn't know for sure how much he'd wind up with or if he'd have wound up with anything at all. Frankly, I don't think he gave a shit about the money because he knew his life wouldn't have been worth much after Hoyt was nailed. That was just something he used to explain why he wanted me down there, why he was willing to give up Hoyt. There's more to it than that."

"It is, of course, possible that the murder of Tommy Pfister had nothing to do with Francis Hoyt."

"I think both of us have been at this long enough—" I flicked my nose with my finger, "—to know when something doesn't pass the stink test."

Manny smiled and mimicked my gesture.

"So, let's assume for the moment that Hoyt instructed Pfister to get me down there. And then let's assume Hoyt had something to do with Pfister's untimely demise. Then we'd have to ask ourselves why? What did he stand to gain from having Pfister killed? And why would he want me to find the body?"

"I believe it could have been done for the sake of revenge."

"That's possible. But Hoyt got out of the joint over two years ago. If he had such a hard-on for Pfister he had two years to act on it. Why now? Besides, Pfister was at least three degrees away from Hoyt getting pinched. It was the fault of those two fuck-ups he had to take along with him. Why not go after them? And if not them why not the mob guy who forced them on Hoyt?"

Manny shrugged. "The criminal mind is not always logical, Charlie Floyd. But you are correct. Where Francis Hoyt is concerned, there is always a reason for what he does or does not do. It is up to us to find out what it is. In the meantime, what did you have planned for us tomorrow?"

"I haven't given it much thought. This kinda changes things, don't you think?"

Manny nodded.

"I believe we could add accomplice to murder to the charges against Hoyt."

"Yes," said Manny. "Now all we need do is find him."

Francis Hoyt

"Francis, baby, you've been in town for over two weeks and this is only the second time I've seen you."

"Gimme a break, Mel. I've been busy."

I grabbed her by the waist and planted one on her. She tasted good. I'd been looking forward to this so I was hoping she wouldn't fuck it up by asking a lot of stupid questions and making stupid demands. I like things simple.

"Too busy to make time for me?"

I told her to meet me on 59th Street on the park side across from the Plaza Hotel and now we were walking into the park. I figured it was a nice day so we'd head up to the Boathouse and have some lunch and maybe, if I was in a particularly good mood, take a rowboat out on the lake. I put my arm around her and pulled her close. She smelled good. Some kind of flowery smell. I always liked the way Mel smelled. Sometimes I put my face close to hers just so's I can smell her hair. I once asked her what she put in it to make it smell that way and she laughed and said, "It's only the shampoo I use, Francis. It's not like I spray perfume in it or anything."

Whatever it was, it worked.

I hated this part of it. The whining, the complaining, the explaining. Why couldn't the part of me I gave them be enough? Why did they always want more? Some people might say, "What the hell are you doing, Francis? Why can't you just pick one woman and settle down? Hell, you've got more than enough dough."

They just don't get it. I don't want to settle down. I don't want just one woman. Yeah, yeah, I know it's all about fear of commitment. You don't think I've heard plenty of that psycho-analytic bullshit all my life. That's what they do when they don't know what to do with you. They send you to a shrink. I been to more shrinks than they have in all of Vienna. Not one of them told me anything I didn't already know. Not one of them changed the course of my life.

"I told you when we started this thing that it wasn't going to be easy. I told you that, right?"

"Yes, but..."

I squeezed her arm. "No buts, Mel. There are no buts. I told you right up front what to expect, that I wouldn't be around all the time, that I might disappear for long stretches, that I wouldn't always stay in touch as much as I should, but that I'd be there when you needed me. I told you that, didn't I?"

"Yes, you did."

"Then I don't think this conversation should go any further."

"You're saying I can't expect things will ever change?"

"You want change, go to the bank and cash in some bills because it's unlikely you'll get it from me. I am what I am and that's all that I am. Who said that?"

"I think it was Popeye."

"Yeah. That's right. Popeye. From the cartoons. What was his girlfriend's name?"

"It's because I love you, Francis. It's because I care about you."

"Olive Oyl. That's it."

"Francis, did you hear what I said?"

"Yeah. I heard."

"What do you say to that?"

"I know what you want me to say. You want me to say I love you, even if I don't mean it."

"Not if you don't mean it."

I shook my head. She was trying to fight it but she was close to tears. That's the last thing I needed, a woman crying. They do it just to control men. I hate that shit.

"I don't know what the fuck love is, Mel. We sure didn't have it in my house."

"I'm so sorry…"

"Don't be sorry, dammit. I'm not sorry. It was what it was. You don't hear me crying about it, do you?"

"No. And you're scaring me a little."

"Sorry. I didn't mean to scare you." I took her arm and kissed her on the cheek. Maybe I loved her a little, maybe I didn't. How would I know? I don't even know what love is, how it feels. All I knew was I liked having her around. But not when she talked like this. When she talked like this I wanted to toss her into the fucking lake that was behind Bethesda fountain that we were approaching. What was that book we had to read in high school about the guy who tosses his pregnant girlfriend into the lake and drowns her? Oh, yeah, *An American Tragedy*. That was it. Pretty good book. I remember at the time I was kinda surprised they'd make us read something like that. About a murder. Of course, I didn't much like the ending with the guy getting convicted and having to sit in the hot seat. He was dumb, though. He didn't have to get caught. It might even have been an accident, though I didn't think so. But he felt guilty about it so he practically led the law to his door. Poor, dumb asshole.

"Let's just get to the Boathouse and have some lunch. I'm sure we can find something better to talk about," I said.

We walked a little further with neither of us talking. But I knew that wouldn't last long.

"I don't care if you don't feel the same way," she said. "I just know how I feel about you and I just want us to be happy. I'll just have to do a better job of accepting you as you are."

I wanted to punch her in the face. I didn't want her to fucking accept me. I don't need anyone to accept me. I just want people to respect me. I want people to give me my due, as they say. I don't want people trying to walk all over me because if they do they're going to learn pretty quick that Francis Hoyt is no pushover. He pushes back when he's pushed. Don't fuck with Francis Hoyt because if you do you're going to regret it.

That's what I want.

That's all I want.

Charlie Floyd

"You wouldn't happen to be Melinda Shaw, would you?" I asked of the woman I knew was her. Matthew Cohan had phoned in the information yesterday, telling me not only where Melinda Shaw resided but also where she worked and who she worked for. She was "special assistant to the Vice President" of a textile company located in the Garment District, Seventh Avenue and Thirty-Eighth Street. This probably meant she was little more than a secretary with a fancy title to make up for being underpaid. But that was her business. Mine was to try to convince her to turn on her lover, Francis Hoyt.

Rather than just march up to her place of business and ask to see her I decided to ambush her as she got off the elevator after work. So, I planted myself in the lobby at a quarter to five in the evening, leaning against a wall while I made like I was reading a newspaper, and waited patiently for the elevators to empty out.

At precisely five-thirty, one of the elevators opened and out walked Melinda Shaw. She was prettier than her photograph, even after a day's work in the rag game rat race. She was of course surprised to be accosted by a complete stranger who knew her name.

"Excuse me?"

"You're Melinda Shaw, right?"

"Who's asking?"

"That would be me."

"Very funny. Who are you and why are you stalking me? I

could call the cops, you know."

"You most certainly could. I like the cops. I used to be one of them. But I think you'd have a tough time convincing them I was stalking you since this is the first time I've laid eyes on you."

"At the risk of repeating myself, who are you?"

"My name's Charlie Floyd and I think we have something to talk about. I noticed a little diner across the street and I doubt this time of day anyone else would be in there. What say we hop across the street and we can talk."

"About what?"

"A friend of yours."

"What friend?"

"Francis Hoyt."

She started to walk away but I followed her.

"I think talking to me might be in your best interests, Melinda."

"I don't have anything to say."

"You're wrong. I suspect you have plenty to say. But why don't we just see by humoring me. I don't think this'll take more than ten, fifteen, minutes tops. After that, I'll be out of your hair forever."

She stopped and turned to face me. "You're not going to give up, are you?"

I smiled. "You've got me pegged."

"And if I do speak to you for ten minutes you'll leave me alone forever."

"Forever and a day, Melinda."

This time she was the one who smiled. The Floyd charm was starting to work its magic.

"You know, I never admitted I know this person you're talking about," she said as we sat across from each other in a quiet booth near the back of the diner, two cups of black, inexpensive, nondesigner coffee in front of us.

"Since I've only got ten minutes, Melinda, I don't think it's useful to waste any of them with this kind of nonsense."

I took out my phone and flashed one of the photos with her and Hoyt.

"Okay, so I know him. So, what?"

"The question is, what do you know *about* him?"

"I know he's good to me and that he loves me. That's enough."

"Ordinarily you'd think so, but in this case, it's not. Francis Hoyt is a dangerous career criminal."

She laughed.

"You think that's funny?"

"Yes, I think the idea of Francis as a dangerous criminal is pretty laughable."

"Would you like to see his rap sheet? Wait, I don't even have to do that. You have one of those smart phones you can just Google him and see what comes up. One of the things you'll find is him doing time for attempted murder."

Yes, I was gilding the lily a little, but so what? Machiavelli would have been proud of me.

The muscles in her face tensed, accentuating her high cheekbones. I could see what Hoyt saw in her, what anyone could see in her. Her eyes were doing pinwheels from one side of the room to the other. She seemed to be gasping for breath. She couldn't look me in the eye. I'd surprised her and it wasn't with a good surprise. You know, like she won the lottery or she snagged the guy of her dreams. I knew what she was doing. Mentally, she was trying to go over all the time she'd spent with Hoyt, trying to make sense of this new information. And I could see it was new. She obviously knew nothing about Hoyt's life of crime.

It was time to pile on.

"He's a thief, Melinda. He breaks into people's home and he steals from them. You get it? He takes what isn't his. That's who Francis Hoyt is. It's not pretty, but there it is."

Finally, she seemed to catch her breath. She shut her eyes and when she opened them she was looking directly at me.

"So, what do you want from me?"

"I want you to give up Francis Hoyt."

"I'm not going to do that."

"Why's that, Melinda?"

"Because...because I love him."

"You think he loves you?"

"I know he does."

"Really?"

"Yes, really."

Here it went. I was going for all the marbles.

I fingered my phone that I'd placed on the table in front of me. "If he loved you like you say would he be playing around with another woman?"

Her eyes went dead. Her face tightened. She was on the verge of anger, an emotion that would, I knew, eventually get me where I wanted to go.

"I don't think so, Melinda. But we're dealing with Francis Hoyt here and he doesn't play by the rules. He makes up his own rules. In his world, you can 'love' more than one woman at the same time."

I picked up my phone and called up one of the photos we had with Hoyt and Evelyn Kerns. I slid the phone over to her. She looked down at the photo but didn't bother to pick up the phone. She pushed the phone away.

"Ever hear of Photoshop?"

"No one tampered with this photo, Melinda."

"It could be old."

"It could be, but it's not. We've got a time and date stamp on the original, if you'd like to see it."

She was silent. Her body sagged. I almost felt sorry for her. She didn't do anything worse than a lot of other women: fell for the wrong guy. And now she was nothing less than another victim of Hoyt's. I felt a little sorry for her but not enough to back off.

She pushed the phone back to my side of the table.

"I know this doesn't make me the good guy, Melinda."

"That's for sure," she mumbled.

"I've got a job to do."

"And you don't care how you do it."

I shrugged. What could I say? She was probably right.

"I'm not going to do what you want me to do."

"You ought to think about it." I took out my renovated card and slid it over to her side of the table.

"You can reach me at that number."

"What makes you think I'm going to have to reach you?"

"It's up to you. But I don't see how you owe this guy anything. He didn't tell you the truth about himself or about this other woman. And I can assure you, there's more than one."

"One's enough," she said. "I'm going to go now."

"Sure. I understand. You need to think about it."

She got up without taking the card. She took a couple steps away from the table then stopped, came back, scooped up the card and shoved it into her purse.

She'd call me. Just a matter of when.

Francis Hoyt

"Why the hell didn't you tell me before this?"

"I didn't want to bother you, Francis. I mean I figure you've got enough going on. And I handled it."

"Jesus, Evie."

She'd called me on one of my burner phones, the number only she had. It was the only way she could contact me and it was supposed to be for emergencies. From what she'd just told me, this was one of them.

"I'm sorry. I really am. But I swear he didn't get anything out of me. Even the second time. But is what he told me the truth?"

"How should I fucking know? I don't know what the fuck he told you."

I stopped myself. I was losing it. Not good. It wasn't her fault. It was that fucking little spic bastard. How the hell did he even find out about her? But now it didn't matter. I had to make sure Evie was on my side. I piss her off who knows what the hell she'd do. I had to make nice, make like nothing was wrong. Damage control. That's what I had to do.

I softened my tone. I pictured Evie. She was wearing a short, tight skirt and black, scoop-necked sweater. Evie was always sexy, but especially when she wore short skirts that showed off her great legs. And she was sweet, in an uncomplicated kind of way. That's the way I like them. Uncomplicated. Just the opposite of me. I missed Evie.

"I'm sorry, Evie. You got me at a real bad time. Work stuff."

"That's okay, baby. I understand. But it's all right if you've been in trouble with the law. I mean, I know plenty of people who've been there. Even me. When I was a kid, you know. Little stuff. Shoplifting. Getting in with the wrong crowd. I'm no angel, Francis."

Jesus, just what I needed. True confessions. But I had to let her talk, no matter how stupid and meaningless it was.

"I'll level with you, Evie. I was in some trouble. Bad trouble. I made a mistake. I was in the wrong place at the wrong time. But I paid my debt to society. I learned my lesson. I'm on the straight and narrow. Honest. But these guys, they won't let me alone."

"I wish you were here, Francis. So, we could talk about it. So, I could support you. So, I could hold you in my arms. Because I know you're a good man. You've always been good to me. No, not just good, great. You've been great to me. You've taken care of me. You've never said an unkind word to me. Now's my chance to do something for you."

The tide was turning. I had her back on my side.

"There's nothing you can do, except not talk to anyone about me. I'll take care of everything else. We'll get through this, baby."

"I know we will. I know it. And I hope you know you can trust me. I love you, Francis."

I knew I was supposed to say, "I love you, too." I knew that's what she wanted to hear and that's what I needed to say. But I couldn't. It's not that I can't lie. I've done plenty of that in my life. It's just that those words—I. Love. You—stick in my throat. So instead, with as much sincerity as I could muster, I said, "Me, too, baby."

When I finished the call with Evie I sat there in my little studio apartment staring at the blank wall. These assholes were beginning to really piss me off. I had to do something about it. Something.

Francis Hoyt

All the houses on the block seemed pretty much the same. On the small side, three bedrooms, tops. None of them shouted out: "I've got valuable stuff. Rob me." But that wasn't the point.

The one on the corner looked to be the most likely because it was set back from the road and had hedges surrounding it. Once past the hedges you couldn't be seen from the street. I called a local real estate agent and asked about the house. Was it for sale? Not at the moment. Did she think the owners might be amenable to an offer? Perhaps, she said, and then she gave me more than enough information about them. They were an older couple who'd been living in the house for six years. Nice, hard-working people. They owned a clothing store in town. That meant they'd leave the house fairly early in the morning.

That's all I needed to know. The rest was up to me.

Manny Perez

I was sitting in the living room when the doorbell rang. Charlie Floyd was in the den, watching a ballgame between the New York Yankees and the Boston Red Sox. Charlie Floyd, as he has mentioned to me many times, is a rabid Boston Red Sox fan.

"How about you, Manny?" he asked before he disappeared into what my wife, Esther, would call his man-cave. "Got any interest in the national pastime now that you're legally one of us. It was part of the naturalization process, wasn't it, choosing a baseball team to root for? Besides, these new Cuban players we're getting up here are really something. What are they feeding them down there?"

"Yes, Charlie Floyd, I am very much a fan. And I am afraid the Yankees, your sworn enemy, are my team of choice, ever since I was a young child. Did you know that I wanted to play shortstop for the Yankees?"

"You're kidding."

"No, it is true. I was an excellent fielder but I am afraid as a hitter I was no more than average. And since growing up there was little chance I would ever play for the Yankees, I gave it up for other pursuits."

"Never too late."

"Ha. I am afraid it is often too late for many things and this is one of them. However, if I watch the game with you, I am afraid I will have to root against your beloved Boston Red Sox."

"That's okay. It's a free country, Manny. But come on,

watch the game with me and we'll make a friendly bet, just to keep the game interesting."

"I believe gambling is against the law in this state, is it not?" I said, with a big smile on my face.

"Five bucks? Just to make things interesting? And if it helps I'll just declare this patch of land as part of an Indian reservation."

I agreed to his friendly wager and told Charlie Floyd that I would be in to watch the game with him as soon as I completed going over my list of possible relevant articles in the periodicals I had isolated that might shed some light on where Francis Hoyt was planning his next reign of terror. It was shortly after 8:00 p.m. when I heard the front door chime. A moment later I heard Charlie Floyd emerge from the den and answer the door. What I heard next stopped me short and made my heart speed up considerably.

"I hear you been looking for me, Floyd. Where's your little spic pal?"

I had heard that voice only once before, in a parking lot of a West Palm Beach motel. It was none other than Francis Hoyt. I jumped up and started toward the front door. "I am right here," I said.

"Well then, I guess the party can begin. You gonna invite me in, or what?"

"Sure thing, Francis, but I'm afraid you're a little late for dinner," said Charlie Floyd in a voice so calm it was as if he were simply inviting a neighbor in for a cup of tea. I do not know how he remained so calm while my heart was pounding and my mind was racing in several different directions at once.

"That's okay, I already ate. Besides, I doubt we have the same tastes. I suspect mine is a little more...refined...than yours."

Francis Hoyt, handsome, short-cropped hair, a face that reminded me of that American actor, Michael J. Fox, the one who starred in one of my favorite American films, *Back to the*

Future, dressed in faded blue jeans and a black T-shirt that hugged his body, entered the house. Charlie Floyd, as any good host would, shepherded us into the living room.

"Good to see you again, Manny. You don't mind me calling you Manny, do you?" said Francis Hoyt. "You'll notice, unlike you, I ring the bell before I enter someone else's private space."

"Something new for you, Francis," Charlie Floyd said.

Anger was boiling up inside me and that was not a good thing, so I decided it would be better if I said nothing and allowed Charlie Floyd handle the situation.

Francis Hoyt took a place on the couch as Charlie Floyd and I flanked him, sitting in two matching easy chairs.

"So, boys, here I am. I'm your wet dream come true." He stretched his arms out wide over his head, then brought them back so that they cradled his head. "I'm here to save you the trouble of having to beat the fucking bushes, looking like the assholes you are, trying to find me. Aren't you gonna say I've got a lot of fucking nerve just showing up like this? Kinda takes the fun out of it, don't you think?"

"I've got to disagree with you there, Francis. I think the fun's just getting started," said Charlie Floyd.

Francis Hoyt smiled. "I stand corrected, Charlie. You're probably right. Wasn't it Sherlock Holmes who said to his pal Watson, 'now the game's afoot'?"

"You gonna sit here making idle chit-chat or are you going to tell us why you're here?"

"What's wrong with your little pal over there, Charlie? Cat got his tongue? Or maybe he don't speakee the English too good."

"Manny speaks many languages, including Asshole. But unlike some people he knows when to talk and when to keep his mouth shut. Listen, Francis, I've got the ballgame on in there and it's a close one and the Sox have a chance to bring justice to the land, so why don't we get down to business. Why the hell are you here and what the hell do you want?"

"Aren't you going to offer me something to drink?"

"Not in this life," answered Charlie Floyd.

I did not wish Francis Hoyt to know that he was discomforting me, so I tried to keep my face as expressionless as possible. The more I did and the more I kept silent the more I knew it would disturb him. I knew he was a man who liked to exercise control over every situation. I have dealt with this type of person numerous times. They like to keep you off balance, to shock and surprise their adversaries. Often, this strategy is effective, but Charlie Floyd is a professional and I was certain it would not take long to thwart Francis Hoyt, then he would be the one controlling the situation. My respect for Charlie Floyd, which was already so high, was growing with every passing moment. I did not yet know the reason for Francis Hoyt's visit, but perhaps he had made a serious misstep in confronting us on our home ground.

"I heard you're looking for me so I'm here to save you some trouble."

"We appreciate that, Francis, especially since I figured you'd be in mourning."

"Yeah? For who?"

"Your pal, Tommy Pfister."

"Oh, yeah, what a shame. I heard he had an unfortunate accident."

"Only if you call a bullet in his head an accident."

"You know, Charlie, I don't read the papers much—there's so much bad news, it just breaks my heart—so I don't know how he died just that he did. But we all gotta go sometime, don't we? Guys like that, guys who are, shall we say, a little shady, who don't always follow the straight and narrow path like you and me, well, you gotta expect some day they might piss off someone."

"He piss you off, Francis?"

"That little worm? What could he possibly do to piss me off?"

"He was partially responsible for that time you checked into the old Graybar Hotel, wasn't he?"

"That's ancient history. Besides, I don't bear grudges. That just gets you into trouble. I don't want trouble. How about you guys? You looking for trouble?"

"Without trouble, we'd be on the unemployment line. Of course, you know all about that kind of trouble, don't you?"

"I'm just a law-abiding citizen. I learned my lesson. I am on the righteous path, my friend." He held up his right hand. "Honest injun."

"If it wasn't about revenge, why did you have him killed? It wouldn't have been to send us a message, would it?"

"I'm here, right? I don't need to send any fucking messages. I'm totally capable of delivering them myself. And I'm offended you think I had anything to do with Tommy's demise. That's not my thing. You should know that. Besides, where would I find someone to commit murder for me? Truth is, guys like him don't last all that long in the business he was in. Maybe he cheated someone he shouldn't have. Maybe he slept with someone's wife. Maybe he didn't pay his gambling debts. There are all kinds of good explanations why someone like him gets iced. You gonna blame me for that? Go right ahead, but that'd be a big mistake because I got an airtight alibi. I wasn't even in Manhattan when it happened."

"You sent word through him to let me know that you were going to be in his office."

"Why would I do that?"

"So, I'd come down there."

"And?"

"I'd be the one to find the body. Nice dramatic touch, Francis."

Francis Hoyt laughed. "You know something, Charlie, you're starting to give me more credit than I'm worth. I mean when it comes to stealing shit there isn't anyone better than me. Ever. Probably never will be. But now you're insinuating that I'm a one-man crime wave, a criminal mastermind, committing murder by what, remote control? If you don't mind me saying, it sounds a little paranoid to me."

"Enough bullshit. Let's cut to the chase. Why are you here?"

"I'm here because I want to tell you you're wasting your time and to keep your nose out of my private life."

"I have absolutely no idea what you're talking about."

Charlie Floyd was playing this with perfection. I leaned back and let him continue.

"Yeah. You do. Your spic pal talks to Evie. You think I don't know everything that goes on in my world? You think I'm some kind of idiot?"

Charlie Floyd shrugged and inside I was beginning to smile.

"It ain't going to do you no good."

"Really? Then why's it bothering you so much?"

Francis Hoyt's faced turned red. He leaned forward and pointed first at me and then at Charlie Floyd.

"I'm warning you, and I'm warning your little spic pal over there. Stay the fuck out of my fucking private life. I know you guys got a job to do but this ain't part of the game."

"So, it's a game we're playing, Francis? Like Monopoly or Parcheesi? You think there are rules we ought to be observing? I've got news for you, pal, there aren't any rules. I'm private now and Manny, well, he can follow the damn rules if he wants to, but not me. My job is to nail you and that's exactly what I'm going to do. You think you're smart, but you're not smarter than me. I'm gonna nail your ass and then let's see how fucking cocky you are."

Francis Hoyt leaned back. He smiled.

"You can give it your best shot. I wouldn't have it any other way. But just remember, you're the one who said there are no rules. I think it's time for me to go. I've made my point and you've made yours. I've got some work—" he smiled, "—to do. Why don't you two lovebirds go back to your ballgame?"

Francis Hoyt rose. Charlie Floyd rose with him. I remained in my seat.

"Let me see you out, Francis."

Charlie Floyd walked him to the door. Before I heard the sound of the door close I heard Charlie Floyd say, "Come back any time. It was a pleasure to meet you. But next time I'll be visiting you and there'll be steel bars between us."

"Just remember this, Charlie. This time I came in the front door, who knows how I'll get in next time?"

"There won't be a next time."

"We'll see about that."

When Charlie Floyd got back into the living room his face was flushed.

"You know what, now I want that little fucker as much as you do."

Charlie Floyd

Holy shit.

That's what went through my mind but not past my lips when I opened the door and there stood none other than Francis fucking Hoyt. He was a lot smaller than I imagined he'd be. He was like the size of a jockey. I know I'm tall but Hoyt, well he's practically a fucking midget. Even Manny seemed to tower over him. No wonder this fucker was so hard to catch. He was fucking hard to see!

But man, was he ripped. He was wearing a black T-shirt and jeans. I could see the well-defined muscles of his arms and chest right through the cotton fabric of his T. And he was much better looking in person than in his mug shots. I'd even say he was movie-star handsome. Not to him, of course.

I'll say this for him—he had a pair of balls on him. I didn't know quite what to expect but I knew I, or rather we, because Manny was now standing right behind me by this time, were in for quite a ride.

Francis fucking Hoyt in the fucking flesh. Now wasn't that something!

He was pissed that we were getting to his girlfriends, which meant we were getting a little too up close and personal. He mentioned Evelyn Kerns down in Miami. Told us we'd better lay off her.

That he was sitting there, in my house, on my couch, indicated we were getting under his skin. He was rattled and when someone's rattled they make mistakes. Yes, even Francis fucking

Hoyt can make a mistake.

It didn't matter what was said. We had now personally engaged and the advantage was ours. But we had to know what to do with it because Francis Hoyt wasn't stupid. He didn't get to where he was by being average, or even slightly above average. He might be the best but even the best sometimes lose. They age out. They run out of steam. They get cocky and make mistakes. Ask any of the big ones. Michael Jordan. Tiger Woods. John McEnroe. Reggie Jackson. Babe Ruth, even. By the end of his career, he was sitting on the bench in Boston rather than in the on-deck circle for the Yankees. Nothing lasts forever. Francis Hoyt was due for a fall. Our job was to give him a little push.

Screw the Yankee-Boston game. After he left, all I could think about was Francis Hoyt. Manny, too. We talked about him. We marveled at his nerve. We talked about what we'd do next.

"You know something, Manny. Hoyt didn't mention anything about Melinda Shaw, just Kerns."

"That is correct."

"You know what, I don't think she told him that she met me."

"I agree. She most certainly did not tell him, or else he most assuredly would have mentioned her, too. And you know why?"

"I think I do. I think you do, too. She's afraid of him. She's not sure what he'd do if he found out. You know what, I think I got to her. I think she's contemplating rolling over on him. I think that photograph I showed her of Hoyt and Kerns shook her up more than she let on. I think if I just lean on her a little harder we can turn her."

Manny had a big, fat smile on his face. And, come to think of it, so did I.

It wasn't till hours later that I realized something was amiss and that's when both our smiles vanished.

A valuable antique silver ashtray, probably one of the few things of value I owned—it was my mother's, who smoked way too much until she gave it up at the age of forty-five—was missing from the end table next to the couch.

I knew where it was. And, so did Manny.

Francis fucking Hoyt.

We'd rattled Francis Hoyt's cage hard enough so he felt he had to do something bold. We had him looking over his shoulder. He was thinking about us. He was worrying about us. Eventually, this would make him take his eyes off the ball. And when he did we'd have to be ready to pounce.

What he'd told us loud and clear, probably without being aware he had, was that meddling in his private life was his Achilles heel. Both Manny and I believed Evie Kerns or Melinda Shaw was going to be our ticket to the show. But we had to act fast. If we were right about Hoyt being behind the death of Tommy Pfister then chances were he wasn't about to leave other loose ends dangling. Hoyt was a man of action.

I didn't trust that PI Cohan as far as I could throw him. He impressed me as the kind of guy who would do anything for money. If he figured out we were going to use Shaw, he might trace the guy in the photo, Hoyt. That is, if he didn't already know who he was and was playing dumb with me. That kind of information would be valuable to Hoyt. If I knew it, so did Cohan. If Hoyt had the slightest inkling that I'd already gotten to Shaw, or that I might somehow find her, he might feel he had to get rid of her. And he would do it without leaving his own fingerprints.

I had to get back to Shaw, push her, and push her hard. And I had to do it quick. If we could get her to turn on him we'd stop Hoyt once and for all. We knew Hoyt probably hadn't confided in Shaw, but we also knew that if we had her on our side we could use her to help build a case against him. She knew more than she thought she did about him. Maybe he'd let something slip. Maybe he'd left something in her apartment. But to find out what it was, first we had to convince her to help us. That was on me.

I also came up with another idea that would open an attack on another front. Hoyt used smoke and mirrors to obfuscate where he was going to hit and we could use the same tactics by letting him know we were not just sitting around with our fingers up our asses. The more he had to worry about, the better the chances he'd slip up.

I told Manny the idea that morning at breakfast.

"Manny, how'd you like to add some frequent flyer miles to your account?"

He smiled. "I love to travel, Charlie Floyd. What destination did you have in mind?"

"I was thinking about the Heartland, you know, home of the Silent Majority."

"Minneapolis, perhaps?"

"Yeah, that sounds about right."

"The sister or the mother?"

"I'm thinking the mother will irritate him more, so let's go with her. You up to it?"

"No one likes to travel more than I do. I have never been to Minneapolis although I have most certainly heard of the fabulous Mall of America. It contains a roller coaster inside it, does it not? And Esther will appreciate the extra miles on our account. Next year, for our anniversary, she has hinted that she would like to visit Rome and meet the Pope."

"Anything to further that dream."

So, it was settled. Manny booked a flight for the next day for Minneapolis. I offered to spring for it but Manny would have none of that so we settled for a fifty-fifty split. "The very same split we will have when we collect the reward," said Manny.

While Manny walked the mile and a half into town to buy a few things for his trip—he insisted he needed the exercise and walking helped him think—I got ready to head back down to the city to have another go at Melinda Shaw.

Just as I was ready to walk out the door the phone rang. It was our local chief of police, William "Wild Bill" Basnight. Billy as I called him, was born for this job. Not only is he a fine enforcer of the law, not that we have all that many problems in our little town, but unlike me he's a people person. Everybody loves Billy, even the bad guys. I tried to pin the name Andy on him, as in Andy Griffith, sheriff of Mayberry, but for some reason it didn't stick. Probably because when needed Billy has a tough side that isn't afraid to knock heads together. Billy can best be described as "a good old boy." But under that veneer of niceness and collegiality is a genuine tough guy. He's a former Marine who saw duty in the first Iraq war.

One job I wouldn't want is cop in a small town, and the only job worse than that is being the police chief of a small town. You have to handle all kinds of little shit, the stuff that would drive me crazy. I like the big shit, which is why I did what I did.

"Hey, Billy, what's up? I was just about to leave the house."

"I'd make sure you double-lock the door behind you, Charlie."

"Why's that? Has a crime wave suddenly hit town?"

"I hope not, but a neighbor of yours got hit last night. All they took was the silver. The good silver. Whoever did it, left a calling card. There was a note taped to the breakfront. It said, 'Fuck you, Charlie Floyd, and fuck you, too, Manny Perez.' Know anything about this, Charlie?"

"I know everything about it. It's Francis Hoyt."

"Fuck me. You're kidding? Hoyt is in town?"

"'Fraid so. What was the value of the stuff taken?"

"Ten, twenty grand, tops. From what I know about Hoyt that's chicken feed."

"He didn't do it for the money. He did it so he could leave that note."

"I take it you and he have a personal problem."

"Looks like. But I'm hoping it's going to be just his problem real soon. Thanks for letting me know, Billy."

"It's my job to deliver bad news, Charlie. You think I should call out the troops and secure the town?"

"I don't think you have to. He's got bigger fish to fry than our citizenry. He just wanted to send a message. In fact, I'd say the last place he's going to hit again is here."

"That's good, because from what I hear, he's a hard one to reel in and you know how I hate to work hard."

"Don't worry, I think we've got a handle on this one."

"Not sure what you mean, Charlie. Didn't you retire last year?"

"I did. But I guess I'm unretired now. I'm working private, alongside a buddy of mine. Manny Perez. He's a Miami cop and he's up here because of Hoyt."

"I wish you guys luck, man. From what I know about Hoyt, you gonna need it."

Francis Hoyt

Those two sad sacks didn't know what the fuck hit them. You shoulda seen the look on the big one's face when he opened the door and there I was, in the flesh. And then, adding insult to injury, to steal the only thing of value that sap had, well that was icing on the cake. Man, I would have loved to see the look on his face when he realized it was missing. And while I was at it, I couldn't resist hitting that house at the end of his block. I didn't get much, a few pieces of silver that might have been a couple thousand bucks. But that wasn't the point. The point was I could do whatever the hell I wanted and where I wanted and they couldn't stop me. In his own fucking backyard!

But there was more to it. I wanted to deliver a message. They already knew about Evie and I figured they weren't about to give up on her. And therein lay a problem. What was I gonna do about her? I didn't think she could or would help the cops, but you never knew. I had to do something about her. So, I sent her some dough and told her to take a little "vacation." She took it pretty good. After all, what's so bad about sitting on some beach in Hawaii, compliments of Francis Hoyt? She's a tough broad and I didn't think Perez or anyone else could get anything out of her, but better safe than sorry.

But what about Mel? Did they know about her? I figured, like Evie, she'd have said something to me, so my guess was they didn't know about her yet. Or, if they did, they couldn't track her down. But they might. And if they did who knows what she'd do. She's already pissed at me for not spending enough time with her and with women you never know what they're thinking, which means you never know what they're gonna do.

I guess I could send her away, too, but the truth is I didn't think she was going to go for that without some kind of explanation. Besides, she's got a real job and can't just take off, and I sure don't feel like supporting her for the rest of her life. What would I tell her, anyway? That the law was after me and that I was afraid she was going to drop a dime on me? I don't think so. I want my women to know as little as possible about me and the life I lead and even telling her that much would be a mistake. Besides, it would give her the kind of leverage I didn't want her to have. Between Evie and Mel, Mel presented more of a problem because she was more stubborn and hardheaded.

Yeah, I'd have to do something about her but I wasn't sure yet what it should be.

Charlie Floyd

We had to work fast. Hoyt is unpredictable. He doesn't run in straight lines. He goes forward, back, then forward again. He's not afraid of doing something outrageous, unexpected...even dangerous. The more outrageous, the more dangerous, the better for us.

"With Hoyt," I said as I drove Manny down to LaGuardia the next day for his flight to Minneapolis, "it's better if we don't play his game or even worry about what his game is. That's not gonna work because he's in control. He knows where he's going and what he's doing and we don't. We have to make him play our game. We have to make him react to us as opposed to us reacting to him. We've got at least a three-pronged attack and I'm betting one of those prongs nails Francis Hoyt."

Manny nodded in agreement. I could see he was thinking about his trip, planning how he would handle Hoyt's mother.

"Eventually, he's going to figure out we know about Melinda Shaw. That's why it's so important I get back to her as soon as possible. Right after I drop you off, I'm heading straight into the city to talk to her."

"I only hope, Charlie Floyd, that he has not already taken care of this particular loose end as I believe he has with another."

Manny was referring to a conversation he'd had last night with his ex-partner, David Chung. He had asked him to keep an eye on Evie Kerns. Evidently, that wasn't so easy. Earlier this morning, just as we were about to leave the house, Chung called. Evie Kerns had disappeared. He couldn't find her at the club where she worked and he couldn't find her at her home. No one had seen her for the day or so. This wasn't a coincidence. Either Hoyt had her eliminated her or he'd stashed her someplace we couldn't get to her. Either way, it didn't bode well for Melinda Shaw. That's why I had to get to her as soon as possible.

Shaw lived in a brownstone building on 71st, between Broadway and West End Avenue. I dropped off my car at a nearby garage and by five-thirty I'd parked myself on the stoop a couple buildings closer to Broadway so I could see her coming down the block. With a copy of the *New Yorker* to keep me company I waited for her to get home from work.

I didn't have to wait long. A few minutes before six, I spotted Shaw heading toward me. She was carrying a Trader Joe's bag and a large purse in one hand and was checking her cell phone with the other. When she got within a few feet of where I was sitting, I jumped in front of her so that her shoulder brushed mine.

"I'm so sorry," she said, as she reflexively took a step back. As soon as she looked up she realized who I was. "What are you doing here?"

"Waiting for you."

"This is harassment," she said as she brushed past me then turned to go up a winding metal staircase that led to the front door. I followed close behind. Halfway up the steps she stopped and turned to face me. "This isn't going to do you any good, you know. And if you keep this up I'm going to call the cops on you."

"You've got the phone in your hand, go ahead. But I don't think Francis would like the idea of you, me, and the cops getting together. Why don't you invite me up for a few minutes and hear me out? Then I promise I'll get out of your hair."

She thought for a moment. "I don't have to talk to you."

"I know."

She put her phone in the large purse she was carrying. "But if I do you'll leave me alone?"

I raised my hand. "Promise."

"Okay, you can come up, but you're on the clock, Floyd. I'll give you five minutes."

"What floor you on?"

"Third."

"It'll take that long for me to catch my breath."

There were two apartments to a floor. She lived in the back apartment. Before she unlocked the door, she turned and said, "I'm not apologizing for anything but the place is a mess."

"You're in luck. I'm not the health inspector."

She was right. It was a mess. She lived in one large room. The bed was a convertible sofa and it was open, a tangle of sheets, blankets and pillows. Otherwise, the room was sparsely furnished, a small table that probably did double duty as a desk and a dining room table, two folding chairs set up on either side of the table, and a dresser with two of the drawers wide open with pieces of clothing hanging over the sides. The walls were completely bare. Melinda Shaw was living a temporary life, waiting for something to change it. Lots of people lead their lives this way: waiting for something better to happen. It almost never does.

"Nice place you've got here."

"Liar."

"That's pretty harsh, Melinda."

"It's the truth. I'd say sit down but then I'd have to make up the couch and there's no point in doing that since you're not staying that long."

She put her purse down on the table, headed toward the small kitchen, and started to unpack her groceries. I sat at the edge of the bed, probably the same bed Francis Hoyt and her shared in the not too distant past.

"You know your boyfriend's a lying, son-of-a-bitch, don't you?"

"If you're trying to get on my good side that wouldn't be the best way to start."

"You're much too smart to go for bullshit. And you know I'm telling you the truth about him. I'm betting by now you've Googled him or whatever you women use to find out about men."

She came back into the room carrying two beers. She handed me one and sat down beside me.

"Thanks."

"Thank my mother for teaching me manners."

"You didn't tell him about our earlier visit, did you?"

"How do you know I didn't?"

"Because we wouldn't be having this conversation if you had."

"What's that supposed to mean?"

"You know exactly what it means. Why didn't you tell him?"

"I didn't want to upset him."

"Bullshit. You didn't tell him because you know all about him now and you're a little scared."

"So what if I am?"

"You're a smart woman. You know enough to fear a man like that when he's backed into a corner. This is not the kind of life you want for yourself, Melinda. It's not the kind of life your mother wants for you either."

"My mother's dead."

"I'm sorry."

"You don't have to be sorry. You didn't know her."

"I'm sorry for anyone who loses a parent. And I'm sorry for you because you don't deserve what Hoyt has in store for you."

"How do you know what he has in store for me?"

"I've been doing this a long time. I've known plenty of Francis Hoyts. They all have one thing in common."

"Yeah, what's that?"

"They're all about themselves. They don't give a shit about

anyone else. He only cares about himself and the minute you get in the way he'll be finished with you. So, if you think you have any kind of future with him, you're wrong."

She began to cry. I don't know what to do with a woman when she cries. When my wife cried, I left the room. That's probably why she eventually stopped crying and left me.

I thought maybe I should put my arm around her shoulder, to comfort her. But then I thought that would be wrong. Let her cry. Let her think about what it meant to be involved with Hoyt. Let her think about the consequences of being involved with a man who steals for a living, a man who has no compunction about breaking into someone else's home and violating their space.

Does this shit make me feel good? No. But I made peace with it a long time ago. It's an ugly business, but that's not my fault. It's the fault of guys like Hoyt and all the other assholes out there who decide it's easier to lie and cheat and steal and murder than to live the way the rest of us do: by the rules. Believe me, I struggle with myself every time I get in a situation like this, a situation where I have to do something hurtful to someone who's an innocent bystander. Women like Melinda Shaw and Evie Kerns are victims just as much as the family that has their privacy invaded, their space defiled, their belongings stolen. But I have a job to do and this, as much as I might hate it, is part of the job. I hate people like Francis Hoyt, not only for what they do to people, but for what they make people like me do to people like Melinda Shaw.

She looked at me. Her tears had made dark streaks, like riverbeds, down her cheeks. She wasn't quite so pretty anymore. She seemed physically smaller, as if she'd shrunk from the tears. I could have let it be but I knew now that I was close, I had to push her over the edge. One day, I knew, I might go over the edge with her. But today wasn't going to be that day.

"The other woman, Evie Kerns, has disappeared. You know what that means, don't you?"

She wasn't ready for words yet so she shook her head.

"It means Hoyt has already seen to it that she can't help us. You're the only one left, and believe me it won't be long until he takes care of you. He'll figure out you're the weak link. Maybe he'll even find out we've spoken."

She looked at me, her eyes daggers. "How would he know that?"

"Maybe he's having you followed."

She took a deep breath. The words I was waiting to hear, bottled up in her till now, were ready to come.

"What do you want to know?"

"I need to know everything, Melinda. I need to know where Hoyt is now, what he's planning."

"He doesn't talk to me about those kinds of things."

"I didn't expect he would. But women know things. I don't know how you know them but you do. You know something that can help me."

She nodded. She got up and went to the small table where she'd dropped her purse. She picked it up and sat back down next to me. She squeezed the purse tightly to her chest. She was still debating with herself as to whether she was going to help me. I knew how this would turn out the minute she got up to retrieve the purse.

"You're doing the right thing, Melinda. The only thing."

"I know," she said in a voice so low I could hardly hear it. This was tough for her but I knew if she didn't do it it would be even tougher. "What's going to happen to me?"

"What do you want to happen to you?"

"I wish I knew."

"You're going through a tough time now. I know that. I've been through it, too. You feel like your life is falling apart. The divorce. Hoyt..."

"I wish I'd never met him."

"That bridge has already been crossed. But now you've got an opportunity to make things right. You can start over."

"I don't know how to do that."

"Getting rid of Hoyt is the first step."

I felt like a goddamn TV shrink, like Dr. Phil, or, even worse, a priest. I didn't know what the hell I was talking about but it sure sounded good. Maybe I was right. Maybe getting rid of Hoyt was the first step in getting her life back on track. It couldn't get any worse, that's for sure. And for that reason alone, I knew I had nothing to feel guilty about. Getting her to betray Hoyt was the right thing, even if she was doing it for the wrong reason.

She opened her purse and stared into it for a moment. Finally, she dug around and came up with a piece of paper. She handed it to me.

"When he was still asleep I went through his wallet. I found this."

I unfolded it. "What is this?"

"It's a motel receipt. Well, it's not actually the receipt because I didn't want to take it because he'd know I did. So, I wrote down all the information. The motel. A name. It's not his name but it must be him."

The name was Michael Leiman. I seemed to remember from the folder Manny gave me that this was one of the names Hoyt sometimes used. I even recognized the name of the motel. The Enchanted Hunter, in Litchfield County, which was a good area for the kind of antique silver Hoyt was interested in.

"I don't know if this helps, if it means anything. It's the only thing I have."

I folded up the paper and stuck it in my wallet. "Yes," I said, "I think it might."

Manny Perez

"I am not here to cause you any trouble, Mrs. Hoyt."

"I know why you're here. It's about Francis. I don't mean to be rude, Mr. Perez, but I don't talk about my son. He forbids it."

"I understand, Mrs. Hoyt, but I promise I will only take a few minutes of your valuable time."

I could see that her Midwest manners would not let her dismiss me without allowing me to talk to her for a few minutes. I know this mindset quite well, since I have visited my wife's family several times. It does not matter what they think of me, they still treat me with respect. I could see that this tiny, frail woman, white-haired woman wearing a tattered housedress and orthopedic shoes was cut from the same cloth.

"My husband isn't home and I don't use Hoyt any longer. I'm Mrs. Johnson and he doesn't like me to entertain strangers when he's not here."

"I stand corrected. I assure you, Mrs. Johnson, that I am perfectly safe." I took out my wallet and showed her my badge.

"Well, I suppose...but only for a few minutes and I really can't speak about Francis. He'd get very upset if he even knew I'd let you in."

She ushered me into the living room, which seemed to be furnished primarily from Goodwill or the Salvation Army. Most of the furniture was decades old, the flower print fabric on the chairs and sofa faded from age, but the house appeared to be impeccably well-kept.

"Would you like some tea?"

"Thank you. That's very kind of you."

A few minutes passed before Mrs. Johnson reappeared with a tray holding two teacups decorated with pink and purple flowers, a matching white pitcher, and a small plate of sugar cookies. She set the tray down on a coffee table, took one of the cups and set it in front of me and poured hot water over a teabag. Before I was able to pick it up she took it from me.

"Oh, no, I'm so sorry. I gave you the wrong cup. Please, take this one." She handed me the other teacup and as she removed mine I could see there was a slight crack running down the side. "Do you take milk or sugar with your tea?"

"This is perfectly fine, thank you."

"Cookie?" she asked, holding up the plate. "I didn't bake them myself, but for store-bought they're really quite delicious."

"Thank you." I took one.

"I'm afraid you've come a long way for nothing, Mr. Perez. I know you think Francis is a bad man, but he's really not. That he got involved in what he did would be quite understandable if you knew how his father treated him. He was just acting out, but now that he's paid for his actions he's a changed man."

"Most criminals have horrendous childhoods, Mrs. Johnson."

"Oh, no, no, no. Francis had a very nice childhood. He had lots of friends. He did well in school. It's just that he didn't get along with his father very well."

I admired Mrs. Johnson for protecting her child and only thinking the best of him. Perhaps she truly didn't believe how bad a man Francis Hoyt really was. There is no one so blind as one who cannot see.

"You do understand why we are looking for him, Mrs. Johnson?"

She hesitated a moment. Would she admit to the faults in her son?

"No, I don't know why, Mr. Perez. He hasn't done anything wrong."

"He has spent time in the penitentiary."

"As I said, that's in the past. Besides, he wasn't guilty of anything other than being in the wrong place at the wrong time."

"He was robbing a house in the middle of the evening along with two other criminal associates. That is a very wrong place at a very wrong time."

She put down her teacup, looked me straight in the eye. "I'm not going to sit here and argue with you, Mr. Perez. Francis has always been a good son. He's taken care of me and his sister. If you're asking me to help you find Francis, I'm afraid you're barking up the wrong tree."

"Helping me find him would be for his own good. He's partaking in an endeavor that can only ultimately bring serious harm to him and possibly others. You don't want that on your conscience, do you? I know you do not wish to see him come to any harm, Mrs. Johnson."

She put down her cup and hung her head. Her voice was nearly inaudible. "I don't want to see him in prison again, either."

I was up against a stone wall. No one is more protective than a mother of a child, even a monstrous child such as Francis Hoyt. But our strategy did not necessarily depend on obtaining her cooperation. All we needed was for her to inform Francis Hoyt that we were doggedly on his trail and that we would stop at nothing to find him and bring him to justice.

"When was the last time you heard from him, if I may ask?"

"Would you like another cup of tea?"

"No, thank you. I'm fine."

"You seem like a very nice gentleman, Mr. Perez, and that's why I don't want to waste anymore of your precious time." She stood up. "I'm afraid I can't give you what you want."

"I fully understand your position, Mrs. Johnson. I, too, am a parent and if I were in your position I am not so sure I would not behave exactly as you are. But I appeal to you as a mother to help us find your son. I promise you that no harm will come to him."

She shook her head. "Francis has always been able to take care of himself, so I don't think he needs your protection or anyone else's. I suppose we could sit here and chat about the weather or the upcoming election, but I'm sure you have better things to do. My husband will be home soon and I haven't even started preparing dinner. So, I'd appreciate it if you'd leave now."

And, so I did.

Francis Hoyt

"Yeah, Ma, I'm glad you called."

"I didn't want to bother you, Francis."

"You're not bothering me, Ma."

"Because I know you're a busy man."

What the fuck. Yeah, Ma, I'm a very busy man. Way too busy for this shit. So, could you just get the fuck off the phone and leave me alone.

"Never too busy to talk to you. I'm sorry he bothered you. It won't happen again."

"It's just that he worried me, Francis. You're not in any trouble, are you?"

"No, I'm not in any trouble. I told you, that's all behind me."

Fucking bitch wouldn't let go.

"I gotta go, Ma. I appreciate you letting me know about this and I'll be sending you a little something very soon."

"You know you don't have to do that."

Then why the hell don't you send the damn money back?

"It's my pleasure. It really is. So, take care of yourself, okay?"

"All right. And remember to call your sister every once in a while, okay?"

"Yeah, Ma. I'll be sure to do that."

Now I was getting pissed. These guys were sticking their damn noses where they didn't belong. Stirring shit up with my mother, what the fuck did they think they were doing? No. Not anymore. I had to put a stop to this. Maybe even a little tit for tat. How'd that little spic like that?

Francis Hoyt

"Francis, I thought you were back up north."

"I am, Artie."

"We're square. You got your money."

"That's not what I'm calling about."

"Knowing you, it's not to find out how I'm doing. But in case you're interested, I got this bronchial thing. Doctor doesn't—"

"You're right, Artie. I couldn't give a fuck about how you're doing. I only care about how I'm doing."

"Then what's up?"

"I need you to do me a favor."

"What kind of favor?"

"I want you to deliver a message for me."

"They got the FedEx for that."

"Don't be a fucking wise guy, Artie."

"You think I owe you a favor? The way you talked to me the last time I saw you? Those threats you made. I mean, that was serious shit."

"That was business. If you'd paid me when you were supposed to pay me we never would have had that conversation. You owe me."

"How you figure that?"

Fucking asshole was enjoying this. He thought he had the upper hand for a change. But that wouldn't hold for long.

"Not only for all the business I brought you over the years, Artie, but let's face it I know enough about your operation I

239

could bring you down with one lousy phone call. You think I don't know about the scheme you been running? The boys don't like that shit. They find out about it you really will be floating in some body of water, but not before they make you *feel* it, if you know what I mean."

The line went dead for a minute.

Good. I was getting through. Who's on top now, asshole?

"I was only kidding, Francis. Of course, I'll do a favor for you. Anything you want, pal. Anything."

"That's what I like to hear. That's just what I like to hear."

Charlie Floyd

We had our first real lead on Hoyt. Either he was staying at that motel or he had stayed there recently, since the date Melinda had copied off the receipt was just two days earlier.

After stirring the nest, Manny was back the next day. He checked his notes and marked off three of the most likely targets in Litchfield County, all of them within five miles of the motel where Hoyt either was or had been staying. We could try to hatch some kind of trap to catch Hoyt with the goods in his hands. We knew how he operated and instead of trying to nail him by putting the house or houses under surveillance, we'd try to talk the owners into letting us inside the house, where we could lie in wait and nab him. Manny in one house, me in another. If we guessed wrong, nothing lost. It was a bold plan, a plan where lots of things could go wrong, but it was the only plan we had.

But with the way Hoyt moved around, I didn't want to limit it to that particular motel and so I went on Google and made a list of at least fifteen other motels or bed and breakfast places in the area.

I called the state police to see if any robberies in the area had been reported. There were none. That meant Hoyt was still in the planning stages, which meant he was probably still around there. Unless, of course, he'd changed his mind and decided to work another state. But I didn't think so. Hoyt was much too arrogant for that. He had to show us how good he was and that meant working right under our noses.

"You know, Manny, he stays in local motels but I'm guessing he has a home base someplace else. It only makes sense. I wouldn't be surprised if he's rented a small place for himself in all four states. He can certainly afford it."

"That makes a lot of sense, Charlie Floyd. He needs to have someplace where he feels safe. A place where he is anonymous. A place only he knows about."

"The question is, how do we find it?"

"If we find him then I believe we can locate his home base. But right now, I think we are best off looking for him in one of the local motels."

The next day we rented Manny a car and the two of us fanned out to each of those places to see if Hoyt might be registered in any of them.

Manny Perez

"Manny, dear, I don't want you to worry."

The moment those words came out of my wife, Esther's mouth, the effect was quite the opposite. I was very worried. Esther rarely calls me during the day unless it is an emergency. The last time she called during the day it was because my daughter, Esme, had come down with something at school and Esther asked me to pick her up and bring her home. I, of course, thought the worst, but it turned out that it was a simple case of strep throat. Esther often accuses me of being overly dramatic, but then I remind her of what I do for a living.

I was in my rental car and was headed toward the first in a series of motels I was checking out to see if Francis Hoyt might have checked into one of them when the call came in.

"Is it one of the children, Esther?"

"Manny, I know how you get and everything is fine now. In fact, it might be nothing at all."

"If it were nothing, Esther, you would not be calling me in the middle of the day. Please, tell me what is wrong."

"Well, Esme was at the mall with a couple of her friends. They had just come out of a movie and they were in the food court, getting a snack. She'd just called me so I was on my way to pick her and her friend up and bring them back here for a sleepover."

"Esther, please—"

"She was carrying her food back to the table when a strange man approached her. He called her by name. She thought she might know him so she said, 'hello.' He asked her about me, how I was—and he called me by name. And then he said he had a message for her dad."

"What was it?"

"He said he knew that you weren't in Miami, that you were 'up north.' She started to get a little scared and began to walk away, but he grabbed her by the arm and said, 'tell your father that this is what it's like when you mind someone else's business.' She was terrified, Manny."

"What did she do next?"

"She pulled away and went back to her friends. I arrived a few minutes later. She was very upset, Manny. I'm sure it was nothing, but..."

"I know who is behind this, Esther, and I promise you it will not happen again. But until I come back home, please do not let the girls leave the house unless you are with them. And I will call David Chung and tell him about this and I am sure he will provide protection."

"Manny, you're scaring me. Is this really that serious?"

"I do not think so, but I do not want to take any chances. Please, listen to what I have said."

"When are you coming home?"

"Within the week. I promise. One way or another I will be home."

Francis Hoyt

At first I was pretty pissed but after I calmed down a little I realized they had to be pretty desperate to go all the way out there to harass my mother. They were frustrated. They didn't know what to do next so they were grasping at straws. I was winning.

I knew exactly what they were doing. They were trying to unnerve me. They probably figured if they do I'll make a mistake. Ain't gonna happen, assholes. Besides, two can play at that game. But I can't take my eye off the ball. I've sent them enough messages so now, while they're busy fucking around at the margins of my life, I'm gonna just get back to doing what I do best. Stealing shit.

But there was one piece of unfinished business left. Melinda. I didn't think there was anything she could say that would help them catch me in the act, but I couldn't take any chances. Truth is she was beginning to become a pain in the ass. I liked her, all right, but it was time to ditch her. But what was I going to do with her? Do I just cut her off? Or do I have to do something more drastic? I had nothing against the bitch. She didn't do anything wrong. But I don't like carrying around any extra baggage.

I had to consider my options carefully. Evie was easy. I'd known her for a while and she'd do anything to protect me. But Melinda hadn't quite bonded with me that tight yet. She could be a loose cannon. And who knew what those two guys might promise her if they found out about her.

There was no point in doing anything rash, anything that

would make things dicier for me. I had to think about it. I had to figure out what the best course of action was.

Meanwhile, it was back to work. I had a much bigger challenge for myself now. I was going to work right under these assholes' noses. Then they'd see how good Francis fucking Hoyt really is.

Charlie Floyd

"Billy, I've got a favor to ask."

"Before I even find out what it is, the answer's yes. I've stopped counting the number of favors I owe you."

"I don't keep count so why should you. Anyway, I'd like to come down there a little later today and I'd like you to deputize me."

"That's gotta be one of the oddest requests I've had in a while, Charlie. I'll do it, of course, but can I ask why?"

"It has to do with Francis Hoyt. If I do catch him doing something he shouldn't be doing, I need to have the authority to bring him in. I also need to have the authority to ask for a search warrant, if that's necessary. And I don't want to be dragging along some poor cop with me."

"I shoulda figured it had something to with Hoyt. You can come on down here right now, if you like, and I'll get the Bible ready for you. I think I've probably got an extra badge hanging around somewhere."

"Great. Now all I have to do is figure out where I want to pin it."

Charlie Floyd

There was the Baymont Inn, the Quality Inn, Super 8, Hampton Inn, Holiday Inn, Tollgate Hill Inn, Heritage Hotel, Farmington Inn, Avon Old Farms Hotel, Inn at Kent Falls, Tucker Hill Inn, Pine Meadow House, and a few others.

We divvied it up geographically. I was on the road, having visited two on my list, when I got the call from Manny. I could hear the anger in his voice before he even got his entire first sentence out. He told me how his daughter had been accosted at the mall.

"That sonuvabitch. I'm sorry about that, Manny. But I promise you, we're gonna find him and put him away."

Hoyt was upping the stakes. Every time we made a move he matched us and then raised. Still, our ace in the hole was that he didn't know that we'd reached Melinda Shaw, that she was co-operating, and that she'd given us a clue as to where he was.

Next stop was the Enchanted Hunter Motel to see if Hoyt was still registered there under the name Michael Leiman.

I parked the car down the road and approached the motel on foot. In case Hoyt was still there I didn't want to run the risk of his seeing me and getting away. I knew him well enough to know he was probably the kind of guy who always knows where the closest exit is.

At first the desk clerk was hesitant to give me any information, but when I flashed my state ID he was a little more forthcoming.

"I believe he left us a day or so ago but I can check if you'd like."

"I'd like."

He stepped to his computer brought up a screen and nodded. "Yes, he checked out two days ago after staying with us only one night."

"By any chance did you check him in?"

"Yes, I did."

"Can you describe him?"

"I usually don't pay that much attention but he was a small man. He kind of reminded me of a jockey and he looked a little like that actor. You know the one I mean, small, has some kind of disease that makes him shake."

"Michael J. Fox."

He snapped his fingers. "Yeah, that's the one. He did kinda look like him. Oh, and his hair was trimmed real short, kind of like he was in the military. What do they call it? A buzz cut, right? Late thirties, early forties. He looked like he was in good shape, too."

"Did you get his license plate number?"

"Afraid not. He said he didn't have a car, that someone dropped him off and someone would pick him up."

I was sure that was a lie, but Hoyt was very careful about covering his tracks so it didn't surprise me that he parked his car away from the motel.

Back in the car, I closed my eyes and tried to think like Hoyt. I figured he'd choose an area to work then case the houses he targeted. But he wouldn't stay in a motel too close to those houses and he would never stay in one more than a night.

It wasn't till I got to the fourth motel on my list, the Super 8, that I hit the mother lode.

A "small man" using the name of Emanuel Floyd, had checked in earlier that day. I asked if the desk clerk thought he was still in his room but he said he'd seen him leave a few hours earlier.

I immediately called Manny.

"We've got him. Meet me at the Super 8. And get here as soon as you can."

Francis Hoyt

"Francis, I wasn't expecting you."

"I'm full of surprises."

"How'd you get in without buzzing?"

"Someone was coming out and let me in."

"I was just getting ready to go out. But so long as you're here, I can change my plans."

"What plans would those be, Mel?"

"I was just meeting a friend for a drink."

"Yeah. Who would that be?"

"You're not jealous, are you, Francis?"

"Do I strike you as the jealous type?"

"I'm not sure."

"What about you, Mel? You the jealous type?"

She thought for a moment, trying to weigh her answer to see if it was the one I wanted. Trouble was, she had no idea what I wanted.

"I guess all women are the jealous type, Francis. We don't like to share." She put a little more emphasis on the word *share*. At that moment, I already knew the answer to my question but I asked it anyway.

"So, any special visitors lately?"

"Special visitors? I'm not sure what you're talking about, Francis."

"I think you'd know. But I can understand why you wouldn't want to talk about it."

"Talk about what? I'm not sure where this is going, baby."

She put her hand on my cheek.

"Why beat around the bush? You get a visit from the law?"

"Why on earth would I get a visit from the law?"

"I don't know. Just asking. But let's say you did get such a visit, what do you think they'd want from you?"

"I haven't the foggiest idea."

"Really?" I stared at her.

"Francis, you're frightening me."

"You don't have any reason to be frightened of me, do you?"

"No."

"But let's just say you did get such a visit, what would you tell them?"

"What could I tell them? I don't know anything. I don't even know where you are when you're not with me, and sometimes even when you're with me I don't know where you are. I don't like the way this conversation is going. I'm getting a little afraid. I think you ought to leave."

"Maybe you're right. But before I do leave, let me give you a little warning. I don't want you talking about me with anyone. You understand?"

She nodded.

"I want you to say it, Mel. Say you understand."

"I understand."

"That's good. I'm glad you understand. Because there are consequences."

"What kind of consequences?"

"The serious kind."

"Now you're really scaring me."

"Good. It's good that I'm scaring you. I'm gonna go now."

She went to touch my arm, but I pulled away. I got what I came for. I knew damn well Floyd or that little spic had gotten to her. I didn't think there was anything she could have told them, but it didn't matter. There were consequences, but I didn't quite know what they were. Yet.

Charlie Floyd

"So, what is the plan, Charlie Floyd?" Manny asked, as we sat at a table in a roadside diner near the Super 8 Motel.

"Good question. I think we should stakeout the motel and wait till Hoyt comes back. We can't get into his room without either a warrant or by breaking in. But that's not the best idea, as I'm sure you can attest to."

Manny smiled and took a sip of his coffee.

"How good are you at tailing suspects?"

"I have driven cars since I was fifteen, Charlie Floyd, and as you can see from my stature I tend not to stand out in a crowd."

"I'll take that as you're going to be the point man. Let's finish up here and we'll go back to the motel. We'll find a good place for each of us to watch him from. Let's try to catch him going back to the motel and we'll wait till he leaves and follow him. It's my least favorite part of the job—staying awake is always a challenge, but it's sometimes the most important."

When we got back to the motel, Manny found a good spot to watch from while sitting in his car. I went back into the motel office to see if the desk clerk had seen Hoyt return. We were in luck. While we were having coffee and hatching our plan Hoyt had, indeed, returned. I warned the desk clerk against letting Hoyt, or in this case Emmanuel Floyd, know we were asking after him, then found a spot far enough away from Manny that wouldn't call attention to me. We now had the motel covered from two different angles. The only way Hoyt could get past us was if he somehow snuck out the back. But eventually he'd have to make it back to the road to his car and if we were lucky we'd pick him up then.

It was close to four o'clock when we began babysitting Hoyt. We both ordered takeout from the diner so that if the wait was long we'd have something to eat and drink. If one of us needed to take a quick bathroom break, he would notify the other. But just in case, we both made sure we had an empty bottle with us. We agreed whoever spotted him first would phone the other and it would be game on.

We'd been there almost three hours when my phone buzzed. It was Manny.

"He is on the move, Charlie Floyd. I just saw him emerge from his room, carrying a small satchel and he's headed toward the road, in your direction."

"Great, Manny," I said, as I turned on the engine. I was parked at a corner and when I looked toward the main road I saw him walking quickly toward me. He was dressed pretty much the same way he was when he visited us, only now he was wearing a blue windbreaker. As soon as he came fully into view I ducked down. He passed by, no more than twenty feet away from me, and kept heading down the road. I waited a moment, keeping him in sight, then I saw Manny's car pull close to mine.

"I will hang back, Charlie Floyd. You take the lead. If, for some reason, he suspects he is being followed and you must pass him or turn off course, I will be right behind you and I shall pick up the tail. And then vice versa."

"Let's just not get too close to him. He's smart enough to know how to spot a tail and we don't want to let him know we're this close. One thing in our favor is that he's so fucking arrogant he can't imagine we'd ever get this close."

"Roger that," said Manny. I could hear him chuckling to himself.

I waited a few more seconds then slowly pulled out. I turned the corner and spotted Hoyt breaking into a jog. Damn, this wasn't going to be easy. He could have parked his car a mile or two away from the motel and he'd certainly notice me if I drove too slowly behind him, or kept passing him. I'd have to be very clever as to how I followed him. I couldn't get too close and I couldn't go past him. Someone like Hoyt, even when they have no reason to suspect someone's on their tail are always hyper-vigilant.

Fortunately, the roads were twisty, which gave me the opportunity to hang back far enough so that I was hidden from his view. I kept about a quarter of a mile back, figuring that he would stay on the main road until he either found his car there or turned onto a side road where he'd parked it.

I was right. I lost sight of him when the road hooked to the right and when I reached that point I saw he wasn't in front of me anymore. I'd either lost him completely or he'd turned onto one of the side roads. I decided to take a chance and so I drove slowly straight ahead, hoping his car wasn't parked too far from the main road.

I got lucky. I'd driven about fifty yards when I saw a car in my rearview mirror. A blue Toyota coming up fast.

I sped up and called Manny.

"I've got him. He's right behind me in a blue Toyota."

"I'm about a quarter of a mile behind him, Charlie Floyd."

I'll stay far enough head so that I can still see him in my rearview mirror. You stay behind him. If he makes a turn note where it is, keep going straight, then I'll double back and pick him up.

We did this for maybe five minutes till we realized Hoyt wasn't headed toward a home in Litchfield, but rather back to the main highway. He was headed south. I stayed in the right lane and let him pass then Manny and I both trailed him. Eventually, he wound up on the Post Road and drove right into the tony town of Westport.

"Manny, I'm gonna bet Hoyt has a place here in Westport. If that's true, we've hit pay dirt. I don't think he's spotted either of us. We'll just follow from behind until he reaches wherever he's going."

"When he does," Manny said, "you drive by him and I'll stop before I reach him. I'll let you know where he is."

Looking back in my rearview mirror I saw Hoyt make a right turn onto a side street. I pulled over to the side of the road. I didn't see Manny coming up from behind me so I guessed he saw Hoyt make the turn.

Manny called a minute later. "He has parked his car, Charlie Floyd. I'm going to drive by and I'll let you know in what direction he walks."

Another minute passed and Manny's name lit up on my phone.

"Yeah."

"I have got him. He parked, walked a few blocks, then went into a small apartment building."

"Bingo. Stay right there, Manny. I'm right behind you."

Francis Hoyt

"Vito, this is Francis."

"Yeah."

"I need another favor."

"What makes you think you got one coming?"

"Two years in the joint is a long time. How about one favor per year. And now that I'm active again I can see they're accruing some benefit to you."

"Yeah? Like what would that be? I already bit one of the hands that feeds me."

"This won't even be a blip on your screen. But I don't think we should talk about it over the phone. The walls have ears, if you know what I mean."

"Then how do you propose we conduct this business? And let me tell you, last time it was a freebie, this time it's gonna cost you."

"Don't worry, I always pay my debts. What say we meet tomorrow, same time, same place."

"I'll be there. Just don't push your luck, pal."

"I only push it as far as I need to. The rest is pure talent."

Charlie Floyd

My cell rang just as Manny and I were about to cross the street, heading into the apartment building where we thought Hoyt might be living.

"You swore you'd protect me. You swore."

I recognized her voice, even if it was distorted from fear.

"Melinda, calm down. What's the problem?"

I motioned to Manny to follow me, as I headed toward the corner. I made a slight turn so if Hoyt happened to be looking out of a window onto the street he wouldn't see us. Meanwhile, Manny positioned himself so he could see the entrance of the building, if Hoyt decided to leave before we crashed his party.

"The problem? You know the problem. It's Francis. You said you'd protect me from him."

"And I will. He's nowhere near you."

"Are you sure?"

"I'm sure. I just spotted him and he's a state away from where you are."

"How do you know he hasn't sent someone after me?"

"Why would you think that?"

"Because I went out to do some shopping and when I came back there was a guy loitering around the building."

"Melinda, you live in New York City. There are guys loitering on every corner."

"This wasn't just any guy. He looked like he was one of those guys you see in the movies, you know, the guys who whack people."

I wondered how much of this was real and how much was imagination run wild. Would Hoyt hire a hit man to go after her? I didn't think so. More likely if he hired anyone at all it would be someone to send her a message, or maybe even get her out of town. Anything more than that, I didn't think so.

"Where are you now?"

"I'm in Trader Joe's. Downstairs. Near the produce."

"Did the guy spot you going in?"

"I don't think so."

"Good. Don't go back home. Is there someplace you can stay tonight?"

"I...I..."

"Forget it. This is what I want you to do. Go down to Grand Central and hop on a train to Westport. When you're on the train, text me what time it arrives. I'll pick you up and you'll stay at my place, with me and Manny. If we can't protect you, no one can."

"Really?"

"Yes. I keep my promises, Melinda. And try to keep an eye out to see if you're being followed. Okay?"

She started to cry. "Yes..." she managed, between sobs. I didn't want to hang up on her but I didn't want to risk the chance of losing Hoyt.

"Don't take the subway. I want you to grab a cab."

"All right," she said, her voice trembling.

"Melinda...will you be okay?"

"Yes," she said. She'd stopped crying now but I could hear her breathing hard. "I...I don't have anything. Clothes. Makeup..."

"Don't worry about that stuff. We've got stores up here. We'll get you whatever you need. But you have to go now."

"I..."

"Do it now, Melinda."

"All right."

"And be careful."

I didn't like the sound of what I'd just heard. She was scared stiff. Would Hoyt really do something to harm her or was he just trying to scare her? Or was she imagining the whole thing?

It didn't matter. I'd put her in danger and she was my responsibility now. I'd figure out what to do with her later. Right now, Manny and I were going to head straight into the lion's den.

Francis Hoyt

Ever get that funny feeling in the pit of your stomach? You know, the one that gnaws at you and you can't quite figure out why you're feeling it. Usually, it means there's trouble ahead, only you can't be sure what kind of trouble it is.

That's what I was feeling as soon as I got back to my little Westport apartment. I'm not saying I'm psychic or anything, but I do believe we have mind powers that haven't been scientifically explained yet. Some call it intuition, or gut feelings. I think maybe they come from way back in evolution. You know, when to survive man had to listen to those signals. Maybe they thought they came from God. You know, the whole voices thing. Me, I just think it's a sense we were given only it's been dulled over the years. The more electronically we get plugged in, the further we get from that instinct. That's what it is. An instinct. An instinct that tells you when danger is near.

I always listen to that instinct, only I don't always know what to do. But something told me I shouldn't be hanging around that apartment for long. I don't know why, but I thought I had to get out of there.

Manny Perez

Charlie Floyd wanted me to take the lead.

"This is your play, Manny. I'm just here to back you up."

"But this is your jurisdiction, Charlie Floyd. You're the one who has to make the arrest."

"I'm happy to take care of that part of it if it comes to that. But remember, we don't have a warrant so we have to have probable cause to take him in. That would come if we can find him with any contraband, but it would have to be out in the open. All we can do is try to rattle him enough so that he does something I can arrest him for."

I nodded. Charlie Floyd was right. We could confront Francis Hoyt but unless there was an opening there would be little more we could do to him. What we really needed to do was either catch him in the act or catch him with stolen property.

Of course, Francis Hoyt's name was not on the nameplates and looking at them we did not recognize any familiar names that he was known to use as an alias. But something caught Charlie Floyd's eye.

"This is it, Manny. Three-B. See, no nameplate. Let's go."

Francis Hoyt

"What the fuck?"

"Trick or treat, Francis?"

"Are you surprised to see us, Francis Hoyt?"

I tried to close the fucking door on them but the little spic was too quick for me, jamming his foot in so I couldn't close it.

"Aren't you going to invite us in?" Floyd said.

"No."

"Got something to hide?"

I decided to let them in. After all, what could they find? It's not like I had a closetful of stolen silver.

"My life's an open book, so come on in, gentlemen."

How the fuck did they find me? My mind raced through all the possibilities. Who knew I was here? No one. So how the fuck did they track me down?

"As you can see, I'm not exactly set up for visitors, which means you won't be staying long. How the hell did you find me?"

"You can run but you can't hide. You should know that."

"That don't answer my question."

"You really think we're going to answer that?"

The little spic started to walk around the room, looking at my stuff, invading my fucking privacy.

"Hey, you!"

He looked up.

"You wanna stay over here, where I can see you?"

I looked back at the big one. "I know you haven't got a warrant or you would have waved it in my face, and I know you don't have probable cause, so what the hell are you wasting my time for?"

"Just being neighborly, Francis. We figured you dropped in on us we ought to return the favor. So, have anything planned for the rest of the day?"

"Yeah. I thought I'd have some dinner and then maybe hit a couple houses tonight. Wanna join me?"

The little spic kept wandering around the apartment, sticking his nose where it didn't belong. He got to my closet and was just about to open it when I stepped over and grabbed his hand.

"You open that door and I'm going to fucking sue your ass off."

"Something to hide?" said Floyd.

"Nope. Okay, Perez, here." I opened the door. Perez peered in to find absolutely nothing but a few things hanging, and my empty backpack on the floor.

"You think I'd be stupid enough to keep anything incriminating around here?"

"I didn't think so. But it seems you forgot one thing."

Charlie Floyd

I couldn't believe my eyes. There it was. Practically in plain sight. Sticking out from under a couple magazines on the night table. It was like a gift from God. If I actually believed in God, that is. But who knows, maybe this will change things.

I didn't say anything to Manny. I just pulled the cuffs out of my back pocket and before Hoyt knew what hit him I'd slapped them on his wrist. Almost as a reflex action he started to struggle. Manny quickly saw what was happening and grabbed Hoyt from behind. He was a strong little fucker, but the two of us managed to subdue him.

"What the fuck is going on?" he shouted. "You got nothing on me. You can't arrest me."

"That's funny, because that appears to be just what I'm doing."

I walked over to the night table beside his bed. There, peeking out from underneath a copy of *Architectural Digest*, was a very familiar item: the silver ashtray my mother had given me.

Hoyt looked stunned.

"You just had to take something, didn't you, Francis?"

"I don't know what the fuck you're talking about."

"Sure, you do," I said, holding up our trophy. "This little ashtray is going to send you away for a long time. A couple years ago I had this appraised and it's worth at least a couple thousand bucks. You know as well as I do that this graduates you to grand larceny. That's a good start, don't you think? And

I'll bet Manny here can find some other charges against you, once we get folks to turn over on you."

He laughed.

"You think it's funny?"

"I think it's fucking hilarious if you think this charge is going to stick. I'll just say you planted it on me."

I shook my head. "That might have worked except that I reported it stolen after you left my house. And I don't think it was that smart leaving that message for us in the house down the block. I'm sure a prosecuting attorney can use that to build the state's case."

"I want a fucking lawyer."

"I don't blame you. I was in your position that's exactly what I'd want, too."

Manny Perez

In my experience criminals catch themselves more than we catch them. Most of them are not very bright or astute. Most of them never finished their schooling. Most of them think they are smarter than everyone else and, in the end, this is what does them in: their own stupidity or arrogance or belief that they are invulnerable. If Francis Hoyt had not given in to his baser instincts and stolen that ashtray from Charlie Floyd's house we would probably still be working on ways to apprehend him and put him under arrest. But you must never underestimate the self-destructiveness of the criminal element. Most of them are criminals because they cannot exist within the rules of civilized society. They must make their own rules and yet their own rules all too often fail them.

Arresting Francis Hoyt for what was a senseless crime was only the beginning. Both Charlie Floyd and I would now, along with the Connecticut, Florida, New Jersey, Massachusetts, and New York authorities, as well as the FBI, be working to put Francis Hoyt away for the rest of his life. I was certain that in addition to all the burglaries he committed, he was also responsible for some more serious crimes, murder among them, though that would be more difficult to prove.

Once my suspension was lifted, I returned home to Miami. I stayed in constant touch with Charlie Floyd and in the back of my mind I had an idea. It was an idea for the future, but I kept it to myself. There might come a time when I would share it with Esther and the rest of my family, as well as with Charlie

Floyd, but right now the goal was to normalize my life and that meant returning to my duties as a detective with the Miami Police Department.

Charlie Floyd

As soon as Manny left town and the furor over Hoyt died down a little—he was now in the hands of the State Police and the FBI—things almost got back to normal.

Melinda Shaw stayed with us for a couple nights, but once she felt safe enough she returned to her apartment in the city. I checked up on her every once in a while, and she had to come back up to Connecticut a few times to be interviewed by the investigator who took my place, John Woycek, and the FBI visited her to get any information they could on Hoyt. They were in the process of trying to track down Evelyn Kerns, but even with Manny's help they weren't making much progress. By this time, Manny had been reinstated and was back to work keeping the streets of Miami safe for its citizens.

My job was done and to be honest, I was left feeling a little down. Being back in the game was good for me. It gave me a reason to get up every morning. And working with Manny showed me that I missed the interaction with human beings other than the postman and the checkout girl at Stew Leonard's.

It was a couple months after the collar when I got a call from Wild Bill.

"Are you sitting down, Charlie?"

"Yeah. Why?"

"I've got some bad news for you."

"Someone making complaints I haven't cut my lawn lately? Truth is, the mower's on the fritz and I'm too damn cheap to pay some kid to do it. Besides, what else have I got to do to pass the time?"

"That's not it. It's about Francis Hoyt."

"Oh, jeez."

"He escaped."

"You're fucking kidding."

"I wish I was."

"How the hell did that happen?"

"He was brought in to make a court appearance. His lawyer had gotten him this real nice suit—"

"Oh, man, I see what's coming."

"Yeah. He asked to go to the bathroom, so they had to uncuff him. They took their eyes off him for only a minute, that's all it took, just a damn minute, and the next thing they knew he wasn't there anymore. Their guess is, dressed like that, he just waltzed out of there like any honest citizen. They probably thought he was just another attorney—"

"Only dressed better, I'm sure."

"I'm sorry, Charlie. We've got a warrant out for him and the FBI is on the case. We'll find him."

"I'm not so sure."

"I'm guessing that reward isn't paid until he's actually convicted."

"I don't care about the reward, Billy."

"I didn't think so. Still, it was probably a nice chunk of change. But it's not over. Like I said, he's going to have to find a very big rock to hide under and I can't imagine he's going to give up the life."

"No. That's not gonna happen. He'll be back robbing houses within a month. But the question is, where?"

"It's not your problem."

"Sure, it is. It's unfinished business."

I hung up and thought about calling Manny, but I didn't have the stomach for it. I was hoping that he was onto something and someone else by now. That he could let go of Hoyt.

After all, we'd proved that Hoyt wasn't as smart as he thought he was. He made a stupid mistake and it got him caught.

Of course, that wouldn't be the way Hoyt would see it.

Sometimes life just sucks and there's nothing you can do about it.

I guessed this was one of those times.

ACKNOWLEDGMENTS

I owe a debt of gratitude to several writer friends who took the time out of their valuable day to read and give valuable feedback and encouragement on *Second Story Man*. Reed Farrel Coleman, S.J. Rozan, Tim O'Mara, David Swinson, Michael Sears, Joe Clifford, Hank Phillippi Ryan, Rosemary Harris, and Mark Johnson. And special thanks to my oldest friend in the world (we can't be that old, but we go all the way back to high school, and that's been a while), Elliot Ravetz, who read this book in manuscript form and also gave me very valuable feedback.

And, of course, a special thanks to Eric Campbell, the founder of Down & Out Books, a writer's dream. Eric has given a home to so many crime writers, and created a community I'm proud to be part of. Thanks to Lance Wright, a self-proclaimed obsessive-compulsive when it comes to finding errors in logic and lets me know when something just plain doesn't make sense, and Chris Rhatigan, who did a great hands-on edit.

And finally, I want to thank Mystery Writers of America, who not only provide a safe haven to crime writers, but also emotional support.

Charles Salzberg is the author of the Shamus Award-nominated *Swann's Last Song* as well as the sequels *Swann Dives In* and *Swann's Lake of Despair*. He is also author of *Devil in the Hole*, which was chosen as one of the Best Crime Novels of 2013 by *Suspense Magazine*. He lives in New York City and teaches writing at the Writer's Voice and the New York Writers Workshop, where he is proud to be a Founding Member.

www.charlessalzberg.com

OTHER TITLES FROM DOWN & OUT BOOKS

OTHER TITLES FROM DOWN & OUT BOOKS

See DownAndOutBooks.com for complete list

By Matt Hilton
No Going Back
Rules of Honor
The Lawless Kind
The Devil's Anvil
No Safe Place

By Lawrence Kelter
and Frank Zafiro
The Last Collar

By Jerry Kennealy
Screen Test
Polo's Long Shot (*)

By Dana King
Worst Enemies
Grind Joint
Resurrection Mall (*)

By Ross Klavan, Tim O'Mara
and Charles Salzberg
Triple Shot

By S.W. Lauden
Crosswise
Crossed Bones (*)

By Paul D. Marks and
Andrew McAleer (editors)
Coast to Coast vol. 1
Coast to Coast vol. 2

By Bill Moody
Czechmate
The Man in Red Square
Solo Hand
The Death of a Tenor Man

The Sound of the Trumpet
Bird Lives!

By Gary Phillips
The Perpetrators
Scoundrels (Editor)
Treacherous
3 the Hard Way

By Tom Pitts
Hustle

By Robert J. Randisi
Upon My Soul
Souls of the Dead
Envy the Dead (*)

By Ryan Sayles
The Subtle Art of Brutality
Warpath

By John Shepphird
The Shill
Kill the Shill
Beware the Shill

James R. Tuck (editor)
Mama Tried vol. 1
Mama Tried vol. 2 (*)

By Lono Waiwaiole
Wiley's Lament
Wiley's Shuffle
Wiley's Refrain
Dark Paradise
Leon's Legacy (*)

(*)—*Coming Soon*

80857139R00171

Made in the USA
Columbia, SC
22 November 2017